THE SOLO TRIP

Leah Battaglio

PROLOGUE

Everyone cheers as we step into the vintage Rolls Royce destined for our swanky hotel suite in downtown Chicago. I look down at my beautiful wedding ring and marvel at its grandeur. My hand is small. I told Jack I didn't need anything too big, but he insisted on the 2.49 carat Cartier square diamond. This is my life now. I have married into one of the most successful law families in Chicago. I have a reputation to uphold. Pictures to take for society pages. Standing hair and nail appointments. An account at Saks Fifth Avenue. All of the designer labels I could dream of. I am now Mrs. Jack Van Horn. I need to live up to the reputation Jack's family demands, but doesn't truly believe his suburban wife can do.

"I can't believe how many people showed up for the reception." I say, trying to pull off my short receptions veil. I switched into a shorter one for the wedding reception. A cathedral length veil is not practical for dancing and other ballroom socializations.

"I can. This was the hottest wedding of the season. My old fraternity brother who lives in Milan flew in just for this," Jack says, nuzzling my neck.

"Do you think the driver will do one more drive around the city? I want to take in this moment with you."

"I want to take in this moment with you in our hotel

suite. Do we really need to do another round?" Jack's chiseled jaw tenses as he softly touches his chin dimple. His looks were obviously what drew me to him, but his need to make me happy kept me there.

"Please, Mr. Van Horn," I say as I pull out the last hair pin from my hair, letting my soft, blonde locks fall naturally.

Jack brushes the loose hair from my face and says, "Anything for you, Mrs. Van Horn. I'd go to the moon and back for you."

"And I you." Jack and I embrace in a romantic kiss as husband and wife and I still can't believe I get to spend the rest of my life with this remarkable man. I must be the luckiest lady in the entire universe.

CHAPTER 1

Divorced. I, Dabney Elizabeth Corrigan am officially a single. I am now a twenty-something woman who sleeps on her best friend, Ruby's, sofa and tries desperately not to drool on the vintage green velvet. I have a small savings account from the advertising job I had before I left to be a social media influencer and doting wife. I miss my bitchy, yet adorable Yorkshire Terrier, Missy, that I walked, fed and cuddled with every day, but since she was purchased by my ex -husband and I didn't have a place to keep her, she stays with him. Despite the many, many things I do not have, I do have one thing—my dignity. I grabbed that as fast as I could before I slammed the door shut on our relationship.

Let me explain a bit more. I fell in love with Jack Van Horn almost immediately. We met one chilly and unexpected Chicago night at a bar downtown. I did know his history of being one of Chicago's hottest bachelors. Somehow, I chose to ignore the rumors that he never kept it in his pants. I just knew we had instant chemistry and when he proposed to me after a year of being together, I did not hesitate to say yes. He was good on paper and good in bed. What was I going to say? No?

Our wedding plans over the next several months were rather hectic and while I thought he seemed a bit more stressed than usual, I figured it was because he had an important case at his law office. He desperately wanted to make partner at the firm and was working very long hours to prove it. I did not question that one bit because all the law shows on television depict lawyers as stressed out and over worked. Despite the stress, we had a gorgeous wedding and my upper middle-class parents finally made it to the society pages. After the wedding, Jack and I had a sun-filled honeymoon in Maui and he barely even thought of work while we were in our wedded bliss paradise. Two weeks of luxurious cabanas and cocktails in pineapples can have that effect on even the hardest of working men.

Once we returned to Chicago however, Jack got back to working late into the night and even some weekends. Many evenings, I sat with Missy on my lap, binge watching Netflix shows, eating dinner via delivery service and staring at my sparkly, Cartier diamond ring...alone.

Fast forward six months to one cold, Chicago evening when I knew he would be working late again. I could not bear the thought of him eating one more Chinese take-out meal at his desk in his cold grey office while I was at home, lounging in my cashmere joggers. Were lawyers allowed to wear casual clothes after hours? Was that a thing? Regardless, I packed up my homemade meal of chicken piccata and angel hair pasta (the only meal I can cook), a bottle of Chardonnay and took a taxi to surprise my husband with dinner.

A surprise indeed.

The security guard let me in, and I pushed the button for the 12ᵗʰ floor like I had done many other times. However, this visit to his office was quite different. I opened his heavy office door and in my horror at the bare ass that stood before me, I dropped the bottle of wine, screamed in shock, and scared the living hell out of the two guilty parties in my presence. It was an embarrassing scene that included the floor's security guard and the building custodian who was lovely enough to mop up the wine and broken glass for me as I rushed out in panic. Jack chased after me once his pants were zipped, but it was too late. The damage was permanently done. I immediately packed my bags and called my best friend for help.

Now, three months later, I still sleep on Ruby's sofa and my ex-husband's mistress sleeps in my bed. The one I picked out from the upscale furniture store because we were *too mature for IKEA now, Dabney*.

***

I wander down the streets, feeling lonesome and lost when I realize I have made it to The Tablespoon, where I am meeting my best friend and savior.

It is a little while until Ruby could meet me at the café to hang out during her break. Ruby is a college professor and teaches English at a private college in the city. I think she enjoys her profession, but it doesn't pay that well, hence the tiny one-bedroom apartment she lives in. It is a cute apartment, don't get me wrong, but not meant for two people, especially for three months. Ruby has been more than gracious though. She spends a good bit of time in her office at work and teaches a few classes at night, so I don't think I get underneath her toes too much...I hope.

While I wait for Ruby to join me, I order a large

latte and a toasted croissant and lightly read through a local Chicago magazine. It is mostly real estate advertisements, articles about up and coming neighborhood restaurants and other local businesses. The café is a favorite of mine. It's close to Ruby's college and unfortunately, close to my old apartment. Nevertheless, I still frequent it. The cozy seats and friendly staff are familiar. They also have a really good avocado toast. Something I didn't order today, unfortunately. Today is a saturated fat and carbs day.

I look up and see Ruby shaking off her vintage tweed coat. "Sorry it took me so long. Our faculty meeting went long as usual. I swear those people became professors because they love to hear themselves talk." Ruby plops down in the opposite chair and waves over the server to order her black coffee with almond milk. Ruby does not consume sugar or dairy, or gluten and eats a lot of trendy, nutritious things like bone broth and unusual animal organs that are high in protein but low on the common food menu.

The waitress comes over to bring me my second latte and takes Ruby's order.

"No problem. I'm just wallowing in my own self-pity." I say, putting another dollop of butter and strawberry jam on my butter croissant as the silver and gold dangly bracelets jingle on my wrist.

Ruby slowly draws the small bowl of butter packets toward her and says, "Judging by the amount of butter you're using; I'm going to guess it didn't go so well?"

"Oh, it went fine. Just as I expected. We didn't fight. He gets everything since it was all his to begin with. I get to keep all of the stuff given to me by him as a gift. I declined spousal support and that was it. We signed our papers and I left. Now I'm here eating fat and carbs as a single woman."

"Wait, you declined spousal support? I thought he offered that to you. I thought it was part of the prenup you signed!" Ruby exclaims, almost pouring her almond milk on the table instead of into her coffee.

"I don't want his money, Ruby. I still have some of my own money that I saved while we were married." It must have been some sort of self-fulfilling prophecy. I saved any income that I made as a blogger and Instagrammer because he paid for everything when we were together. It's not like I've won the lottery, but it's getting me by for a bit.

"Well, if you say so. I understand not wanting his money, but life isn't cheap. Also, you have champagne taste, Dabney. That savings of yours will go quick."

"I know. And don't worry, Ruby. I won't be on your sofa forever. I'll figure something out. I know it's been a few months now."

"I know you will. You always do. But in the meantime, my sofa is all yours." Ruby says nonchalantly as she sips her unsweetened coffee. She really is a champion.

I hold back a tear at my friend's selfless generosity and get out a, "Thanks, Ruby. That means a lot."

Ruby, sensing my near meltdown instantly tries to fill my cup back to half full, rather than empty.

"You know what you need, Dabney? You need to get away somewhere. Get out of the city. Rent a cabin or something," Ruby says, trying to change the subject a bit.

"Rent a cabin? Can you imagine me sitting alone in a cabin? I'd lose my mind. A getaway might be nice though. I don't know. I don't even know where I'd go."

I look down at the magazine I had been reading. In the bottom right-hand corner, is an advertisement. "Irish Eyes Adventures...We help fill your bucket." It lists a website for inquiries as well as a local Chicago number.

"What about this?" I show the Kelly-green advertisement to Ruby, who has been checking her work email during our discussion and getting more and more annoyed.

"Huh? Sorry, I'm responding to a student who has asked me the same question three times now in three different ways. What's this?"

"I'm not sure but it looks like some sort of Irish vacation. A Bed and Breakfast tour group or something? Maybe I shouldn't rent a cabin. Maybe I should get out of the country for a bit? Do you want to come with me? Please? Pretty please? You know I'm not a good solo flyer. I get very confused in airports and have extremely awkward conversation with strangers. I need a travel buddy. Please?"

Ruby puts her phone down and furrows her brow. "I wish I could Dabney. But this semester isn't close to being over and I can't just leave. That's very frowned upon for non-tenured professors."

"Sure, I understand." The thought of taking a trip out of the country makes me want to vomit. I don't even like going to the movies by myself. I mean, there's nobody to poke when something really good happens. Or laugh at me when I can't help but cry because despite what the rest of the theater thinks, it is a really sad moment.

"Dabney, I have to get back to the office. But I think you taking a trip to Ireland is a fabulous idea. Check out some flights, look into an Airbnb or maybe a cute Bed and Breakfast. Email that company and find out what they're all about."

Hmm. I pull out my phone to check flights to Ireland and realize I have seven text messages from Jack. Yuck. My stomach immediately sours, and I begin to regret that last pat of butter...or two.

Dabney, I want to give you some money. Can we meet?

A few minutes later another text...

Why are you being so stubborn. You don't have any money! Just take some. You deserve it.

A couple minutes later...

Fine. Be stubborn and poor.

Are you seriously not going to meet up with me?

Five minutes after that...

I'm sorry. I don't mean to harass you. It's your decision.

Ok, I know you're at the café we always went to. I'm coming there now.

Are you still there? Don't leave. I really need to talk to you.

"Oh good. You're still here." My now ex-husband barges into the café like someone who has been running from the bulls of Pamplona.

"What the hell are you doing here? I put my phone away for a few minutes and have seven text messages from you! And how do you know where I am?" I ask, furious.

"Find my iPhone app. We're still on the same account until the end of the month."

Aw shit. I forgot to get a new phone and new phone number. I meant to do that but then went to get a Mani/Pedi instead.

"Ok stalker. Lose my number and I still don't want any of your money."

"I'm not taking no for an answer. This bullshit of you not accepting spousal support is one thing, but you should at least take something from me. For fuck's sake, Dabney, you're sleeping on your best friend's sofa. At least take some money to get settled into your own apartment or something. I've had closets bigger than Ruby's apartment." Jack is starting to raise his voice in frustration and I can see the tiny vein on his forehead getting bigger.

"Ugh, you always were such a snob." I roll my eyes and turn to my faux diamond encrusted phone to delete his messages. "So again, why are you even here? Are you concerned for my welfare? You think I can't make it on my own without my Sugar Daddy to care of me? My life choices are none of your business now."

"Of course, I 'm concerned, Dabney. I'm not a total asshole. And I'm not your Sugar Daddy. I'm only six years older than you," Jack says, running his tanned manicured hands through his thick layers of blonde hair. While Jack may not uphold the solemn vows of marriage, he does take his weekly manicure at the local nail salon very seriously.

"Well, whatever. You can't just pick and choose when you care about me, Jack. I'm going to be fine." Truth be told, I am not sure how fine I will be, but I don't want him to know that. Again, it is all none of his business.

"I'm writing you a check for $50,000. It's out of my trust. It's enough for you to pay some rent and start a new life. Please Dabney," Jack says pleadingly.

Fuck you. Fuck you, I want to say. I want to spit in his beautiful face, a face that after rushing around the streets of Chicago still looks as handsome as ever. But then something occurs to me. I do deserve something. I deserve to take a fabulous trip to Ireland or anywhere. I deserve to get away from all the bullshit that he has created for me. And while I would never admit to Ruby or Jack, it would be nice to sleep in a real bed for a while.

I look him in the eyes. "Fine. I'll take your stupid money. Then please, forget this number. I'm getting a new phone and a new number. You have absolutely no reason to ever contact me again. Do you understand?"

Jack looks startled. He knows I am completely serious, and he can tell I mean every word.

"Fair enough. Here. Take this." He hands over the envelope with a check for $50,000. "And Dabney, for the record, I'm sorry."

I watch him slowly walk out of the café. I want to hate him. I want to hate him so badly. But mostly, I just feel immense pain and emptiness.

CHAPTER 2

When one doesn't have much to begin with, it doesn't take a lot of effort to decide what to bring on an Irish adventure. I simply pack everything, which now that I look at it all, may actually be a lot.

"Have I told you how proud I am of you? I can't believe you're actually taking this trip alone," Ruby is, unfolding and refolding the clothes I am packing into my suitcase. "Tightly roll, Dabney. That's how you get the most bang for your buck with this suitcase. Yes, that's it."

Ruby is a champion packer. She once went backpacking in Europe for eight weeks with one large backpack. If I spent eight weeks in Europe, I'd need an entire suitcase set. Well, maybe not. I now know how to pack, thanks to Ruby. But I do have the biggest suitcase I have ever seen to fill. I've borrowed it from my mother, who I assume has the same travel anxiety as I do when it comes to needing to pack everything. As a kid, my father used to always fuss at her about brining too many bags when we would go on vacation. She'd say, *'You fuss now until I've packed something you need later.'*

My other reason for packing a lot of clothes, is I just don't know what the weather will be like. Sure, it's spring, but spring in Ireland might be a lot different than spring in Chicago. Maybe it will rain a lot. Maybe they will have an odd heat wave. Maybe it will be really cold one day. I would rather make sure I have all of my seasons covered. Sure, I can go shopping while there, but I don't want to be desperate while shopping. That's just asking for trouble. Do you know how many ugly shirts or other items of clothing I have purchased because I spilled coffee on the shirt I was wearing and had to pop out of the office to the closest luxury discount store? I will save you the trouble of guessing. It's a lot. Like, more than ten a lot. I am rather accident prone. One of the benefits of quitting my office job and becoming a social media influencer is working from home. Now when I spill something on myself, I can just change. I think it's saved me a ton of money.

"Ruby, I wish you could come with me. I'm still nervous. I've never traveled by myself."

"I do too. But I think this what you need. You're going to come back a stronger, more confident Dabney. Just you wait and see. And don't worry. You can call or text me anytime if you feel lonely."

I know Ruby means well, but I also know how busy she is. With the time difference and her work hours, I will be very limited as to when I can call her for moral support. No, this trip will definitely be a test for me. It will force me to step out of my comfort zone and get comfortable with myself. My single, self-employed and somewhat lost self.

"Okay, I've packed all of my clothes, my essential toiletries and accessories. I've also packed snacks for my carry-on bag in the event I am stuck on the plane and the snack cart is out of service."

Ruby picks up the check list. "Chargers packed?"

"Yep! Phone, iPad, Kindle, and portable chargers all charged and packed," I say confidently. In fact, I have checked and rechecked several times now.

"Extra change of clothes in case you spill something or have a pee accident?"

"Yes. But why would I have a pee accident? Do you question my bladder control? I can assure you I have not peed my pants since the field trip in first grade." And in my defense, that was not my fault. Mrs. Granger wouldn't let me use the restroom at the pumpkin patch.

"It's always a good idea to have a spare set of clothes. All clothes. You just never know, Dabney."

"Uh huh. Okay well spare undies it is!" I grab a pair of underwear and roll it up into my large zipper lock plastic bag that is part of my carry-on bag. I put in a spare pair of shoes as well, just in case the ones I am wearing don't look right with the new outfit I may have to change into.

"And most importantly," Ruby holds up an empty plastic bag and says, "do you have your essential three-ounce items in your quart size plastic bag? Moisturizer, hand sanitizer, facial spray, lip balm, facial wipes?"

"Ruby, you know me so well. Of course. I also packed my multi-purpose cheek and lip stain and travel size BB cream." Ruby is very low maintenance. She's a tinted moisturizer and lip balm kind of gal. Her skin regime consists of just a few things; cleanser, tinted moisturizer and tinted lip balm. Whereas mine amounts to approximately ten. I am a self-proclaimed and proud beauty and skin care junkie. Since my separation, I have had to cut back on some of my luxuries because now I pay for them myself. $300 moisture cream is not in my budget any-more—unfortunately. I still have my luxurious creams but save them for special occasions. Now I use a stand-ard $15 moisturizer with plenty of hyaluronic acid for day and a cheap retinol serum for night.

I zip up my oversized suitcase and pull it to the door. It's rather heavy and I am hoping I don't have to contend with a flight of stairs during my journey. I don't think I could do it. I mean, I'm not trying to be a Negative Nelly, but I honestly don't think I could physically pull this bag anywhere that does not accommodate wheels.

Ruby dips her organic tea bag into the steaming hot water of her favorite mug. "Do you want me to come with you to the airport? For one last goodbye?" (maybe switch order of these two sentences.)

"No, no. I know you have papers to grade. I can do this. I'm actually getting excited for my adventure. In fact, I should probably order a ride soon. I don't know what traffic is like getting out of the city. It is less than twenty miles out to the airport and should take less than thirty minutes, but you just never know. Not to mention, O'Hare International Airport is one of the busiest air-ports in the country."

"Okay, well let me say my goodbyes then. Text me when you get there. I don't care what time it is. I want to know you've arrived and gotten to your Bed and Break-fast."

"Will do! Don't worry, Ruby. I've got this." I give Ruby a big hug and start to pull away when she stops and looks at me with complete focus.

"I know you do. Have a great time, Dabney. I mean it. Enjoy yourself. Go out for a day without makeup. Take advantage of the fact you don't know these people and you won't ever see them again."

I laugh. "Jeez, Ruby. I said I'd get out of my comfort zone, but go out without makeup? You're asking a lot." I'm still laughing as I head out of the door. "

"You know what I mean!" She shouts out the door as I walk down the hall to the elevator.

The driver helps me get my suitcase into the trunk of his car and says, "Right, so O'Hare Airport. Which terminal?"

Which terminal. Good question. I actually forgot to check that. I quickly scramble to get my phone out of my bag, while the driver rushes out of the temporary zone into busy traffic.

"Terminal? Do you know?" He asks again.

"No, I'm sorry. Let me find my flight."

"Who are you flying?" The driver asks while honking his horn and swearing at the driver who cut him off.

"Aer Lingus." I can at least answer that question.

The driver swishes through more traffic and replies, "Yeah that's terminal five," he says in a thick Chicago accent.

I finally get my app to pull up and decide to discreetly confirm he is correct. He is.

"Didn't believe me huh?" He laughs and continues to swear at drivers. Forget being a lawyer, I think being an Uber driver is much more stressful. Second to being an

Uber passenger.

Once the car stops, I rush to get out, feeling a bit queasy from car sickness…and maybe nerves.

I drag my suitcase down the walkway and into the departures area to check in and drop off my bag. I honestly can't wait to drop off the monstrosity.

"Next." The check in desk attendant motions me over. I lug the suitcase onto the scale and take a deep breath. Please don't be too heavy. Please. Don't. Be. Too. Heavy.

"I'm sorry but your bag is too heavy. It's 54 pounds." The lady just looks at me for a minute and then says, "If you'd like to take some things out you may. Or it's a $100 fee."

I most definitely will not be taking four pounds of stuff out of my suitcase and carrying it around for a day. However, I don't want to spend $100 either. So, I quickly open the bag and pull out a sweater, tie it around my waist, roll up a pair of jeans and toss it in my carry-on bag, along with a hairbrush and flat iron. I also grab the pair of Hunter boots and socks and replace my flats with them, hoping that covers the four pounds.

"How's that? Did I make the weight?" I ask, nearly pleading and definitely out of breath.

"No. I'm sorry, but it's still too heavy. One and a half pounds to be precise. Is there anything else you can pull out?" The airline employee asks impatiently because there is now a long line of Asian tourists behind me wondering what on earth this crazy American lady is doing pulling out everything from her bag.

"But I can't possibly pull anything else out. There's no room and my carry-on bag is really heavy."

The airline employee looks again at her ever increasingly impatient line. "Have I suggested the $100 fee? That may be a better option for you at this point."

I look down at my mess of a suitcase that was once so neat and tidy. Ruby worked so hard on it and now I've made a complete disaster of it all. Then I make the mistake of looking behind at all of the people who have been watching this debacle.

"Sure. I'll pay the fee." I pull out my debit card and hand it to her. The airline employee hands me my bag check ticket and my passport and sends me on my way.

Walking away to the security gates I can hear a man shouting, "Panties! Ma'am! Panties!" I look back to see an Asian man waving a pair of black lacy thong underwear. *My* black lacy thong underwear. Oh my god. They must have fallen out when I was digging through my suitcase trying to pull out heavy items.

Keep walking Dabney.

"Ma'am!" He's now running after me, waving my underwear in the air as I run even faster through the airport toward security.

As I approach the security line, a security officer stops me.

"Ma'am, stop. I think that man is trying to get your attention."

At this point, I am in the presence of hundreds of people waiting in line to go through security. Everyone is looking at me wondering what in the world is happening. Have I been pulled out of line because the security dog has sniffed cocaine in my carry-on bag? Am I carrying a gun? Did I shout about a bomb? Am I a potential terrorist? No, I am none of those things, but I am the lady who dropped her black lacy panties in one of the busiest airports in the country.

The Asian man, who is out of breath simply says, "Ma'am, your panties," while handing me my underwear. Then he turns and walks away as though I had dropped my keys or left my cell phone behind.

Now, everyone is not only looking at me, they're either embarrassed at having to see my underwear, laughing because they saw my underwear, or are completely appalled at seeing my underwear. Either way, it is terribly embarrassing for me. I only hope none of these people are on my flight to Dublin I think to myself as I shove the underwear in my purse.

I finally get through security and make my way to the gate for my flight after a quick stop for magazines and coffee. It doesn't matter what time of day I fly, I have to get a coffee. It's just a tradition of mine.

Once I've gotten my necessary flying supplies, put on the sweater I had wrapped around my waist, I walk to my gate and have a seat. It looks like I've received an email from the tour guide people. They're very nice. Their names are Sam and Cassie and they're actually American. They have a place in Chicago, but maintain most of their time in Ireland. Sam is a travel writer and Cassie is a former stay at home mom/financial adviser. The story is, they met through a mutual friend who just finished her aunt's bucket list and moved to Ireland. Feeling inspired, they decided to move as well and set up a bucket list travel service along with their Bed and Breakfast. I sent them some places I might want to see or do around Dublin, but to be honest I really have no idea what to do or see. This trip has been put together on a whim. I'm kind of excited to meet some new people while I'm there though. I don't want to feel completely alone. I had enough of that when I was married to Jack.

I read the email to find that they are picking me up at the airport, so I send them my flight info. I planned on taking a taxi, but I'll take the free ride into town. My mother says I'm far too trusting of people, but I'm fairly certain they aren't psychotic cult leaders. They are simply providing me good customer service. I hope. If I'm wrong my mother will never let me live it down.

I told you Dabney, never accept rides from strangers and especially attractive men.

While I finish my email to Sam and Cassie, I hear my name being called over the loudspeaker. Startled, I look around and see my name is up on the board. Shit, I think to myself. I don't know why, but I always assume I'm in trouble. It must be the Catholic kid in me.

I walk up to the front desk. "I'm Dabney Corrigan. Is there a problem?"

The attendant laughs and says, "No, there's no problem. Your upgrade request has been approved. You've been upgraded to First Class!"

"Really? This never happens to me! Wonderful!"

"Yes, we had a last-minute cancellation so you're in luck. Here's your new boarding pass. We'll be boarding in about 15 minutes. You get first-priority of course."

Fifteen minutes later, I am sitting down in my own personal little cubby and get comfortable. For some reason, my mind immediately goes to Jack's new girlfriend. I've heard she's very superficial. More than me. I will freely admit that I like nice things. So far, they've completely re-done the apartment we were in with even fancier furniture and appliances than we had. I've heard from Amanda, a mutual friend of mine and Jack's, that she insisted they put in all Sub-Zero and Wolf appliances before she would even move in. Apparently, she fancies herself an amateur chef and requires only the best in her kitchen. Amanda sent me a DM one night asking if I was okay. She'd heard about the divorce and was shocked when she and the husband were invited to a housewarming party—again. This time for the mistress.

Alas, I will not be thinking of my past anymore. I will put my Bose headset on, catch up on some movies and perhaps take a nap since it will be morning by the time I arrive in Dublin.

A flight attendant taps me on the shoulder and asks, "Prosecco?"

I never say no to free alcohol. Especially on a long flight.

"Yes, please." As I sip my bubbly wine, I try to relax and think about what I will do while I am in Ireland. That is one nice thing about this travel service I have booked. They do most of the thinking for me. I am looking forward to seeing some history and beautiful scenery—rolling green hills, but not handsome Irishmen, despite the divinely sexy accent. In fact, I am resolving to make this trip a discovery of Dabney and Dabney only.

CHAPTER 3

After a very long flight, all I want to do is get to my room at the B&B, take a shower and relax. I think it's going to take a while though. The line to get through customs is miles long and moving at a snail's pace. In front of me is a family with five children who are less happy than me to be in the never-ending line. How anyone could have that many children let alone travel with them is beyond me. I plan to only have two children max. After all, any more than that and a parent team is outnumbered. That doesn't seem too smart to me.

What feels like hours later, I finally reach to front of the line.

"Next!" A rather stern looking man motions me to him. "What are your plans while you're in Ireland?"

Realizing I don't really have an 'plans' I stumble out, "Well I'm going to first take a nap and then see some of the local sites maybe. I'd love to do some shopping."

"Address of where you're staying," he asks, without actually forming it in a way that one would think it was a question. More of a statement really.

"Oh, err, I'm staying just outside of Dublin."

The stern man huffs impatiently and says, "Address."

"Oh well I don't have the address memorized. Let

me see if I can find it. It's in my phone somewhere. I didn't think I would need it since the B&B hosts said they'd pick me up. Just a sec, I start rifling through my oversized purse looking for the phone, I honestly just dropped in.

"Very well. You don't seem to be a danger to Ireland, so I'll let you in. Off you go then. Have a nice stay."

Feeling somewhat offended, although rather relieved, I follow through with his request and go on my way. I thought Irish people were friendly, but they certainly do not act that way when your passport is stamped.

Cassie, my point of contact said she would pick me up. Once I've gathered my bags, I look around to see a lady with a sign bearing my name. I've always wanted to be picked up at the airport like that. Like someone important. Alas, I don't see anyone holding up a Dabney Corrigan sign anywhere. Perhaps she is just running late.

The busy baggage claim area scatters as nearly all the bags are retrieved from the carousel. I sit on my oversized suitcase and look around. I watch families meet up and hug as they walk to their cars, they talk non-stop about what they did and what they've missed while they were away. I see people walk with determination, knowing exactly where they're going. Probably to a taxi line or a parked car that has been waiting for them. I watch and watch, realizing I have nobody waiting for me and I suddenly feel quite lonely.

I dig through my purse and find my phone this time. I scan through my emails, looking for Cassie's contact information and to confirm my plans. I read the email, correctly didn't I? Someone was coming to get me. Right?

Then it occurs to me. What if I have been scammed? What if this travel company was just a stupid scam? I only paid my accommodations up front and the fee arranging things. But still, something is definitely wrong.

Fighting back tears, I start to put in Cassie's phone number when someone approaches me.

"Excuse me, are you Dabney?"

I look up to find a rather tall man with short, messy black hair and crystal blue eyes staring down at me. His arms have a few tattoos with designs that I'm not familiar with but assume are Celtic and his rough looking hands don't look like they've been manicured ever. He's wearing a black t-shirt and jeans with black work boots.

"Huh? Oh, yes, I'm Dabney. Who are you?"

"I'm Simon and I'm here to pick you up. Can I get your bags? I hate to rush you, but I'm in a bit of a hurry. I have a shift that starts soon and it's a match day."

"Oh, excuse me. I've been sitting here for an hour waiting for someone to pick me up, but let me rush for you by all means," I say in a huff. Who does he think he is?

Seeing my annoyance, he blushes a bit and says, "Err, I'm sorry about that. Cassie had an emergency and needed someone to help her out. I was next door at the pub getting ready to start my shift, but I couldn't leave right away. But now that I'm here, can we get moving?" He motions toward the exit doors.

I hop up in a rush as the Simon fellow grabs my large suitcase from underneath me and heads toward the exit.

"Hurry up, then. Deacon and Tilda are on their own

with a new guy. I'm the only cook today which means Deacon is in the kitchen. He might be the owner, but the guy knows nothing about keeping a tidy kitchen."

"Oh, are you a cook then?" I ask, feeling somewhat winded by the pace I'm having to keep. My legs are about half the length of Simon's, who is extremely tall and possibly an Olympic sprinter given how fast he can walk.

"I'm actually a chef. I have a Culinary Arts degree from the DIT." He casually lifts up my giant suitcase. "Aw bugger, me. It's too fuckin' big."

I watch Simon try to maneuver my suitcase into his tiny automobile to no avail.

"Well can you put it on the roof?"

"No, I can't put it on the roof. What am I going to tie it up with? Your scarf?"

It's a pashmina actually, but I don't bother to correct the ruffian.

"Well what am I going to do?"

"It looks rather old and beat up. Why don't you just dump in the boot and leave it?" He says, pointing to the trunk of his tiny clown car.

I look at him stunned. Does he honestly think I am going to dump all of my personal items in his trunk?!

"I'm not dumping my stuff in your car. I will have you know I have some rather expensive pieces in this bag. Not to mention the suitcase doesn't even belong to me!"

"I'm sure they would understand."

"Oh, I'm sure you are wrong. You have never met my mother. You don't know how understanding she is and furthermore I'm offended you would even—"

"Look, I already told you. I'm in a hurry to get you back. I don't know what else to do. Your bag is gigantic and doesn't fit in my car."

"Fine. I'll take a taxi. There must be large taxis that accommodate people like me. In the meantime, maybe you should think about getting a bigger car."

Simon slams the trunk shut., "Fine. Suit yourself. Taxi line is that way. It's about to rain though. Are you sure?"

"Oh, I'm quite sure." I yell, briskly walking out of the parking garage toward the taxi line downstairs. Thankfully, there is an elevator.

I approach the line, which now has several people waiting. The morning air has turned cold. A sudden breeze sends a chill through my bones. Thankfully, I still have my sweater tied around my waist. As I pull it over my head, I look up to see the dark clouds hovering over my head. In an instant, the sky opens, and the clouds release the fastest and hardest rain I've ever felt in my entire life. At the same time an attendant appears.

"Miss, that's a rather large bag. You might have to wait for the larger taxi to come. Would you like an umbrella? I have a spare."

"Yes, thank you that's very nice." I open the umbrella, although it's really too late. My perfectly curled blonde hair is dripping wet, my clothes are soaking wet and my first day in Dublin is turning out to be miserable. I want to march right back into the airport and buy a ticket back home to Chicago. Sleeping in a bed is not worth all of this.

But I don't.

This trip is to prove to myself I can do things. Travel alone. Not rely on a man for help. I've already proven I do not need a specific arrogant Irish man to drive me places.

The larger taxi arrives. I get in and tell the driver the Bed and Breakfast address. I feel a sense of relief when we arrive. I simply can't wait to shower and get out of my travel clothes. There's a cute pub next door as well which I have to say works out perfectly. Besides a shower and sleep, I think I need a pint or a rather full glass of wine.

I pay the taxi driver and give him an extra tip (due to the massive and heavy suitcase) and head into the B&B. It is actually quite charming. There's a cozy fire lit for this wretched rainy day. I always picture B&Bs to be full of gawdy floral wallpaper, cats and old lady chairs, but this is rather modern and chic.

A young lady, perhaps in her late teens or twenties, greets me as I drag my suitcase through the door. "Hello, you must be Dabney. We've been looking forward to your arrival! Let me help you." She's petite, with light brown hair and warm brown eyes. She has the typical, Irish cream complexion with adorable dimples when she smiles.

"Oh, thank you. This suitcase is terribly heavy. I hope I don't have too many stairs to drag it up."

"We have you on the second floor but not to worry. I'll call on Donno to help you with it. Just give me a second. He's helping out next door at the pub."

The young lady, who I now see is named Maura according to her name tag, takes out her phone and calls the Donno gentleman who arrives in a matter of minutes.

The large, dark haired man, possibly in his thirties greets the young lady and says, "All right, Maura?"

"All right, Donno. Is it busy over there?"

"Not too bad. Heard anything about Cassie yet?" The tattooed gentleman asks as he picks up my suitcase like it weighs ten pounds.

My ears perk up at the mention of Cassie's name. I've been wondering what big emergency would have caused her to leave me to be taken care of by that ghastly Simon. Ghastly Simon sent her company down a star in my mental rating book.

"No news yet. Sam texted and said she's got a ways to go yet. But things are processing nicely. Are the boys doing okay over there? Send them back if you need to. Anyways, Donno, if you could take Dabney to her room upstairs in 202, I'd appreciate it. She's come a long way from America."

"Is that right? Welcome. Place is full of Americans now. You should feel right at home," I watch Donno easily carry my suitcase up the steep stairs. Sometimes men are good to have around, I suppose.

"We've got a pub next door that serves food and drinks. Good family establishment. My brother-in- law Deacon and his wife, Tilda, who's American, run it. I help them out when I can. I mostly do fix-it stuff around the two buildings and help out in the kitchen."

I pull out a few Euros to hand him as a tip and settle

in once he leaves. The room is mostly white, with crispy linens on the bed and light, flowy curtains. The day is so grey and gloomy, but the bright clean room is comforting. While part of me wants to lay right down on the bed and sleep, I know the best thing to do is stay up. So, I head to the bathroom to take a quick shower. It is small, but it has an adorable claw foot tub and shower, pedestal sink and a basket of organic toiletries for guests. I decide to take a relaxing soak and plan my next move.

A pint it is.

But first I need to call my mother and text Ruby to let them know I'm alive.

"Yes Mom, there's a proper lock on the door." I say, on speakerphone while I try to scrape the last tiny bit of my Crème de La Mer moisturizer from the small travel container. It's all I have left of the extravagant beauty cream. I still have the La Prairie caviar eye cream though. I gently tap it under my eye then take the jade beauty roller and glide it across my lush skin. I push the last of the Chanel travel foundation out of the small packet I received from my previous order of makeup from my favorite department store. I won't be ordering any more Chanel anything in the future. In fact, my latest foundation is the highest end I could possibly find from my local drugstore. Budgeting is the worst and something my mother always tried to teach me—to little avail, I'm afraid.

"I know you think I'm paranoid, Dabney but you're a pretty young woman in a new country all alone. I wasn't happy about you taking this trip. It's important to make sure all safety precautions are made."

"I know Mom. Don't worry. If anyone barges in, I'll knock them down with your ginormous suitcase. Do you know how much trouble that's caused me?" I say, still fuming about my encounter with Simon.

"But you got everything you needed in it didn't you? You sound just like your father. He has complained for twenty years about that suitcase, but he never needed to make a late-night trip to the corner store on our vacations because I always packed well."

"Sure, Mom. You're right." I bid my mom adieu and finish getting ready. I suddenly feel anxious about the idea of going to a pub by myself. Where do I sit? At the bar? At a table? Who am I going to talk to? Do I watch the television there? Or stare at my phone? If I stare at my phone, nobody will want to talk to me. But do I want anyone to talk to me?

Okay, Dabney, enough internal conversation. Get yourself together. It's just a pint.

Once I finish putting on my makeup, I put on my favorite comfy chic outfit. Dark blue skinny jeans that have been tailored to the perfect length. My go-to pima cotton tee shirt with my cashmere long cardigan. It has finally stopped raining so I put on a pair of pointy toe Louboutin flats that I purchased a month before I knew I would be poor.

I send Ruby a quick *hello I've made it text* and head downstairs for the pub.

"Hi, Maura. Just popping over for a drink. Any recommendations?"

Maura looks up from watering one of the many fresh flowers in the foyer. "When in doubt, go for a Guinness.

My cousin, Deacon calls it 'The Nectar of the Gods.'"

I've always been more of a sweet cocktail kind of gal, but when in Ireland...

I walk next door to the pub. It is exactly what I hoped for. Cozy, warm, and friendly feeling. I am not sure how one can feel friendliness in an instant but that's what it feels like here. Seeing that the bar has open seating, I opt for a seat up there.

A kind looking lady smiles at me and approaches me with a menu. She has long dark brown hair that's been put up in a top knot and is wearing a flowy black blouse.

"Hello! I'm Tilda. What can I get you? Is this your first time to The Stag's Leap?"

"Yes. In fact, I just got off the plane a while ago." I suddenly yawn. I realize I'm beginning to feel the effects of jet lag.

Tilda looks at me with excitement. "You're American! You must be Cassie's guest!"

"Yes, but I haven't had a chance to meet her." I did meet a rude man named Simon, however.

"Ah, well, she went into labor almost a month early. Her husband Sam took her to the hospital not long before you were supposed to land, I'm afraid." Tilda's expression suddenly went from jubilation to worry at the conversation regarding Cassie.

"Oh, I hope everything is ok. I have very little experience with labor and children. I have a niece and nephew but my sister in law had no complications. Both her kids were scheduled C-Sections, to fit her Type A personality of wanting everything planned ahead of time. I don't know Cassie, but I do hope her delivery is free of any major drama."

"I'm sure it will be. Cassie is amazing. She was also very excited for your arrival and feels terrible about leaving you. I hope Simon took good care of you?" Her kind brown eyes show that this Simon character knows how to take good care of anybody.

I twitch slightly. "You know Simon?"

"Well, yes he's our chef here. Deacon just hired him a few months ago, but he's been great. It was hard for Donno to keep up with everything, and to be honest, he wasn't excited to cook full time. Deacon wanted to make the kitchen a bit more upscale, so we hired Simon."

Not wanting to see Simon for the rest of my trip, I now realize I've stepped into his place of work, where he's likely working this very moment.

The thought makes me nauseous. "Tilda, could I have a pint of Guinness please?"

"How rude of me. All this talking and I forgot to get your order. Of course. Good choice. Deacon calls Guinness the Nectar—"

"—Of the Gods." I smile and say in unison. Yes, I've heard." I hope this Guinness cures me of the internal dread.

I take a sip, cough and realize I must not be one of the gods.

Tilda pours a drink for a customer and then comes back over to me. She whispers, "I don't like it either. Can I get you a glass of wine or something?"

I breathe a huge sigh of relief and say, "Yes please. A glass of chardonnay please. Could I also get an order of fries? I mean, chips? Wait, no I change my mind. I'll have a salad with an oil and vinegar dressing please."

"Coming right up." Tilda pops back to the kitchen to put in my order and I wonder if my salad will be made by my new Irish foe, Simon.

The pub is lively. Tilda brings me my wine. I sip it, and people watch. There is a mixture of young and old at The Stag's Leap. Most are watching the football match, but some are chatting with one another. How wonderful, I think, to have a local place to come and socialize. Sure, we have restaurants and bars in Chicago. The feel of this pub is different though.

"Here is your salad, Miss…Oh, it's you." Simon says, standing in front of my plate of roughage.

"Oh, hello. I don't know why you're surprised to see me. It shouldn't be too shocking that I'm able to get my own taxi and manage to walk next door for food. Or is it?"

"No, it's not. Listen, I'm sorry for what happened earlier. I really am."

"It's fine. I managed." I take a bite of my salad and look back at my phone that has been alerting me of messages and I'm not happy to see who they're from. All the while, Simon continues to stand there.

"Can I buy you a drink? As an apology?"

"I have one, thanks." I say as my phone continues to beep with text messages. "Why can't men get the message??" I blurt out loud.

"Sorry, I won't bother you anymore." Simon says in an offended tone.

"Huh? No, I'm sorry. I wasn't referring to you. It's my ex-husband. He keeps texting me."

As I send a quick *Go away* text to Jack, a man from the kitchen shouts for Simon to come back and help.

"Be there in a minute, Deacon!" He shouts back.

"So, I'd like to apologize properly. I'm off tomorrow. Why don't you let me show you around the city a bit? I know Cassie had plans for you and your trip must seem a bit scattered now."

Feeling rebellious, I say, "Yes." My mother, who is overly cautious about everything would not approve of me going out with a perfect stranger in a city I don't know. Granted, I don't know Cassie or Tilda either, but they seem to trust Simon so maybe I can too.

Pleased with my acceptance, Simon releases the first smile I've seen since I met him and says, "Right then. I'll meet you at the B&B at 11:00 tomorrow morning. That should give you enough time to get ready."

"Because you think I'm high maintenance?" I ask, waving my jingly bracelet wrist in the air.

"No. I assume you'll be tired from travels." Simon smiles again at me and says, "See you in the morning," and heads back into the kitchen.

Great, Dabney. You've already broken your promise of not associating with any handsome, Irish men. Oh well, he must be better than the handsome American who I just told to get lost.

CHAPTER 4

After work, Simon walked home to his flat. A flat that still needed unpacking. It had been nearly three months since he moved into his new place and nothing really motivated him to make it a home. Not until he met the extremely aggravating, blonde American woman, that is. Why on earth she was a motivating factor was beyond him. It wasn't like he was inviting her over anytime soon. He didn't even know how long she was staying. Judging by the size of her suitcase though, perhaps a year.

That damn suitcase and his stupid small car.

He could have at least helped her get a taxi to accommodate her. But he just left in a huff like the petulant child she was acting like as well. It wasn't his fault his car was too small. But it wasn't hers either.

Simon reached for and opened up the box of photos and letters stored in his nightstand. He kept the letters from her to remind him of happier days. Even on her worst days, she wrote him a letter every single day. Not wanting to go down memory lane, he closed the box back up.

"Maybe another day, my dear."

Simon instead, fed his cat her nightly dinner and heated up some food he brought back from the pub. Deacon and Tilda didn't pry into his personal life, but they knew enough to always make sure he had dinner to bring home and an open invitation to their house whenever he wanted.

While he ate, Simon thought about the ad he had seen in the local paper a few months ago for a head chef at the small pub. He jumped at the chance. Deacon was impressed with his credentials and hired him immediately. He also directed him to a nice lady who had an available flat close to The Stag's Leap. He enjoyed his new job from the start. Now that he had met Dabney, he was even happier he jumped at the job change.

"Well, Cleo, what should I take Miss Dabney tomorrow? No idea? I have a few, but I'm not sure she'll take to them. What's that? We should give her the benefit of the doubt. Not sure I agree Cleo, but very well. A walking tour around the south side of the city it is."

The next morning, Simon packed his backpack with waters and sandwiches for his tour of the city and went along to meet Dabney at her B&B.

"Bye, Cleo. Wish me luck."

CHAPTER 5

Although extremely tired, I had trouble falling asleep last night. It is no surprise when I wake up at 10:30 in the morning, completely unready for my outing with Simon.

"Dammit, how did I set my alarm for 10:30 p.m.?" I fuss aloud to myself while jumping into a cold shower since I don't have time for the old plumbing to warm up enough to take a hot one. Once I am done and wrapped up in the white fluffy towel, I look out the window on my way to the closet. The weather looks clear and dry today, although it is still somewhat chilly.

I opt for some jeans, a light blue sweater that I think brings out the blue in my eyes and slim white t-shirt underneath. I'm not sure what kind of walking we will be doing so I will go with my white leather sneakers. Super comfy and still quite stylish. No time for a blowout, but I do have time for dry shampoo that I am extremely thankful that I packed. Ponytail it is! I quickly do my layers of moisturizer and makeup, feeling a bit sad that I don't have time for my relaxing two-minute morning facial massage. It's very important for my blood flow and collagen regeneration.

Once I am dressed, I add my gold hoop earrings and silver and gold bracelets to finish off my look. I give myself a once over in the full-length mirror and I head downstairs to meet Simon in the lobby. He is there, right on time. Although I am still not sure what to make of his personality, he is rather handsome. His light, milky complexion against his dark hair and blue eyes are quite dreamy, I hope he doesn't notice me taking him all in.

"Hi, I hope it didn't keep you waiting long. I didn't set my alarm right." I say, somewhat embarrassed at my ineptness.

"I just got here. Are you ready?"

"Yep. But I'd love a cup of coffee." I look around to see if there might be a coffee machine somewhere.

"Maura?" Simon calls to the back to the kitchen.

"Hi, what's up?" Maura asks coming out from the kitchen.

"Is there any chance Dabney can get a coffee to-go?"

I can't help but notice Simon is looking rather handsome today, much to my dismay. He seems to prefer wearing black or similar neutral colors and it works on him.

"Sure! Do you like cream and sugar, Dabney?"

"Yes, please, Maura."

Maura brings out a piping hot cup of coffee for me in a to-go cup.

"Here you go, Dabney. Have fun today!" She says before heading back into the kitchen.

"So, Simon, what do you have planned for us?" I really have no expectations since I've barely read my travel book about Dublin. I remember seeing some museums to explore and of course the Guinness factory, but that's about it.

"Well, it's a nice day for the time being so I thought we could do a walk around South Dublin. There's quite a bit to see. I packed a couple of my famous chicken fillet rolls to eat as we walk."

"It seems you have everything covered. Too bad I'm don't eat carbs. Ever." I say coolly.

Simon's face drops to a whiter shade of pale.

"You don't...eat carbs?" He asks, putting his bag down on the floor, looking defeated.

I laugh quietly, "No. I just wanted to see you squirm for a second or two." I do refrain from eating carbs as much as possible because they make me bloated. But in all honesty, I love bread and sometimes it hard to say no.

"Nice." He says with a smile. "Shall we carry on then? I've parked outside. We can drive to the neighborhood and then walk around."

"I'd like to take some photos for my Instagram page. I'm starting a new topic about travel and trying new things."

"Instagram, huh? What have you tried so far?" The way Simon says 'Instagram' I don't get the feeling he terribly impressed by my social media presence.

"I came here all by myself for a start. I don't do things by myself."

Simon scrunches up his face in disbelief and asks, "Ever? Like a movie or dinner?"

"Nope. Once I had a date cancel on me when I was

waiting for him at the movie theater and I walked out. I had paid for my ticket and everything." The date was actually the guy I was kind of seeing before I met Jack. That same night, I went out with some friends and met Jack and the rest is history. I never called the other guy again. I wonder what he's up to now.

"I can't believe you don't do anything by yourself. That's ridiculous. I do things by myself all the time."

Oh well good for you. It's probably because nobody likes to hang out with you, I think but don't say.

"It's not ridiculous! I just know what I like and what I don't like. There's nothing wrong with not liking to be alone. I like people and most people like me. You've been an exception."

Simon smirks as he turns the corner into the city. "I didn't say I don't like you."

"Well you weren't very welcoming yesterday." I look outside the car window at the city scenery. It's mostly a lot of old stone buildings and mature trees. It has turned rather grey since I got dressed this morning, but I find it rather cozy. I hope it doesn't rain, however. I didn't dress for rain and I assume Simon didn't pack an umbrella with his famous sandwiches.

Simon does a deep sigh and says, "I apologized for that. You caught me on a bad day."

"I suppose we can start over today. You can show me you aren't a complete and utter asshole." I say, wondering why I agreed to this, whatever this is.

Without missing a beat, Simon replies, "And you can show me you aren't an entitled American."

"Are you kidding me? How is not wanting to dump my entire suitcase into a stranger's car entitled?"

"You're the one that brought a gigantic, oversized suitcase that couldn't fit into a typical car. You just expect everything to fit like the world revolves around you."

At this point, my blood is boiling, and I am ready to hop out of the car and take a taxi back to my room.

"Well for someone that says he doesn't NOT like me you sure have some strong and negative opinions about me!"

Calmy he says, "I'm just saying that's how you came across on first impression. I was an asshole according to you, yet you're still here." Simon parks the car and turns off the ignition.

We get out of the car and walk towards a park that is absolutely breathtaking. Everything is so green, just like a person would imagine an Irish park to be.

"This is St. Stephen's Green. It's been around since the 1600s. When I was having a difficult time in my life, I'd come to this park every day to walk and contemplate for a short while."

"Even on rainy days?" I ask, looking up at the grey Dublin sky.

"Ah, rainy days are the best days to walk and contemplate."

I look at Simon and try to figure him out. He's acted like such a jerk off and on in the last 24 hours that I've known him, yet I find him intriguing. I don't ask him what his difficult time was because, to be honest, I don't think he'd tell me.

We walk near a bench in the lovely, green park. Simon puts his backpack on the bench and pulls out two sandwiches wrapped in parchment paper.

"These are my specialty so if you don't like it don't tell me. I can't handle the rejection." Simon hands me a sandwich. I'm starving since I didn't eat anything but salad for dinner and I missed breakfast this morning, so I unwrap it quickly and take a bite.

"Oh my god. This is delicious, Simon." It's a simple sandwich of breaded chicken-fillet, cheese, lettuce, and mayonnaise on a baguette but it's possibly one of the best sandwiches I've ever had.

"Yeah? Thanks. I'm glad you like it. You can't come to Ireland and not have a chicken-fillet roll."

"You know, this is only my second day here, but I feel so relaxed. I love Chicago, but I don't have the same feeling there."

Simon tosses his sandwich trash in the nearby bin and says, "So, while you're relaxing here in Dublin, what's your plan? Sightseeing?"

"I don't really have a plan. Maybe to find myself again? Truth be told, I'm escaping my life."

I cringe as I say it out loud. It was such a spur of the moment decision to pack up and take this trip. I think Ruby was actually in shock that I went through with it. My mother, on the other hand, was more concerned and convinced that I would get myself lost in the airport and never get to my destination.

"Well this is a good place to do it. C'mon. Let's walk."

We head down Grafton Street and approach the famed Trinity College. I marvel at the beauty and history as we walk down the cobblestone pathways.

"I can't imagine attending a school that once had Oscar Wilde and Jonathan Swift as students. It's simply incredible."

I stop to take pictures with my iPhone for my Instagram page. I feel so fortunate to be here.

"Will you take a picture of me? I'd like to try and get one by these gigantic doors."

Simon laughs, as I hand him my phone.

"Do you think it's stupid? Instagramming?"

"I don't follow social media. I think it's a waste of time. Who would care what I'm thinking or doing? I don't care what they're doing."

"Well, I've gotten some decent paychecks from being a social media influencer, you know. You would be surprised how much people want to know what you're doing...It's not stupid, if that's what you're thinking."

"Ah, Dabney. Don't assume to know what I'm thinking. Now, go stand by your door so you can get your winning photo."

I touch up my makeup and head over. In a quick shot, before more people walk in and out, Simon gets my photo, and we make our way down another street.

Simon points ahead and asks, "How about we pop in here for a whiskey?"

We approach a bar called the Dingle Whiskey Bar. It's dark and brooding and I love it. Although I hate to tell

Simon I don't love whiskey.

"Do you think they have chardonnay?" I ask, in a whisper.

"It's a whiskey bar. Why would they want to serve you wine? Don't worry. I'll find you something, that doesn't set your throat on fire...too much anyway."

We find a table and Simon goes to the bar to order us our whiskey. I'm terrified. I hate whiskey and the mere thought of having to drink it makes my stomach churn.

"Here we are. Now, this isn't one of your sorority parties. You sip it." Simon says, handing me my glass.

"The last time I had whiskey, I had broken into my dad's liquor cabinet when he and my mom were away for the weekend. I was in high school and my friends dared me to have a shot. I had several and thought I was going to die. I never touched it again."

"Just sip it." He says again with a slight smile.

"Okay." I take a deep breath and sip the Irish whiskey. As soon as it makes its way down my throat I cough. But surprisingly, it isn't anything like my dad's liquor cabinet elixir. It's much smoother. I feel instantly calmer and my fear of it has dissipated. My warm and tingly feelings elude me however, when I get another text from my ex-husband.

"Not bad, eh?" Simon takes another sip of his whiskey. I'm not drunk but after several more sips, my inhibitions are slowly leaving me, and I want to tell him how beautiful his blue eyes are. They're like swimming in the blue sea.

"Dammit! Why doesn't he leave me alone?" I say in

frustration. The lawyer in Jack definitely shows up when he doesn't get his way. Obviously trying to ignore him does not help.

"Someone bothering you, Dabney?" Simon asks, trying to get a glimpse of my phone. I decide now is as good a time as any to enlighten my new friend.

"You know how I said I was trying to escape my life? A few weeks ago- I signed my divorce papers, thus making me a twenty something year old divorced woman. I couldn't even make it work until I was 30!"

I take a large sip of my drink and try to bury my head in my sweater.

"Is that who's texting you? Your ex? Does he want you back?"

"Yes and no. He's already living with the woman he cheated on me with, so I don't think he wants me back. But for some reason, he can't seem to accept that I've moved on and don't need him."

"Does he know you're here?"

"No, I haven't responded to any of his texts. Well, except to tell him to get lost."

"Hmm. Maybe you should call him." While I am somewhat curious as to why he keeps bothering me, I have absolutely no interest in calling Jack. I don't want to see his text messages, let alone hear his voice.

"Why? Won't that make it worse? I don't understand why he's texting me at this time of day anyway! It's like 7:00 in the morning there."

"Shall I talk to him?" He asks casually.

I laugh at mere idea. "Are you serious? He'd be flabber-gasted! Maybe we should." I look at Simon, like a mischievous child. Simon orders another round of drinks while I get the courage to dial Jack's number.

Simon takes my phone as it rings. Jack presumably answers as Simon, who is laying on his thickest Irish accent says, "Good morning! Is this Jack? This is Simon, Dabney's mate from Ireland." Simon pauses for what I assume is Jack's response. "Yes, that right. She didn't tell you. She's in Dublin visiting me and she wants you to know she's having a wonderful time...No, we didn't meet on the internet. We've been friends for longer than you, mate. She'd like you to know she's just fine and she doesn't want to talk to you. Something about you being a total wanker. Take care, mate."

And with that, he ends the call and hands me back my phone. I'm dumbfounded and utterly elated.

I take a large sip of my drink. "Simon. That made my day."

"Right, lets finish up your drink then. I have another place I want to take you. But we'll need to drive I think."

We finish up our drinks. I'm feeling a bit tipsy at this point because I rarely drink hard alcohol. We finish walking through Trinity College and St. Stephen's Green and find Simon's car. Only to see it has a flat tire.

"Aw bugger me. I just replaced this tire. I must have run over something on the way here."

"Do you have a spare in the trunk."

"I did. But I changed it and never replaced it. Shit."

Simon makes some calls while I post some images of

Dublin to my page. In about twenty minutes, a man pulls up, brings a new tire, and helps Simon change it. Then, like a fairy godmother, the man leaves as though he were never there.

"Who was that? He came and left quickly." I say, admiring the hint of perspiration and tire grease appearing on Simon's face.

"He was my uncle. He's not really a man of many words so I didn't introduce you. I'm sorry, is that rude?"

"Well it's not like we're dating or anything, so I guess not." I suddenly get a jolt of panic as I wonder if this was, is, indeed, a date.

Simon's eyes drop for a moment. "No, I don't suppose we are, err, dating." He looks up at the ever-graying sky. "We should probably head back. It looks like it's about to rain."

The conversation back to my B&B is quiet. I can't help but wonder if it's because of my comment about us dating. I mean, we barely know each other. But did I offend him?

Simon pulls up to the B & B and looks at me. "This is where we depart Miss Dabney. I have some errands to run. I also owe my uncle a pint when he's done with Sunday dinner. Will you be around the pub tomorrow?"

"I probably will. Truth be told, I'm a bit lost. Cassie had plans for me all set up, but with her having the baby early everything seems to be a mess."

"Sounds like this might be a good opportunity for you to find yourself doing things you wouldn't normally do."

The thought of doing any of that makes me feel sick.

Going to the pub yesterday by myself was a huge step in the new Dabney process.

"Yeah, maybe so." I say, trying to sound as upbeat as possible.

As I get out of the car Simon smiles at me, seemingly seeing right through my bravado and says, "I'll see you soon, Dabney."

"See ya, Simon. Oh, and Simon, thanks for today. It was nice."

Simon waves bye and rushes to his car in the cool, afternoon rain.

"Hi Dabney, did you have a nice visit of Dublin?" Maura asks, as I walk through the door.

"Yes, it was lovely."

"Simon showed you a good time, then? He must like you. He's never that friendly with guests that I've seen." Maura walks past me casually, bringing one of the guests her cup of tea with some cookies.

I don't bother telling her that it's highly doubtful that he likes me in that way. We've only just met, and he's still been rather critical of my ways. But we did have a nice day.

Not wanting to be subject to more comments about me and Simon, I order a pizza for my dinner and hide away in my room. The B&B offers a light meal for guests, but I feel like being alone for the night. I have planning to do. I also really need to apply a detoxifying mask to help my skin get back to normal from my travels.

First things first. What do I want to see?

I go into my email and see the list of things Cassie suggests. In Dublin, she suggests a tour of Trinity College and The Book of Kells. She also suggests the Guinness Storehouse. Apparently, there is a magnificent view once the tour is over. That might be interesting, but it would entail me drinking more Guinness. Maybe it's an acquired taste. Cassie also recommends the National Gallery Museum. That might be something I can do alone without feeling lonesome and looking like a loser.

So, it's settled. Tomorrow I will figure out how to get to the National Gallery Museum and have a solitary adventure.

CHAPTER 6

    This morning I wake up much earlier than yesterday. My room offers a Nespresso machine and creamers so the first thing I do is make a coffee. Since I'm on my own schedule, I decide to start my morning casually. I usually have a cup of coffee with Ruby in the mornings and I can't help but miss having a friend to chat with while I sip my coffee. I look out the window, seeing people walk, some alone looking perfectly content. Not feeing content myself, I decide to finish getting somewhat presentable for breakfast downstairs. Now, I would normally never go out in public without doing my makeup. Hair can be put in a messy top knot and look trendy —but no makeup? Absolutely not. However, this trip is about doing things I wouldn't normally do. So, after I apply my serum, moisturizer, perform the quick two-minute facial massage and then do a light layer of foundation, I simply add a few layers of mascara, tinted lip gloss to my lips and a light tinted cream for my cheeks. After a quiet coffee, I slip on some cozy joggers and a hoodie then head downstairs for some breakfast.

    When I get down to the bright and white dining room, I see a man rushing around, delivering coffee and looking somewhat frazzled. I feel kind of bad for him because he appears to be the only one around and judging by the number of tables that are occupied, the B&B must be full.

I take a seat near the big window as the frazzled man approaches me in a rush. He looks to be in his late forties with wavy brown hair. He is wearing dark jeans, and a polo shirt with black and white Adidas Sambas.

"Hi! I'm Sam. Can I get you a coffee or cappuccino?" he asks, briskly.

"Oh, a cappuccino would be awesome. Thank you."

"Coming right up. I'm sorry if it takes a bit longer than expected. Maura is off today and normally it's Cassie and I, but she just had the baby and is occupied at the moment."

I realize this is the second half of the B&B owners.

"Sam! And Cassie! Of course! I'm Dabney! Most of my emails have been with Cassie about my trip from Chicago. She's doing well then? And the baby?"

"Yes, thank you for asking. The baby was almost a few weeks premature, but he is doing great. He just needs to stay at the hospital for a couple more days. I'm so sorry about the lack of communication. I've asked Maura to give you a discount on your accommodations." Sam seems to relax a bit as we talk about his family.

"No problem. These things happen. Can I help you out at all? I have some barista experience from working as a coffee girl at a country club for a summer." I suddenly feel a shock of surprise at my offer, but I feel so bad for Sam.

"Oh, I can't ask you to do that." Sam says, looking terrified at the room of people. "Okay, I hate to say this, but I think I might need some help. If you could make cappuccinos, I can bring them to the tables. I need five."

"You got it. I'm happy to help."

I get up from my table, realizing that I look rather schleppy. I mean I'm not even wearing foundation with my blush, but I decide to ignore that fact since I'm doing something nice. I walk over to the coffee machine and start brewing my espresso and steaming my milk.

Five cappuccinos turn into ten, which then turns into me helping Sam with the omelet bar. Before I know it, breakfast is over and it's 10:00.

Sam picks up the last of the dishes off the table and says, "Dabney, I can't thank you enough. There is no way I could have gotten through this morning without your help."

"It was actually kind of fun. But I must ask, do you have help for later? Don't you put out food in the evening?"

"We do but it's mostly light snacks. Happy hour type of things. I put out some wine and socialize with guests. I will miss Cassie though. She's good at chatting with everyone. Finding out where they're from and why they chose Ireland...that type of thing."

"I can help out. I'm doing a museum tour today but that's all I have planned." To be honest, I'm lucky I have that planned. I've never not known what to do so much in my entire life and I've only been here a few days.

"Are you serious? I don't know. It seems inappropriate for me to ask my guest to work. I can see my stars dwindling by the minute." Sam smiles wryly as he picks up empty plates and cups. I am literally following him around the room.

"What?! No way. I wouldn't do that. Tell you what. I'll work for complimentary cappuccinos." I have decided to add my star back since Simon has redeemed himself a bit and Cassie and Sam were in a dire emergency.

Sam mulls it over for a second, knowing that he doesn't really have any options, unless he wants a repeat of this morning. "Okay, if you could be back here at 4:00, I should have everything prepped. I just need help with drinks and picking up dishes...and maybe conversation."

"I'll be here. And I promise I'll look a little less disheveled." Sam laughs with me as he makes his way back to his office, which makes me wonder how disheveled I look since he didn't disagree.

I turn to go back upstairs when Simon walks through the door, his arms full of baguettes. I'm sweaty from working, and to be honest, there's a good chance I haven't even brushed my teeth yet. I was not anticipating actual conversation with people, especially Simon, who I've had on my mind for an unusual amount of time.

His face lights up as he says, "Good morning, Dabney."

"Good morning." I mumble, wanting to hide my face inside my hoodie.

"How are you this morning?" Simon appears to be rather cheerful first thing in the morning.

"I'm good. I've been helping Sam, which is why I look like this." I say, feeling the need to explain my appearance.

"Look like what?" He asks, confused. How can he be

confused? I'm in worn out Birkenstocks, grey joggers and a very old but super comfy hoodie. Thank god I'm wearing a bra.

"Like this obviously." Is he blind? I look like I just crawled out of bed.

He gives me what feels like an extra-long once over and I feel a pang in my stomach. I really wish he was less attractive because, when I am around him, I feel less focused and a lot more confused.

"I don't see anything wrong with the way you look. Anyway, I'm here to drop these off for Sam. Is here around?"

"Um, yes I think I saw him go back to his office. I'm going to be back here later to help him with happy hour."

"Are you? That's nice. Maybe I'll see you later then. I work until 8:00. You should come to the pub and hang out. Deacon sings tonight. It'll be a good night."

"Okay, maybe you'll see me there." I make my way back upstairs before Simon sees me blush three shades of pink.

I want to call Ruby but it's still way too early. I imagine this is what it feels like when you go to the movies alone and something good happens and there's no one to laugh with. That is why I don't go to the movies alone.

After a warm shower, I take the time to blow dry my hair and softly curl it. Then, I put on my layers of serum, moisturizer, eye serum, eye cream, primer, foundation, blush, translucent loose powder and finally a finishing spray. It's a lot of work, but it's worth it. I want to look nice for this evening when I help Sam. I resolve that is the only reason I want to look nice. There is no other reason. At all.

I pick out an outfit to wear to the museum. It's cold today so I find some comfy black leggings, my go to pointy flats, a loose soft pink blouse and my favorite striped blazer. I also wrap my grey pashmina around my neck for this chilly Irish spring day.

I make my way downstairs and try to find a rideshare. After a few minutes of failure, Sam sees me and orders a taxi.

"Rideshare isn't quite as reliable here for some reason. So, you're headed to the museum today, huh?"

"Yes. I'm embracing my loneliness and exploring options that are partial to be being alone." I say proudly.

"Hey! That's great! Good for you. My friend Tilda did something like that a couple years ago. She had her late aunt's bucket list to do. I didn't really know her before the list, but I think it did wonders for her confidence. You should talk to her about it. She's an owner of The Stag's Leap next door."

"I've met Tilda! She's super nice." I say, recalling her giving me complimentary wine to replace my not so favorable Guinness.

"Have you met Deacon? He's Tilda's husband. Deacon sings in the pub a lot of nights when he's not in the kitchen helping out Simon. That guy is an amazing singer and songwriter." I can see Sam is in awe of Deacon as he refills the display of local sites and entertainment ideas with brochures.

"Simon mentioned Deacon might be singing tonight and that I should stop by." I try to hide my interest in the name Simon. I am not sure why I feel a hint of excitement at the mention of his name.

"You definitely should. I'd pop in, but I've been going to the hospital at night with the boys when I'm done here." Sam explains that he is also stepfather to Cassie's two twin boys, Jameson and Michael from her previous marriage.

"Oh, Sam. I'm sorry that you can't be with Cassie more."

"It's okay. We're making it work. You, stepping in tonight to help is a huge weight off my shoulders, trust me. For now, though, it looks like you need to be on your way. Your taxi is here."

Feeling excited about my new task tonight, I get into my taxi destined for The National Gallery museum.

While in the taxi, I use my phone to try to order my ticket, but it seems they don't require one. In fact, the museum is free. It is donation based. Not wanting to be a free loader, I immediately make a donation to the museum online and then tuck my phone safely back in my bag. I have a terrible habit of losing my cell phone in public transportation.

When we arrive, I go up the grand stairs to look for the European art. Early Renaissance art has always been my favorite. I walk through the Grand Gallery to find a myriad of intricate and elaborate paintings along with a cheeky statue of a nude man. I wonder how long it took for the paintings to be completed. How long must have those people stood for their portrait? I just push a button on my cell phone and we're done. The result is far less beautiful and meaningful, though.

I find a seat in one of the rooms and sit for a while to marvel. I don't think I've been to a museum in years. Perhaps since college. I wish I had remembered how relaxing they are. Chicago has many museums I should have visited during my divorce drama.

After about 15 minutes, I get up and finish my tour of the museum, and head back out the busy Irish streets. Realizing I'm in the same area I was yesterday with Simon, I decide to pop into a few of the shops I saw to find some gifts for Ruby and my mom. A quick search shows me a Starbucks not far from where I'm exploring, so I must get a coffee and then Instagram it. I caption it, "An Irish coffee…"

I see a cute baby shop and decide to get a gift for Sam and Cassie's baby. Hmm. Was it a girl or a boy? Crap. Sam mentioned it but I can't remember. Next on my list of self-improvement items, be a better listener. I tend to get distracted by my own thoughts and don't always hear everything in I'm supposed to when people talk to me.

Perhaps a plushie will suffice. Baby boys or girls play with them. Right? Is a plushie safe for a baby? I decide to follow my instinct and pick out the sweet looking elephant sitting on the full shelf of equally adorable plushies.

Once I leave the pretty shop, I have absolutely no idea what to do next. I decide to call Ruby and check in on how she is. I miss her and wish she could have come on this trip with me. I think Ruby would love all of the history in the city.

"Hi Dabney! How's Ireland??" Ruby says, huffing and puffing. "Sorry if it's windy, I'm walking to work."

"Ireland is wonderful. I miss you though."

"Well of course you do. I'm equally as wonderful. I thought you might be mad at me though." Ruby says, nervously.

"Why would I be mad at you?"

"Because I may have accidentally, kind of, told your ex-husband where you are?" I can feel Ruby squirm through the phone. I feel stupid that I didn't even consider where he would have gotten the information from.

"Ruby! It was you?"

"Yes. He called me when I was off-guard and extremely busy. I fussed at him to leave you alone and then said you had gone to Dublin to escape him and everything else for a while. I am so sorry. It's none of his business and I know you want to keep your life private from him now."

"Well, he has been bothering me, but I think I've taken care of him for a while. I had my new friend Simon talk to him." I look down at my manicured fingers that are sans a wedding ring now.

I hear Ruby groan and then she says, "Simon? Have you met a man, Dabney?"

"Yes, but it's not like that. He took me on a little tour yesterday but that's it. There's nothing going on." I'm using my most serious voice. It's true, nothing has happened.

"Dabney, is he handsome?" Ruby asks, probably already knowing the answer.

"Well, I guess it depends on what you find handsome. Some people don't like tall, dark and Irish."

"And handsome?" She asks again.

"Yes, he's handsome. But don't worry, Ruby. He's rather grumpy," I say, recalling some of my first impressions of Simon.

"Oh wonderful. So, he's handsome and brooding. Dabney, please don't fall for this guy. You're only there for a couple of weeks and you're supposed to be finding yourself...alone."

"I am, Ruby. I just spent the whole day by myself. I won't be getting drunk and kissing any guys on this trip. Trust me."

"Dabney, I've seen you kiss guys and be perfectly sober. There was a reason we called you The Kissing Bandit in college. Listen, I'm not trying to 'Mom' you. I just want you to make the most of this trip. I know you aren't over what happened with Jack."

Feeling a punch to the gut with my tough love from Ruby, I am instantly sent back to the time I knew my marriage was over.

"Ruby, I've got this. I'm having a great time and I've met some nice people. None of whom want to sleep with me." I am fairly certain Simon, especially, thinks I am a silly American who likes to dress nice and post pictures on social media.

"Okay, Dabney. I trust you'll make good choices. I have to go now. I have a class starting soon. I need to prep."

"Okay bye, Ruby," I say, missing my best friend more than ever.

"Bye, Dabney."

On the taxi ride home I think about what Ruby said. Why doesn't she think I'll make good choices? I know she said she trusted me, but Ruby does the mom thing sometimes. Like, she knows I won't, but she wants to plant the seed in my head that she believes in me regardless.

Dammit. I'll prove to her that I can have a completely platonic relationship with a handsome Irish fella. I don't have to jump into the bed with the first hot guy I see since my divorce. Besides, he *is* rather grumpy. Maybe he doesn't have any feelings like that for me. Maybe he was just being nice. He did seem to feel guilty about our first meeting at the airport though.

Lost in deep thoughts about my love life, the short taxi ride back to the B&B was even quicker. After I tip the cabbie I go to my room and catch up on social media. I also freshen up a bit. Walking around the city all day wreaks havoc on a lady's makeup and hair.

Once I determine I'm happy hour ready I leave to go downstairs to meet up with Sam. Looking anxious, he meets me as he walks out of his office.

"Hi Dabney! You're still sure you can help me out? It's from 4:00-6:00 but some guests stay and hang out. Don't feel obligated to stay though. I usually leave what's left of the wine out for them. We have a couple guests that I believe are still out on day trips, but the others will probably come down. Come with me and I'll show you where it all is."

We walk back to a small kitchen that has a refrigerator, sink, dishwasher, and prep area. Sam hands me a few bottles of wine and we walk back out to the front.

"Do we have a limit?" I ask, having never served a free wine bar before. Well, unless you include Sorority parties. But they never have limits and at some point, we all just served ourselves, repeatedly.

"No, not really. I just let the guests enjoy themselves. Simon should be here soon with the food. I've had him put out a cheese and meat tray along with some other things. He likes to try out new recipes on the B&B guests sometimes. They're always delicious."

"Oh! I almost forgot!" I pick up the gift bag that I left on by the front desk. "I got a little something for your baby."

"Dabney, that's so nice. You didn't have to do that, but it's appreciated. I'll bring it tonight when I go see Cassie and the baby. So, do you have any questions? If guests have any issues with anything beyond food and drinks, just let them know to email me. I think everyone knows what's been going on around here. Do you want me to stay until Simon gets here?"

"No, no. Go be with your family. I've got this. Don't worry."

Sam gives me his phone number and rushes out, excited no doubt to see his wife and baby.

I open a bottle of each red and white wine and set out the glasses that Sam showed me. Typically there are specific glasses for each type of wine, but I don't think this is the kind of crowd that worry about that. It's a very casual and comfortable atmosphere.

Some guests start to come downstairs and I greet them as though I'm an actual employee. I remember some of them from this morning's crazy breakfast. I suddenly hope they don't think I'm an employee because I looked like a total slacker this morning with my messy hair and comfy Birkenstocks.

I can tell they're enjoying the wine but are looking around for food. Where is Simon? If I don't feed them soon, they're going to be dancing on the tables.

Almost on cue, he rushes through the back door that attaches to the pub with multiple trays of food.

"Dabney? Where's Sam?" Simon asks, as he places the platters of food on the counter. I must say, he's looking good tonight. He has a tight black short sleeve t-shirt on with slim, dark jeans and boots.

"Oh, he left to go see Cassie and the baby. Remember, I'm helping out tonight." I say proudly.

"Ah, right. I forgot. Okay, well I have the meat and cheese tray, some cheese puffs and some bacon-wrapped dates."

"It all looks delicious." I suddenly remember I forgot to eat lunch when I was at the museum. I am starving.

"All right then, I'll leave you to it. I've got to get back to work. Will I see you later?"

"I think you might."

Simon smiles. "I'll see you later then...maybe."

I respond, nonchalantly. "Maybe."

"Miss, are the hors d'oeuvres ready to be distributed?" A rather hungry looking lady asks. She's on her second glass of red wine so I understand. The bacon smells quite good as well.

"Yes, ma'am! They just got here. Sorry, I'm helping out tonight so I'm trying to figure everything out."

"Uh huh." She says, filling her plate with prosciutto and cheese. I'm still starving, and the bacon wrapped figs look divine, but I don't think it's very professional of me to eat while I'm serving drinks. Maybe I can sneak one when nobody is looking.

I notice a group of bicyclists coming in from the street. It's a rather large group of mostly tall, skinny men, with a couple women.

"Oh! We almost missed happy hour! We'll be down soon. Save some food for us. We're famished!" A skinny, muscular looking man says as the group races upstairs.

"Miss, can I have a glass of white wine please?" There's a lot of older people here. Not that there's anything wrong with that, but they definitely expect their service prompt and orderly.

"Absolutely! Coming right up!"

The group of senior citizens get their drinks and food and gather over by the fire. Even though it's April, the fire is cozy and warm.

I sit down to chat with a small group of people when we all hear a shriek from a room upstairs.

The sound shrieks, stops and then shrieks again. Suddenly, the skinny, muscular looking man runs down in his bathrobe.

"Miss! Can you come up please?!" He is soaking wet and hysterical.

The group of senior citizens look at me in horror. Possibly because there is a naked man under that robe or possibly because they expect me to solve his problem.

"Miss! Please there's a water emergency! The shower won't shut off or turn now and it's dumping out scalding hot water!"

In a panic I just say, "Sure!" However, I have no idea what I'm supposed to do. I don't want the other guests to think Sam has left them in some amateur's care, so I put on my most mature tone of voice and get to work, following him up the stairs.

"Right. First things first. Are you hurt, sir?" I think in an emergency you're supposed to ask that.

"No, no I'm ok. But this bloody water won't shut off. I can't get it to turn or anything. Can you fix it?"

Apparently, this guest assumes that when one is in charge of a B&B happy hour, they also possess plumber skills. Again, not wanting to let on that I have zero plumbing skills, I carry on with the mature tone and say, "Okay. It appears the knob is stuck. Let's just try and... yes, err, hmm. Okay it's quite stuck, isn't it?"

The man looks at me dumbfounded and simply says, "Yes."

I remembered once in the apartment Jack and I lived in, the shower wouldn't adjust correctly. Jack had to pull off the knob and manually do it. I took about three cold showers before he actually fixed it. Jack is one of those men who refuse to call the Super if it can be fixed easily by him. So annoying.

So, I pull off the loose knob and try to see if I can adjust it. No use. It needs some pliers or something.

"I'm going downstairs to get a tool. I'll be back."

I run downstairs and into the office, hoping to find some sort of toolbox. Lo and behold, in the corner of the office= is a metal tray with several different tool-like devices. I grab the pliers and another tool that looks like something a plumber might carry, according to television and movies.

I run back upstairs, knock on the door because I most definitely do not want to catch that naked towel man getting dressed. Thankfully, he had done so already.

"Right, I'm going to see if I can get it to work with my tools. You may want to stay back. I wouldn't want you to get wet."

"Um, okay. Do you mind if I go ahead and meet my friends, downstairs for happy hour?"

Feeling relieved that I can tend to this plumbing disaster without prying eyes I tell him he should absolutely go downstairs and enjoy himself. "You'll just have to pour your own wine, I'm afraid."

The man disappears and I head to the bathroom shower to tackle the water disaster. The water is so hot that the bathroom has turned into a sauna. Any chance that my loosely curled blonde locks and freshly applied makeup will survive this is slim to none.

I get the plumber tool thing and start twisting. I continue to twist until the steaming hot water slowly cools down and the rush of water becomes a slow stream. Finally, I get the water to stop. I did it. I actually did it!

I grab a towel and wipe down the bathroom floor. Between the heat and water pressure, water has collected all over the black and white tile floor. This guest will definitely need more towels because I've used most of them to wipe up the slippery floor.

As I reach for one last towel, my foot does something out of the ordinary and I end up falling on the floor, right on my back. Every part of my body is wet.

"Shit!" I say out loud. I'm not hurt, just a little sore, but I look a mess.

I pick up the towels and tools and head downstairs where I see the entire room looking at me. I must look awful, I think, as I limp my way towards them.

"Did you fix it?" One of the senior citizen ladies asks in hopeful anticipation.

"Yes, I think I did!" I say, proudly.

"Ooh, well done, miss!" Another senior citizen lady says.

The room lights up with a cheer at my announcement. Especially the skinny muscular man.

"I'll have to bring you up some towels though, sir. I used them all to clean up the mess."

"Not to worry, young lady. I'm just glad you were able to fix it! Now sit, sit! Have a glass of wine! I'm Trevor by the way. We're part of a bicycling group that travels around the British Isles." Trevor brings me my glass of wine and I sit and relax for a little while.

I feel such a sense of relief, but I am exhausted. I'll

have to tell Sam what happened however, I don't want to bother him while he's with his family. To be honest, I'm still shocked I was able to fix it-- although I won't let anyone know about that.

I get up to gather the empty wine bottles and clean up a bit. I'm so tired. I can't imagine getting dressed up again to go next door to the pub. But I told Simon I would maybe come, which was totally a yes.

I find some clean towels for Trevor and say goodbye to the rest of the group.

"Are you going next door later? We hear it's a good time." Carole, the obvious leader of senior citizen group asks. She is short with light blonde hair that she keeps short and lightly curled. She is wearing a tie-dyed t-shirt and sparkly sneakers that light up when she walks. Her overall ensemble is bold and totally adorable.

"Oh, I don't know." I say casually. Truth be told, I do want to go but I'm not sure it's a smart idea. I have Ruby's voice of reason trailing in and out of my head.

Carole, who is having none of my silliness says, "Nonsense! You must! We're going over in a bit. That cute chef who brought the food over earlier said they have a singer later. We love live music."

Suddenly, I realize that the senior citizen group is much livelier than I am; which means I need to have a cup of coffee in my room and get some energy back. I can't have a bunch of seventy-year old's showing me up.

I go to my room, turn on the Nespresso machine and make myself a cup of coffee. I put on some lively music and take a quick shower, even though I practically got one in Trevor's bathroom.

"Now, what to wear, Dabney." I pick through my things and settle on a pair of dark skinny jeans, my big oversized black turtleneck sweater, and black flats. I dry my hair a bit and put it up in a bun. I take a makeup cleanser wipe to my face and redo my makeup with a quick layer of tinted moisturizer, blush, and mascara. Very low maintenance, I think, proudly to myself. I finish off my look with a pair of dangly Kendra Scott pink earrings. I grab my small black Chanel bag and head out the door. I want to curse it because it was a gift from Jack, but I can't...because it's Chanel.

I arrive at The Stag's Leap around 8:00. It's a lively crowd for a Monday night. When I walk in, Carole and her group spot me immediately and direct me to come sit with them.

"Oh love, you came at the right time. The singer lad is about to come and sing."

"Ah, yes, Deacon. I think he's the owner of the pub and he's married to Tilda." I look around for Tilda but don't see her.

"Yes, I've met them." Paulina, one of the other ladies says. "She has four kids. Can you believe it? Twins to boot!" Paulina is taller and slimmer than Carole. She has dark shoulder length hair with wispy bangs and glasses. She is also wearing a tie-dyed t-shirt, but Paulina has opted for ankle boots instead of the sparkly sneakers. The two ladies are quite the pair.

Then Carole says, "Ooph, that's too many kids for my taste. I had two and was done with that! She must be so tired. Do you have any kids, Dabney?"

"Me? No. I'm not married." I look at my lonely ring

finger that once boasted a 2 karat Cartier diamond. It seems so odd not to wear it anymore. Jack insisted I keep it, but I have no desire to wear it. In fact, I should probably sell it and makes some extra money.

"I saw you talking to that cute chef earlier. He's quite the looker." Carole adds. These ladies are insufferable. I am enjoying their company though.

"Speak of the devil, here he comes. Look natural ladies." Paulina says as she adjusts her top.

"So, you made it Dabney. Nice to see you ladies." Simon is wearing some black pants and a snug t-shirt that hugs his slim but muscular frame.

"Dabney was the hero of the night. Fixing poor Trevor's faulty shower. She came down a right mess but now look how lovely she looks. Right Paulina?" Carole mentions loud enough for Simon to hear.

"Yes, Carole. She looks lovely." Paulina says in agreement.

"Can I get you ladies a drink?" Simon asks.

"We're fine, love. But Dabney needs something," Carole says as she pats me on the shoulder.

Simon smiles back and says, "I think I know what she'd like. I'll be back. Save me a spot eh, ladies?"

Paulina takes a sip of her drink and says, "Ooh Dabney, I think he likes you. If I was much, much younger, I'd give it a shot. He's lovely."

"I'm only here for two weeks! I can't get involved with anyone. But yes, you're right. He is rather lovely to look at, isn't he?" I whisper to the ladies.

Simon returns with a glass of whiskey and a glass of white wine.

"Here you go. I thought you could start off with a whiskey and chase it down with some wine."

"Simon, are you trying to get me drunk?" I ask with a laugh. I can honestly say, I have never paired whiskey with wine. Something new to try while I'm here I suppose.

"Absolutely not. Just trying to get you cultured."

"With wine and whiskey?"

"Yes. Now shall I sit down and enjoy our upcoming musical event with you?"

I scoot over towards Carole and let Simon sit. I feel like he is dangerously close to me. Every once in a while, his thigh hits mine and my hearts skips a couple of rapid beats. I am brought back to the night I met Jack and take another sip of my whiskey, followed by another gulp of wine.

"So, tell me more about this heroic thing you did tonight?" He asks, trying to talk over the loud voices in the pub.

"It was nothing really. Our guest had a shower that wouldn't stop shooting out scalding hot water. I found a wrench and some pliers in Sam and Cassie's office to fix it. Anyone would have done the same."

Simon looks at me and says, "Wow. Quite impressive! Good for you, Dabney."

I start to say something when Deacon comes out with his guitar. His microphone is already set up and he sits down in front of it. The once lively room has quieted to a whisper.

"Good evening, everybody. I've written a new song that I'd like to share." Deacon picks up his guitar and begins. He honestly sounds like someone I would hear on the radio.

I whisper to Simon, "He's wonderful. How is he not famous?"

"I haven't a clue. The guy writes and sings his own songs. It's just a matter of time, I reckon." Simon relaxes a bit, and we have a brief period of time where we stare at each other.

I want to grab his face and give it a huge kiss. But I don't...because I'm not The Kissing Bandit anymore. I am a respectable woman who knows how to behave herself around hot Irish men.

In fact, in a moment of clarity I say, "Will you excuse me for a minute? I need to find the ladies room."

The moment passes and he scoots out the bench to let me out.

I find the restroom and call Ruby immediately. I have finished my whiskey and wine and now must make an emergency call for back up.

Ruby answers the phone and says, "Hi Dabney! Two calls in one day. What's up?"

"Ruby, I want to kiss him."

"What?! No. You can't."

"But you don't understand. Do you know how long it's been since anyone kissed me? A long time Ruby. A loooooong time." Not really seeing the signs, Jack and I went months without kissing beyond a hello and goodbye before I saw why. He was too busy passionately kissing someone else.

Ruby sighs and says, "I do understand, Dabney. That's why I'm telling you no. You want me to tell you no, right?"

I think about her question for a second or two. Ruby is my voice of reason. The adult in our friendship. She is who I should listen to. Not my lady parts that are burning like cherries jubilee.

"Yes, that's why I called you."

"Okay. But Dabney, I can't always tell you what to do. You have to listen to your own heart and instincts. What do they say?"

"They say I want to kiss this guy and have a major make out session."

Ruby laughs. "Well, Dabney. Maybe you should listen. But you're leaving soon. If you fall for this guy it's going to be hard to come back to Chicago alone."

"Aaaaaargh! You're right! Thanks, Ruby. I gotta go. I'm missing Deacon's show. I wish you were here."

"Me too. Okay, go have fun and let me know what happens. No judgement. Love you, girl!"

"Love you, too. Bye."

I go to the bar to order another glass of wine when Simon approaches me.

"I've gotta head back to the kitchen for some orders since Deacon is out. I'll talk to you later tonight?" He asks, invading my personal space just a smidge. It's like he can feel the heat I'm giving off and is drawn to it.

"Oh, yes, I'll be here for a bit longer. I forgot to ask Sam if he needs help tomorrow so I might be getting up early. I'll um, probably leave soon."

Simon goes back to the kitchen and find my seat again with the Carole, Paulina and the other ladies.

"He watched for you the entire time you were gone, I will have you know." Carole says, giving me a nudge.

"He did?" I ask, coyly.

"Yes! Are you gonna snog or not?" Paulina asks, taking a gulp of her Guinness.

I laugh. "I'm not sure if we'll, er, snog or not. You'll be the first ones to know, though, if we do!"

I decide this is my opportunity to do the responsible thing. I bid my new friends, adieu, tell them I'll see them in morning and walk back over to my room next door... alone.

CHAPTER 7

Simon finishes his last order of the night and casually comes out to the dining room. No sign of Dabney anywhere. He wasn't in the kitchen that long, but it appears it was just long enough.

"Where is Dabney?" He asks the table of ladies with whom they were both sitting with.

The lady named Carole says, "She had to leave, love. Something about having to get up early in the morning. You'll see her again though, I imagine."

The ladies smile as though they are in on the secret. What the secret is, Simon has not quite figured out yet.

"Can I get you ladies another drink?" He asks, pointing to the bar.

"Oh no love, we have a long tour tomorrow. We're going to kiss The Blarney Stone." Paulina says.

"And we have some planning to do. We're only here another two days. That's not a lot of time to help you and Dabney find your way together."

Simon laughs nervously. "Me and Dabney? Oh ladies, I think that's a far-off plan. She's only here for a couple weeks."

If only the ladies knew. He wanted to hold her close

and kiss her every single second they sat next to each other earlier. But that would be irresponsible for him and for her. When he looked into Dabney's beautiful blue eyes, he wondered if she was thinking the same thing.

"A lot can happen in a couple of weeks." Carole says.

"Yes, when it's meant to be, it's meant to be." Paulina says.

"What are you two, a couple of cupids?"

"Perhaps. We've been around for a long time. We know when the arrow has struck, and it has struck for you two." Paulina says adamantly.

Simon picks up the group of ladies' empty glasses and says, "Well, who am I to argue with Cupid's messengers?" He smiles at them. "But for tonight, I guess I will say goodnight and see what tomorrow brings me."

The ladies smile back in agreement.

Simon goes back to the kitchen with the empty glasses and helps clean-up for the night to get his mind off the charming, American, Dabney.

CHAPTER 8

I wake up first thing in the morning to shower and get myself ready for the day. The morning sun is shining through the narrow window in my room and I can't help but feel its cheer. I have determined that a make out session with Simon is ridiculous. I should focus my energy on more important things--like helping poor Sam and Cassie.

When I go downstairs, in more professional attire, slim black pants, a pink t-shirt and grey wool blazer along with my signature bracelets, I see Maura is there. Perhaps Sam doesn't need my help after all?

"Good morning, Dabney! Can I get you a coffee?" Maura asks cheerily.

"Good morning, Maura. Yes, please."

I accept the warm cup of coffee and pour my cream in slowly. Maybe this will be a quiet morning after all.

"Sam said you helped out yesterday morning and last night. That's so nice! I felt terrible taking an extra day off, but I had a test to take to get into some classes at school. I'm starting university next fall and I've been taking some prep classes."

Sam walks in, looking exhausted and says, "Good morning, Dabney."

"Good morning, Sam. How are Cassie and the baby?"

The exhaustion fades from Sam's face at the sound of Cassie's name.

"They are doing spectacular. In fact, they're coming home today! Doctor says everyone is perfectly healthy."

"That's wonderful news!"

"I've been so busy with taking care of the B&B, Jameson and Michael and then going to the hospital life has been a bit chaotic. It'll be nice to have Cassie and Miles at home."

"I wanted to broach something with you. I'm here alone and don't really have any specific plans, why I don't I help you out while I'm here?" I have only been here for a few days, but my loneliness makes me restless.

"What? No. I couldn't expect you to work on your vacation."

"I know it's a bit odd. But to be honest, Sam, working here yesterday was the best time I've had in a while. I haven't been very productive back home and while I agree, it is my vacation, I'd like to have a bit of purpose."

"What was the point of coming to Ireland if you didn't want to explore the country?"

"It isn't that I don't want to see Ireland, I do and will. But my main purpose of coming here was to get away from my life in Chicago. Have some 'me' time. I just got divorced, you see... and well, I'm still a bit lost."

"I'd have to run it past Cassie since she's my partner in all of this. How about you take the day off and go on the Blarney Stone trip today? I have a bus chartered for the group and I'm sure there's room for one more. I'll talk to

Cassie and let you know."

"Sure. I'd like to see the Blarney Stone and spend more time with Carole and Paulina. I'm sure this adventure will not disappoint."

"Great! It's settled. You have some fun today and then tomorrow we can find you some work to do. I'm sure Cassie won't mind but I'll text you to let you know for sure. Oh, and thanks again for your plumbing work last night. I have a plumber coming today to check out what happened, but it sounds like you saved the day."

"I hope that's okay. I just didn't want to bother you. Something similar happened back home so I thought I'd try."

"Well it worked! Now, why don't you enjoy some breakfast and let us serve you?"

Sam leaves to attend the omelet bar and I suddenly feel like he might think I am crazy. I mean, who would go on vacation and then ask for a job? I nibble on my croissant and strawberries alone at the table when Carole and Paulina approach me.

"Good morning, love!" Carole and Paulina are both wearing bejeweled t-shirts with matching track suits and sneakers. They take a seat with me with their breakfast.

"Good morning, ladies," I reply, feeling distracted by my thoughts.

"Ooh why the sour face?" Carole asks.

"Oh, sorry. Just have some things on my mind."

Carole takes a bite of her whole wheat toast and says, "It wouldn't be that handsome, Simon would it? He seemed quite disappointed you snuck out last night?"

"Really?" I'm surprised. "Actually, no but it's nothing really. Good news though, I'm going on your trip to the Blarney Stone today!"

Paulina claps her hands together and exclaims, "That's wonderful! This our first time going to the Blarney Stone. Actually, would you believe it's our first visit to Ireland, at all?"

Carole adds, "It's true. We're both widows of men who never liked to travel outside of Yorkshire. Now that they've passed on, we try to make a trip somewhere new at least a couple times a year."

"Oh, I'm so sorry your husbands have passed away. But I'm happy you're here now. You've added some much-needed company for me." I say, finishing my coffee. I look at the two ladies and wonder if Ruby and I will have a friendship like theirs when we get older.

"And you for us. The other ladies we've been with are a separate group. From the Isle of Man, I believe. They're a bit more subdued." Paulina says taking a bite of her omelet.

"Which means they don't like to drink like us." Carole whispers. Those ladies are not far from our table.

"Are they going on the trip today as well?" I whisper back.

"Oh no. They can't make it up castle stairs and bend back to kiss the stone. I think they're going to do a walk around Dublin. See the Book of Kells, that sort of day."

"Well, I need to get back to my room and change my shoes if I'm going to make it on time for the bus departure. I hear it takes a few hours to get there."

"Okay, love. We'll see you in a bit."

Carole and Paulina finish their toast and eggs and chit chat while I go back to my room to finish getting ready for my day trip. I am assuming wedge sandals are not appropriate for walking around an Irish castle in Spring.

I change into some black Lululemon yoga pants, my hot pink Nikes, a long sleeve t-shirt and a light pink workout jacket with a hood in case it rains. I'm opting for comfort today. A three plus hour bus ride will also include me catching up on some Netflix shows. I should be reading my book, but I'm too distracted today for some reason.

I pack some snacks and a water in my bag and go downstairs to catch the tour bus. Carole and Paulina are downstairs already waiting for it.

"Maura, I don't suppose I could get a to-go coffee for the road?" I ask Maura as she delivers a drink to one of the guests.

"Of course!" Maura says, happily. She's so sweet and cheery all the time. Even at 8:00 in the morning. Her long ponytail bounces away without a care in the world. Oh, to be a teenager again.

Maura brings me a coffee in a to-go cup, and I walk over to meet up with Carole and Paulina.

"So apparently, this bus will be full of guests from other B&B's." Carole says, suspiciously.

"Ooh, I hope the seats won't be full when we get on. I don't like sharing seats with strangers." Paulina says.

"I agree. Remember when we took that train ride

from Florence to Livorno last year? There was not a seat in sight. We had to stand half of the trip. Can you imagine, Dabney? Two old ladies having to stand on a busy train from Florence all the way to the coast? That'll teach us for catching a last-minute train I suppose." Carole says, obviously still upset from reliving her Italian adventure.

"Don't worry, ladies. I won't let you stand on the bus. There should be plenty of seating."

The bus arrives and thankfully, for Carole and Paulina's sake, there is plenty of seating. I find a seat to myself and settle in with a good Netflix show to binge for a few hours.

Once we get to the castle, I find myself getting excited. This is my first tour of a real castle. When we get closer though, I see that castle is only partially intact. The grounds are beautiful and green, however. It is just what one would expect Ireland to look like. I zip up my jacket to protect myself from the cool breeze that hits me. I show the attendant my ticket, which I booked on my phone this morning and enter.

I decide to explore the gardens first. Although there is a crowd of people, I find walking through the green peaceful and relaxing. I see it's a hike to the Blarney Stone, where there is already a line forming. I am still on the fence as to whether I want to kiss it. How many people have kissed it? Is it full of germs? Does it get wiped with an anti-bacterial wipe? Will it really give me the 'gift of the gab' as I'm told?

All these thoughts spin through my head as I see I have a text message from none other than my ex-husband,

Jack.

Who is Simon? And why are you in Ireland?

None of your business. Leave me alone. You divorced me, remember?

I never heard you mention any friend from Ireland.

Again, it's none of your business. Now kindly fuck off. I'm about to kiss The Blarney Stone.

Dabney, I'm concerned.

I am too. A lot of people have kissed it already.

Dabney.

Jack, please go away.

I am so mad that Jack has ruined my peace and tranquility. I march over to the tower to climb the stairs for the stone. There's a long line, but I wait patiently until it is finally my turn.

The stone, which is built into the wall of the actual castle, is not terribly easy to get to for a smooch. It's rather high up and as I watch people hang off the castle in order to receive their 'gift of the gab' I find myself rethinking my decision. Unfortunately, it's quickly my turn. Not wanting to be shown up by the tour group of senior citizens that succeeded before me, I reluctantly lay down on my back while a man holds my torso. I lean back while holding on to the iron rods for safety and give the magical stone a kiss. The man helps me up and that's it. I did it. I kissed The Blarney Stone! I try not to think of the millions of people who have kissed the stone prior to me as I walk over to the nearby café for a coffee.

While I sit and relax, I get a call from an unknown

number that looks to be a local Irish number. I go ahead and answer since I'm curious who would be calling me.

"Hi! Is this Dabney?" The female voice on the other end asks me.

"Yes?" I say, confused.

"It's Cassie from the B&B. First off, I want to apologize for having my baby early. It was not in the plan."

"Oh, my goodness, Cassie. Please don't apologize. I've had a wonderful time so far."

"I appreciate your helping out. Is this something you really want to do though? On your vacation?" She asks, perplexed and probably trying to figure out if I'm crazy or not.

"Cassie, I just feel bad that you guys don't have any extra help. I think it would be fun actually."

"If you could help out with breakfast that would be amazing. It would be nice to have Sam at home in the early morning. At least while we get a routine down. The boys are still in school, so I need someone to help me make sure they get out the door on time."

"If you need me to stay more than a couple weeks, I'm happy to adjust my flight plans. I don't really have much in Chicago to go back to right now."

"Ah, it sounds like there's a story there."

"Yes, but not one I'd bore you with. You're far too busy." Plus I really don't feel like going into the long story of my dysfunctional love life.

"Well maybe another day. How about this? I comp your stay at the B&B for work?"

"That seems like a lot."

"Don't worry about it. Listen, how about you meet me at the pub around 7:00? I'll take a little break from home and we'll go over the specifics. I'm coming home this afternoon from the hospital."

"Cassie are you sure?? You just had a baby a few days ago!"

"This is my third kid. We live right around the corner and I wouldn't mind some socialization actually."

"Okay, I'll meet you tonight at The Stag's Leap at 7:00!"

I finish my phone call as Carole and Paulina come in. They've been doing a tour of the gardens and are exhausted.

"I have good news, ladies. I don't know the specifics, but I'm going to be an employee of the B&B!"

"But you're on your holiday! Why would you want to work?" Carole looks perplexed which is not unexpected. I myself am a bit shocked at my offer.

"I came here to find myself. Do things I wouldn't normally do."

"So, making coffee and omelets is out of the ordinary for you?" Paulina surmises.

"Kind of, yes. I need to do something. Helping out strangers appeals to me. I've been too wrapped up in my own problems. It feels good to be doing something useful for someone else."

"Plus, it will keep you working close by 'you know who.'" Carole adds, practically swooning.

"Carole, I'm not concerned with 'you know who.' If you must know, I've decided to be single. Indefinitely."

Carole and Paulina look at one another and laugh.

"My recent annoying text messages from my ex-husband has led me to believe that all men are nuts. I'm better off alone and I don't need them."

"My dear, we were both married for many, many years. Our husbands drove us crazy. But I will speak for Paulina when I say, we needed them every day and they needed us. You just haven't found the right man."

On the long ride back to Dublin, I contemplate Carole's advice. I am sure they mean well and perhaps they are correct. Jack was not the right man. However, even if I stay a bit longer than two weeks, there is no way I can figure out if Simon is the right one either. Not that I'm looking for him to be. Do I deserve a fling? A simple excuse to have fun with zero strings attached?

These are all questions that I might need to figure out if Carole and Paulina are correct...if Simon does have his eyes on me as much as I've had mine on him.

CHAPTER 9

I head over to the Stag's Leap at 7:00 to meet up with Cassie. I don't know what she looks like, but when I walk in, I see a lady I haven't seen before at the bar, talking to Tilda. The pub is quieter than previous nights, so I assume it might be Cassie.

"Hi Tilda, may I have a glass of Chardonnay, please?"

"Hi Dabney, of course you may. Cassie, this is Dabney." Tilda points to the auburn-haired lady sitting next to me.

"Just the lady I've been waiting for! Nice to meet you, Dabney." Cassie has light makeup on, her hair pulled back in short ponytail. She actually looks great for just having a baby four days ago. She's wearing a long sundress with cute sneakers and a light denim jacket. Hmm. Did I pack my denim jacket?

I reach out my hand to shake hers and say, "It's nice to finally meet you too, Cassie."

"So, what do you do in Chicago?" Cassie asks, sipping her soda.

"I used to work in advertising. But when I got married, I quit my job and focused on, um, Instagram full time."

Cassie ignores the Instagram profession and asks,

"Your husband didn't come with you on this trip?"

"No. We're divorced now," I say quietly.

"Ah, I see. So, you came here on your own for a vacation from it all, eh?" Cassie says this in an understanding tone.

"Yes, kind of. Things have kind of been up in the air since my separation and divorce."

"Say no more. If you're up for it, I'm sure there a lot of things we could find for you to do around the B&B and The Stag's Leap. Sam said you did quite well the night you helped out so he could visit Miles and me at the hospital."

"It was fun. I got to know some of the other guests—"

"And showed off your plumbing skills!" Cassie adds.

"Skills I didn't know I had until then." In fact, I don't think I have ever even used a wrench before.

Cassie smiles as though she has come up with a brilliant idea, "What do you think about working between the B&B and pub? We could find you odd jobs to do around here and in return, you can stay at the B&B and we'll pay you some on the side?"

Tilda returns and says, "Sorry to intrude on your conversation, but we could definitely use some help around here. Doris, our assistant manager, has been out with back surgery and I've had to work extra hours. If you can start now, I could use someone to help with the kitchen duties. Simon has been back there alone, and the dishes are piling up."

"You mean, right now?" I ask, surprised.

"I'm sorry. You don't have to. I don't want you to think we're taking advantage." Tilda looks somewhat frazzled as she fills another pint of beer for a patron.

Cassie laughs and says as her phone beeps with text messages. "Well, that's my request to get back home. Have fun, Dabney!" Cassie waves goodbye to me and makes her quick exit.

I look at my outfit, casual yes, but I don't want to get grease or dirty water on my clothes...

Tilda grabs a clean apron and says, "I have a long apron for you. If you want to. Only if you want to though."

I take the apron and say, "Show me what you need help with."

Tilda walks me back to the kitchen where Simon is finishing up a plate of food for a customer.

Not looking up he says, "Tilda, I'm nearly done with Table 5. I can start on the dishes so you can go home on time tonight."

"No need, Simon. I got you some help."

Simon looks up, shocked at seeing me. "Dabney?!"

I finish tying up my apron and say, "The one and only. I'm here to help!" I mean, how hard can it be?

"To help do what, exactly?" He asks.

Tilda points to the pile of dishes and says, "Wash dishes, silly."

Simon, still confused by the situation says, "There really isn't that much to do."

"Simon, we're almost out of glasses. And we haven't caught up on the big pots and pans from dinner." Tilda points to the empty racks of glasses at the bar.

"Tilda, if you can just show me what to do, I'll get started on it all," I offer.

"You just have to load the dishes and run it through the dishwasher. These big pots will have to be soaked and scrubbed though. If you could do the glasses first, I'd really appreciate it."

"Absolutely. I'll get right on it."

Once I worked in a restaurant for a week, until I deemed it way too much work. My younger self would be so shocked to see me rolling my sleeves up and getting down to work like this—almost as shocked as Simon.

"What is going on? Why are you working here? I thought you were on your holiday. All you've done since you've been here is work."

"That's not true. I kissed The Blarney Stone today. I've walked around a museum. And don't forget, I did a nice little walk around with you."

"You thought our walk was nice?" Simon asks, with a coy smile.

I choose to ignore him. "Besides, it sounds like Cassie and Tilda need some help. They seem nice and I feel like giving my fellow Americans a helping hand. Do you have a problem with that?"

"Nope. Here's another pan. It's quite greasy, so watch out for your manicure."

I look around the shelves, "Don't you have gloves? For washing greasy dishes?" I say, finding nothing but scrubbers and soap.

"Nope. Here's another one."

There goes my manicure.

"I can't help but feel like you're enjoying this a bit too much, Simon."

"Sorry, but it is rather humorous. You just don't come across as someone who would work in a kitchen."

"Why not?" I can't help but feel somewhat offended by his remark.

"I don't know. You're just a bit, prim and perfect. Your perfect manicure, the way your hair is always put together even when you're trying to look messy. Your shoes always match whatever you're wearing. And I have never seen anyone wear so much jewelry. But it seems to work for you, I guess."

"Hmm. You make a lot of accurate points. It seems someone has been paying attention to me. But what you don't know is I'm more than the layers of jewelry and a perfect manicure." I dip my hands in the water to wash the dirty pot and make a mental note to ask Maura where the closest nail salon is the next time I see her.

Simon gets closer to me, to hand another pan to me, I presume. "I guess I'm seeing that." He's so close to me that we can't help but gaze into each other's eyes. Until I break the spell by opening a steamy dishwasher that has just finished washing Tilda's glasses.

"I'll take those out to Tilda. You can work on the pots and pans." Simon says as he takes the tray of piping hot, clean glasses out front to the bar.

Simon comes back and finishes up some small order of fries and then comes over to help with what I have left.

"You finished everything?" He says, surprised.

"Yes, I have washed pots and pans before, you know." To be honest, I rarely wash dishes, opting to use to the modern technology of dishwashers.

Looking flustered he says, "I'm sure you have. I just thought there were a lot of pots and pans to wash, that's all. Thank you…for your help."

"You're welcome. I'm happy to be here. What else is there to do?" I ask, looking around the kitchen.

"Well I think we just need to sweep the front." Simon hands me the broom with a smile, his dimples on full display.

I sweep up the kitchen and front room, while Simon cleans the grill and what is left of the kitchen mess.

"I can mop if you want to get back to your room," Simon offers as he continues scrubbing the grill.

"It's ok. I can finish helping you. Unless you want to be rid of me."

"No, it's nice to have you here," he says, not looking at me.

"Really?"

"Yes, Dabney." Simon says, carrying on with his cleaning duties.

"So, Simon, are you from around here? I feel like you know a lot about me, and I know nothing of you."

"There's not much to say. Yes, I'm from around here, sort of. Here, why don't you grab this bucket, and you can mop out front and I'll mop in here. Then we can finish even quicker."

Simon fills up a bucket and scoots it over my way with a mop. Realizing I'm not going to crack this nut tonight, I follow through with his request and go out to the front to mop.

Tilda, who has probably listened to all of this says, "Give him some time. He's not much of a talker. But I'll tell you this, anytime we've needed anything from him, he has obliged without a scowl." She smiles and continues, "He has taken to you quite quickly I must say."

"So, Tilda, how did you end up here?"

"I met an Irish guy back home and fell in love. So, watch out!" She laughs as she brings the last of the dirty glasses back to the kitchen to wash up.

I finish mopping up the front room and behind the bar. It's fine to do this once in a while, but I think I might hate to do this kind of work forever. Cleaning up dirty messes. Yuck.

I walk into the now spotless kitchen to let Simon know I'm all finished and slide all the way across the floor.

"Hey! Caught ya!" He smiles and grabs my arm to hold me up. "Probably not the best shoes for working in a kitchen."

"But I didn't know I'd be working in a kitchen tonight." I never would have worn my Louboutin flats had I known I would be working in a pub kitchen, trust me. I decided last minute to change out of my travelling clothes into something new to meet Cassie, which may not have been the best idea after all.

"Tonight, has been full of surprises," Simon remarks thoughtfully.

"Yes, it has."

He's still holding me and staring into my eyes when he says, "Would you like me to walk you back to the B&B? It's rather late?"

"You mean, the B&B that's next door?" I ask, not really understanding why Simon would want to walk me to the next building over.

"Yes," he says simply, not breaking eye contact with me.

"Yes, I think I do. Would you like to come to my room for a drink?" I say, not even thinking twice about my request.

"Yes, I think I would."

Aw shit. I just invited him to my room?! Is he going to think that means sex? Furthermore, did I pick up my dirty clothes earlier? Do I have hair and makeup products all over the place? Also, what do I think I'm serving him? All I have in my room is a bottle of spring water from my trip to Blarney Castle!

"Let me just let Tilda know we're finished. Do you want to me buy a bottle before we go?"

"Um, okay? I know I invited you over to hang out, but I have nothing to serve you except water and a half-eaten bag of Walkers crisps."

"No worries. I'll get something from Tilda."

He comes back with a bottle of, of course, whiskey and a couple of plastic cups.

"I figured you didn't have cups either."

"No, you're right."

We walk out and go next door to the B&B. I punch in the code to enter and we quietly walk up the dimly lit stairway.

"Wait." I say realizing I am about the let him into my most intimate space, well, almost. "Can you give me a minute to pick up a few things?" I whisper when we get to my room.

"Sure." He whispers back.

I rush into the room, pick up my change of clothes, underwear and bra from earlier in the day and throw them in my suitcase. I move the makeup bag into the bathroom and throw away some tissues.

"God!" I say to myself quietly, "I'm kind of a slob." Then I take a quick peek in the mirror, smooth my messy hair as much as I can, and let in my handsome new friend.

"Come in." I say, casually.

"Nice room. I've never seen what they look like from the inside before. Shall I sit here?" Simon finds a spot on the small settee next to my bed.

He pours a cup of whiskey for me and for himself. God, I hate drinking whiskey. Why am I even doing it? Oh well, yes. Because of the hot guy who poured it for me.

Simon hands me a cup and says, "So, Dabney, have you heard anymore from the ex-husband of yours?"

"Yes, actually. Today! I thought he might have gotten the hint when you spoke to him, but I think it made it worse unfortunately. I believe he thinks I'm unstable now."

"Sorry. I thought it would help."

"It's fine. He needs to stop harassing me though. I don't know why he keeps contacting me." I wince as I take a drink of the strong elixir that Simon seems to adore.

"Maybe you should ask him. Maybe he's still in love with you."

"Oh no. He's already got his new lady living with him. He's quite over me." At least I thought so?

"Fair enough. But that still doesn't explain why he's so worried about you."

"I don't know. Let's talk about you Simon. Simon...I don't know your last name."

"O'Connell. It's O'Connell."

"So, Simon O'Connell. I know nothing about you and here I have let you into my boudoir. How unladylike of me." In a bold move, I go to sit down next to Simon on the settee.

"I don't find you unladylike whatsoever. In fact, I think you are quite the lady."

"Really?" I feel my lips quiver as he softly touches my cheek with his hand to brush a piece of how out of me eyes. "I think you're avoiding the topic of me getting to know you, Simon O'Connell."

"Perhaps. But fine. What do you want to know?" Simon says, getting himself comfortable on the settee.

"Okay, well, how old are you?" I look at him, trying

to guess myself. He doesn't seem like someone in their twenties, although he doesn't look like he's in forties.

"How old are you?" Simon asks, promptly.

"I asked you first. Also, you can't ask a lady how old she is."

"I am 32. I just had a birthday in March."

"Do you have any siblings?" I continue the fast-paced questions and answer session.

"Nope. Single child."

"Have you ever been married?"

"What? No."

"It's not an odd question. I've been married."

"True. Okay. It's my turn."

"Fair enough."

"How old are you?"

"I'm 29. I'll be 30 in one month and a couple of days in fact."

"Do you have any siblings?"

"Yes. I have an older sister and brother who are far better at adulting than me." It's true. My sister has been married for five years now to a perfectly boring but faithful and decent man. My brother is also married and has two children. My siblings pay their bills on time and never ask my parents for anything. I, on the other hand, have to borrow things like giant suitcases because I'm just not quite that adult yet. I only have weekend bags.

As I sit and ponder my failures compared to my brother and sister, I see Simon deep in thought as well.

"Do you think you'll fall in love again?" He asks me kindly, yet inquisitively.

"That's a rather personal question." I say, wincing at another gulp of my drink. "I just asked you basic *questions.*"

"Do you?"

"Ugh. I suppose. It's scary though. The thought of giving my heart again to someone. What if they take it and throw it down the garbage disposal like Jack did? I don't think I can handle that again."

"Ah, that's the scary part about love. You never truly know what you're getting yourself into until you're knee deep in it."

"Have you been in love?"

"Yes, of course. My last relationship was three years ago. I was going through a difficult time in my life and I couldn't be the man she needed me to be. So, we broke up."

"Do you have regrets?"

"No. At the time I did what I needed to do. It just wasn't meant to be."

"Sometimes I go on Facebook or Instagram and see what Jack and his new girlfriend are doing. It's so unhealthy."

Simon looks at me like I'm mad and says, "Dabney, I don't recommend that at all. I have no idea what any of my old girlfriends are doing."

I get my phone out to show him.

I see the latest photo is of Jack and the mistress in a

restaurant. It looks recent and when I get a closer look at the caption, it tells me everything.

It reads, *'I said yes!'* I don't need to scroll to the next photo, but I do. It's a close up of her ring finger.

"Oh, my god. He proposed to her. Simon, he proposed to her. We've been divorced less than a month and he's already engaged to a new woman!

"Shit, Dabney. That's why it's not good to look on an ex's social media!"

"Simon, can you fill up my drink? I hate this stuff, but I need another." I don't know why I would be surprised that Jack has continued to quickly move on and replace me. I mean, he was cheating on me forever possibly. It still hurts nevertheless.

"Sure." Simon pours more whiskey into my clear plastic cup and I take a big gulp. "Woah, there. Take it easy," he says as I continue to drink more.

I take another gulp. And then another.

"I don't understand what she has that I don't." I have seen her and she's not any prettier than I am.

"Nothing. Obviously, no morals if she was shagging him while he was married to you. Not to mention, he has no fucking morals. Fuck them, Dabney."

"You're right. I know you're right. I guess I'm just in shock he got engaged like, right after we officially got divorced. Part of me thought she might still be a fling. But maybe he loved her when we were married." I start to whimper a bit when I think of Jack's infidelity. I really am over him, but the betrayal still hurts a bit.

"Come here." Simon takes me and holds me while I let

out a whimper of a cry. I try desperately to hold it back.

"I feel like such a cliché. Like, what am I doing? What am I doing here? What am I going to do?"

"Well, tomorrow you're going to go downstairs, help out the B&B or the pub and make yourself useful. But for now, we should just come up with a plan of how you're going to get yourself out of this rut."

"Thank you, Simon. For being here for me. For being a good friend. Can you please excuse me for a minute? I think I might need to puke."

Yep, I definitely need to puke. I run to the bathroom just in time.

"Are you okay in there?" Simon asks from the other side of the door. So much for me trying to seduce him tonight. "Maybe I should be going."

"No, please! Please don't go yet."

I wash my face and brush my teeth quickly and go back out to my room. Simon hands me a bottle of water and smiles.

"I'm sorry, Dabney. Maybe whiskey was a bit too strong for tonight. We should stick to wine from now on."

"It's me that's sorry. I've ruined tonight."

"Ruined it? How?"

"I decided last minute that I should seduce you." I believe it was somewhere between sip two and gulp one.

Simon spits out his drink, presumably at my honest declaration.

"Shit, Dabney. I've never met a woman so open and

forth coming."

"It's probably the whiskey. I'm sorry."

"Don't be. Perhaps I had the same idea." He says cringing. "Is that creepy? I wasn't trying to get you drunk though. More to give me the courage."

"What a bunch of losers we are!" I laugh at what could possibly be the least romantic evening I've had yet.

"Maybe I should be on my way."

"No, wait. I know the moment has passed. But don't go. Stay with me. Please?"

Simon's blue eyes gaze at mine and I can see him mulling over what may or may not be a terrible idea.

"Please, Simon. I don't want to be alone."

"Okay. But try not to seduce me. I'm quite sexy in my boxer shorts you know."

"Haha. I'm going to put my pajamas on."

I go to the bathroom to change and wonder what the hell I've just done. How am I going to sleep next to him and not touch him?

When I'm done getting ready for bed, Simon goes into the bathroom. He comes back out, in nothing but his boxer shorts. What I assumed was a tall and lanky body is smooth and muscular.

We get into bed and I turn out the light.

"Goodnight, Simon." I say as I turn over to face the opposite side.

"Goodnight, Dabney, he says as he moves his arms around me and holds me. I don't flinch. The feeling of his arms holding me on the second worst night of my life is comforting to me.

It's going to be a long night.

CHAPTER 10

I wake up and look at the clock. It's 8:22 and yet I feel like I can barely move. I roll over and quickly remember I have a man sleeping next to me. My movement wakes Simon, and he slowly opens an eye which reminds him, as well, of the night before. He doesn't look surprised or alarmed though.

"Good morning," is all he says.

"Hi. How did you sleep?" I ask, not really knowing what to ask in this somewhat awkward moment.

Simon smiles and replies, "I slept well and you?"

"I did too. Surprisingly. Can I get you a cup of coffee? I have a machine in the room."

"Ah that would be excellent." He says, sitting up.

"I just thought of something. How are we going to get you out of here without the entire B&B knowing you stayed here last night?"

"Nobody cares, Dabney. I'll just walk out through the front door."

"Yes, but Sam will see you. And Maura. And what about Carole and Paulina?"

"Carole and Paulina have been trying to get us together since I met them. They'd be pleased, I imagine."

"But nothing has happened. We haven't even kissed."

Still sitting in bed, he says, "Would you like to remedy that? I'm feeling rather lively this morning. Hence, the lack of movement from your bed."

"Simon!" I say with a blush.

"Sorry, just trying to lighten the mood."

I hand him a coffee and sit down next to him.

"I think we could sneak you out if I keep a lookout. If everyone is busy in the dining area, perhaps nobody will see you."

"Or I could sneak out the window," he whispers.

"Yes! The window!"

"I was joking, Dabney. I can't fit through that tiny window." I look at the narrow window in my room and nod my head in agreement. Plus, I'm on the second floor. I'd feel bad if he slipped and broke his neck trying to sneak out of my room.

"Maybe I shouldn't worry what people think. Maybe that needs to be a new part of my finding myself."

"Well, I don't think that's a bad idea. Nevertheless, I'll sneak out as discreetly as possible—for your sake."

"Thank you, Simon."

"You're very welcome, Miss Dabney." He says staring at me with intense passion. I can do nothing but stare back at him with equally intense passion.

Simon puts his coffee down and seizes the opportunity to make a move. He gently pulls me toward him and kisses me. His lips are forceful with desire, yet soft and gentle. It's in that moment that I seize my opportunity and roll onto him. I pull off my pajama shirt and let him make the next move. He takes no time and pulls the rest of my pajamas off.

I'm about to pull off his boxer shorts when a knock at the door interrupts us.

"Dabney? It's me Maura. I was just wondering if you were coming down this morning. Sam had to leave abruptly to help Cassie with the boys. Something about a diaper disaster. So, it's just me."

"Seriously?" Simon whispers in pain.

"Oh, Maura, of course! I fell back asleep this morning. I'll be down there in ten minutes!" I shout through the door.

"I think I might need more than ten minutes." Simon says, not moving.

"I need to go help her. I'm sorry."

"No, no I understand. Just give me a minute."

I rush into the bathroom and get ready as quick as possible. Doing my makeup in record time. Strike two at trying to seduce Simon.

Once I've finished in the bathroom, I rush out and say, "Again, I'm so sorry. Can we have a do-over?" I ask, putting on a pair of sneakers.

"I'm off tomorrow. How about I take you on a proper date? And then we'll see where that leads us."

"Ooh, a date. That sounds serious. Okay, I'd love that. I just need to see what Cassie and Tilda need me to do. We haven't really discussed an actual schedule."

"I just realized I don't even have your phone number."

"Oh here, give me your phone. I'll text myself and you can save my number. I'll talk to Cassie and Tilda today." I pick up Simon's phone and tap in my number to text.

Simon takes his phone back and puts it in his pocket, "Perfect." Simon then kisses me, which turns into a lingering kiss that is extremely difficult end.

"Simon. I have to go and so do you." I say, still attached to his perfect lips.

"I know. Dammit."

We stop kissing and I start to go downstairs first. My plan, is to keep everyone that is in the dining room, occupied, so Simon can easily slip out.

"Hi, Maura, I'm here!" I say loudly to let Simon know to go ahead and leave.

"Thanks so much, Dabney. Can you bring these coffees to the table over there?"

"Of course." As I take the coffees over to the table of lovely German tourists, I can't help but hear loud talking in the stairway.

"How nice to see you, Simon!" I know that voice. It's Carole. We've been busted by Carole and Paulina.

"I was just stopping in for a coffee, Carole. It's nice to see you as well."

"You look like someone the cat dragged in, love. Been out, late have you? Well never mind, why don't you sit with Paulina and me and we'll have a nice chat."

Simon mouths help to me and I can't help but laugh to myself.

I pick up some dirty dishes on the tables, then go over

to their table to see what I can get for them. The breakfast is self-serve, but Sam said they like to offer to get drinks and whatever else the guests might need.

"Good morning, ladies. Can I get you a coffee? Oh, Simon, I'm surprised to see you here so early, this morning."

"Dabney, dear, Paulina and I need a couple of those cappuccinos. Simon, do you want a coffee, love?"

"Yes, please Dabney. A coffee would be wonderful." Simon says as he rubs his face in embarrassment.

I make the coffees and think about how I'm going to miss Carole and Paulina when they go back home to England. They have been a lot of fun and rather decent wing women for me. Watching them chat with Simon as though he's one of their sons is adorable. It's also sweet the way Simon lets them boss him around and ask him rather personal questions like,

'Where've you been all night, love? You look a wreck.' And my personal favorite, 'Have you noticed how lovely Dabney looks first thing in the morning?'

It's quite funny and I am j really going to be sad to see them go.

I bring Carole, Paulina and Simon their coffees and clear the rest of the dirty plates off the remaining tables. Maura goes back to start washing up and I help her pick up what's left of the food that's out. By 10:30, we've picked up all the tables cloths and linens, thrown them in the wash and set out new tablecloths for the following morning.

"Maura, what else do you need me to do for the B&B?"

"I think that's it for now, Dabney. We have a cleaning crew that comes each day to change the linens in the rooms and clean the rooms. I have a couple of guests checking out and a few more that are coming later today."

I should pop over to the pub to find out if Tilda needs any help, but instead I sneak upstairs for a nap. I'm hungover from the drinking and exhausted from the lack of sleep. As it turns out, having a hot guy sleeping next to you all night is not conducive for a good night's sleep. I wanted to have sex with him all night long but didn't want to make a move. So, I suffered and didn't sleep so well.

Once I've gotten a few extra winks of sleep, I go over to the pub to find out what Tilda would like me to do. I guess I'm kind of like Donno, the handyman who does a little bit of everything around the place.

I walk into the pub to see Tilda at the bar pouring drinks and wiping down the counter. "Hi, Tilda how's it going?"

"Hi, Dabney. How are you?"

"I'm good. I was wondering if there was anything you needed me to do today?"

"Oh Dabney, if you could keep an eye on the twins over there, I'd love you forever. I had to bring them in today because my nanny's car broke down. Honestly, I feel like everything is going wrong lately.

"Um, like babysit?"

"Well, yes, I suppose. Have you babysat before?"

Have I babysat before? It's a simple question. I mean,

most young girls chose babysitting as a teenage job. I, however, was not one of them. Truth be told, kids scare the crap out of me. I feel like they're just waiting for way to outsmart me. And kids are so fast. One second of checking my Instagram account and they could be out the door taking a taxi to the local nightclub.

"To be honest, Tilda, I don't have a lot of experience with kids."

"Oh, I'm not worried. Let me introduce you. These are my twins, Brennan and Brianna. They're almost three years old. Brennan has stopped putting things in his nose now. Thank goodness. Brianna is my quiet one. She'll just sit and color and draw pictures."

"Cute names." I say, while trying to not show my fear.

"Thanks. I had a favorite great aunt named Beebie. So, the two B names are kind of take on her name."

"Wait, is this the late aunt who had the bucket list?"

Tilda wipes Brennan's face and says, "Yes, how'd you hear about that?"

"Sam mentioned it the other day. I'm thinking of putting a list of things together that would better me. You know since I'm on a journey of self-discovery and all."

"I definitely discovered myself that's for sure. It was mostly things I had absolutely no desire to do. Like pose naked for an art class, ride in a hot air balloon. But once I did them, I felt I had accomplished something huge."

"I don't even know what I would do." I have never thought I was perfect by any degree. However, the idea of putting together a list of my flaws has never occurred to me. Does it occur to anyone?

"Maybe make a list of things you might not want to do but know would make you a better and stronger person if you do. Does anything come to mind?"

"Just silly things. I don't like to be alone. I don't like to eat alone, go to the movies alone, shop alone, really."

"Well you came on this trip alone. That's huge." Tilda looks over at the man sitting alone in the corner.

"True. It still shocks me at times to realize I did that."

"Hang on. I need to get a refill for Barney." Tilda goes back to the bar and I sit with Brennan and Brianna.

"Hi, I'm Dabney." I say to the two kids. They just stare at me for what seems like a very long second.

"Hi." Brennan finally says. Brianna just looks at me indifferent to it all.

"Can I draw a picture?" Brianna asks.

"Of course. What would you like to draw?"

"I like buildings. Big, tall buildings." I watch her draw a magnificent three-year-old version of the Empire State Building.

Tilda returns and says, "Oh isn't she amazing? She started watching YouTube videos of famous buildings and then started drawing them. When I was her age, I was probably picking my nose and watching cartoons!"

Brennan, who shows no interest in his sister's brilliant drawings, is watching a cartoon on his iPad.

"Brennan likes music. Listening to songs, making music with anything he can find. But mostly, he likes to watch cartoons."

"Is there a nearby park or somewhere you'd like me to

take them?" I ask in a moment of bravery.

"There's a park right around the corner, down the street. They would love that. Are you sure? You might need the stroller."

"I think I can handle it. If you trust me, that is." I think the bigger question is, do I trust myself to keep two lives safe for an hour? I have never even taken my niece and nephew for the day before.

"I have a good sense of people. I trust you. If you could just be back by noon? I think their nanny should be here by then and they can eat lunch and take their nap. I'll give you my phone number in case you have questions."

"Sure, I can do that."

I get the kids in their double stroller, and we go outside to find the park. It's actually a rather nice day. I have found the weather here to be quite pleasant when it's not pouring down rain.

"Swings!" Brennan shouts when he sees the small park.

"I want to slide! I want to slide!" Brianna claps her hands excitedly.

The two kids wiggle so much I think they're going to pop out of their strollers. Maybe we should have walked. But then that might have been even more difficult to keep them corralled.

"Okay kiddos let's play!" I unbuckle them from the stroller and they both run in completely different directions. How am I supposed to watch them both when they're in two different places? What do moms do? Maybe I will switch my plan to only having one kid.

"Dabbey! Swings! I want to swing!" Brennan shouts again at the swings while I run to help Brianna get on the ladder to slide.

"Hold on Brennan, I'll be there in a minute!" I shout over to him but it's too late. He's headfirst in the mud that sits underneath the swing.

"Oh shit." I whisper to myself. I don't think Tilda was expecting them to come back in need of a bath! She'll never let me watch them again.

"Dabbey! Look! Mud!"

Then I hear Brianna shout back to Brennan, "Mud! I'm coming!"

Before I can catch her, Brianna is in the mud now. What the hell? Why can't kids come and play on the equipment?!

"Wait, guys, wait!" I look in the bag Tilda gave me for some towels or wipes. Something to clean up the mess. "Brennan and Brianna, I think we should go play somewhere else that's less muddy."

The twins scream in unison and then run away...in different directions...again.

I decide to stay calm and remain in one place to see where each one goes. Can I see them? Are they doing something dangerous? Can they get up the ladder with their muddy shoes and not slip off, possibly breaking their necks?

It is decidedly so.

But then I hear a cry. Is it Brennan or Brianna? Please be okay. Please be okay. If I've let one of Tilda's kids get hurt, she might never trust me again. I might actually have to leave Ireland early instead of staying longer.

I run over to find Brianna has gotten to the top of a slide and now refuses to go down. She's not hurt at all. She's just scared.

"Brianna, come on down. I'll catch you." I shout.

"No! I don't want tooooooo!" She cries.

Brennan runs over to our side of the play structure and climbs up to find Brianna. He takes her hand and helps her climb down. It's the cutest thing I have ever seen.

Now that Brianna is on solid ground, she's perfectly fine. I look at my phone to see it's nearly noon so I get more wipes from the bag and try to clean the kids up as much as I can. They are still a muddy mess but at least it isn't as bad as it was. Tilda might trust me with her kids again...maybe.

"Okay it's time to go now. We have to eat lunch! Are you hungry?"

"No." Brennan says.

"What about you, Brianna. Are you hungry? It's time to get back in the stroller to find your mom."

"No!" Brianna shouts.

I can't get either one of them to get in their stroller. Instead, they run off and get dirty again.

"Come on, you guys. Help a lady out. Please get in your stroller."

"No. No. No. No." They sing together. Apparently, they think this is some sort of game.

"Yes, it's time to go. Now get in your stroller right

now. You don't want your mommy to be cross with Miss Dabney, do you?"

"Cross! Cross! Crossy cross!" They sing back to me. Shit. What am I going to do now?

Not wanting to manhandle someone else's kids, I decide to try chasing them into the stroller.

Nope that doesn't work.

Then I try to bribe them.

Nope that doesn't work. Especially when all I have to bribe them with is a stick of gum and an energy bar.

"Okay, look!" I finally shout, "Your mommy wants you back home right now. So, get in your stroller and let's go!"

They stop what they're doing and burst into tears and climb in the stroller. Great, Dabney, now you made them cry!

"I'm sorry! I didn't mean to make you cry!" I plead with them to stop but they just cry harder. Then, I start to cry because I have absolutely no idea what I'm doing and realize I may never be a mother because I'm terrible with children and no man wants to be my husband anyway!

The crying must startle them because they stop crying and let me buckle them up in the stroller. I sniffle my way back to the pub, with the two traumatized toddlers in tow.

"Oh, you guys are back! Was it fun?" Tilda says excited to see her kids.

Deacon is now in the front and says, "Bloody hell,

what did they do to you, Dabney?"

I must look a hot mess.

I tear up and say in blubbers, "I'm so sorry. They got into the mud under the swings and then they wouldn't listen to me and then they started to cry and then I started to cry. I understand if you don't want me to help you anymore," I cry out.

Deacon and Tilda look at each other and burst into laughter. How is this funny?

"Dabney, they're toddlers. They're going to get dirty and cry and not do what you tell them to do." Deacon says sympathetically, unbuckling the muddy kids out of the stroller.

"But they're so dirty." I say, trying to wipe the mud off myself.

"I should have warned you. They love getting dirty. I always keep a spare change of clothes for both of them everywhere I go. It's fine, Dabney. They look like they had a great time." Tilda says, taking Brennan and Brianna to the back of the pub. "Deacon, watch the front for me while I get them cleaned up?"

"Of course, Tilda." Deacon heads to the bar to get a drink for a customer.

"Well, I might go ahead and get cleaned up, too." I wave goodbye to Deacon and start to turn around when Simon comes in for his shift.

"Good god, Dabney, what happened to you?"

I sigh and say, "Simon why do you always seem to find me at my worst moment?"

"Ah, it's a gift. But seriously, why are you all muddy and such?"

"I'm afraid it's my fault, Simon. My kids got hold of her. A park visit with Brennan and Briana will do that to a person." Deacon laughs.

"You took the kids to the park? How nice!" Simon says, trying to hold back his laughter.

"Why is that so funny?"

"Have you taken kids to a park before?"

"My brother has a kid you know...but no. No, I haven't. Does it show?"

Simon wipes away what I can assume is dirt from my eyebrow and quietly says, "You look beautiful, Dabney. Even with mud on your eyebrow."

Gulp.

Fearing Deacon and Tilda might see that something is up, I take a large step back from Simon's personal space. They don't notice though because they have actual work to do.

Simon takes my hand and leads me toward the kitchen and says, "So, did you ask about getting tomorrow night off?"

"No, I forgot. I'll ask her before I leave."

He puts his apron on, ties it around his waist and says, "I can take you somewhere later that night if you have to work."

"Oh, where would that be??" I say in a salacious tone.

"A late-night pub." He says with a wink.

Oh, obviously. Damn, Dabney. Get your mind out of the gutter. Just because we nearly did the deed this morning does not mean he's planning on taking me to his apartment to finish what we started.

"Well, I should leave you to get your work done. I'll see you later."

"See you, Dabney."

Tilda walks into the kitchen and says, "Dabney, are you still here? Did you want to stay for lunch?"

"Thanks, Tilda. I should probably get cleaned up though. But I was meaning to ask you, if you were going to need me tomorrow night. I might have plans, but if you need me then I can rearrange—."

"No, I think we actually have tomorrow night covered for once. Our new hire seems to be working out, so I have her on the schedule." She says, as she makes cheese sandwiches for Brennan and Brianna. "Simon, Donno will be coming in tonight to work in the kitchen with you. Deacon is singing and working the bar for a few hours."

"Oh! I might come by to listen later after I help out with happy hour next door."

Tilda lights up at conversation about Deacon. "You should come by later! It's a school night so I'll be home with Logan and Livia, and the twins of course."

"You know what? I should Instagram live part of his show! You should follow me, Tilda."

Tilda gets out her phone and opens up her Instagram, "Sounds fun. How do I do that? Where do I find you?"

"I'm in there as Dabney E. Corrigan. Will he be upset if

I Insta him tonight?"

"No, I don't think so. I've seen drunk ladies record him before. I have no idea where the videos go though."

I leave Simon and the rest to their work and go back to my room. I'm helping out with happy hour, but I am so exhausted from the children I have to relax for a bit before I do anymore work.

Once I get to my room, I take a hot shower and wash all the mud off my body. I am thankful the B&B has clothes washing services because my clothes need a lot of soapy love.

Since I don't have anything to do until 4:00, I decide to have some much need relaxation time and make a list of things I should try.

Hmm. I can't really think of anything I don't want to do. Okay, that's not really true. But the thought of making a list of things I have avoided most of my adult life is rather daunting. Tilda at least had an aunt who did it for her. I am having to start from scratch! And it's much easier to do things that other people tell you to do rather than making yourself do it.

"Okay, Dabney. Let's get this list put together." I say to myself.

1. Go to a scary movie alone.
2. Find a new restaurant and eat a meal alone.
3. Babysit Tilda's kids again.
4. Go deviceless for 24 hours.
5. Go without makeup for an entire day.
6. Cook a new meal for a friend.
7. Drive a car on the other side of the road.

Okay, I have a week's worth of things to do. And they are all terrifying. I need a rest after making this list, but I am so excited about my first step of growing as an adult, I decide to call my mom instead.

"Hi, Mom, how's it going?"

"Dabney, what a nice surprise! How are you? I've been so worried about you."

"Why mom? I'm fine." Sometimes I think my mom has no confidence in my ability to make it out the door without falling on my face. When I told her I wanted to move out to live in the city she thought I was going to get mugged the first night I was there.

"I'm just imagining you there all alone, not knowing anybody. It must be so lonely for you."

"Actually, Mom, I've met quite a few people. Some are guests of the B&B, but a lot of them work here."

"Are they respectable people?" She asks suspiciously.

"Mom, are you asking if the staff are like Carnies? That's so rude."

"Dabney, it's not rude. I'm just being honest."

"Yes, they are very nice and quite respectable. Anyway, I wanted to tell you what I've done! I made a list of things for me to do while I'm here. To make myself a more confident adult."

My Mom is silent.

"Mom?" I ask, making sure she's still on the line.

"Dabney, I don't think you should be taking any big risks while you're in a country all alone."

"Do you want to hear my list?" I let out a deep breath in

frustration. I feel like my mother never believes in me. It's as if she thinks the worst possible thing will happen with anything I do.

"I don't know, do I?"

After I read my list of things I'm going to accomplish, my mom goes silent again.

"With all the Uber taxis why in the world would you try driving on the opposite side of the road? You have a hard-enough time driving on the American side, dear."

"Mom! I'm trying to better myself. Why are you so negative?" Ugh! I am so tired of my mom raining on my Dabney parade.

"Dabney, I love you and I'm just being realistic. I have not seen you leave the house without makeup since you were 15. I am just wondering if you're setting yourself up for disaster. And considering how many fender benders you have been in, well, I just I don't think challenging yourself to driving in a new country is smart. Do you even have car insurance now that you live in the city?"

Now I can hear my dad in the background. He's an accountant who just retired, but still works from home so he's available to enter the conversation of my life's demise.

"What's Dad saying?"

"Your dad says the same thing. If you don't have insurance, then you can't drive anywhere. We can't bail you out of anymore driving disasters. This is tough love, Dabney. We just watched a Suze Orman show that talked about this. Something about letting your adult children pay for their own disasters, or something like that."

Suze Orman, a fellow Chicagoan, is very popular in my parent's house. As far as I'm concerned, however, she has nothing to do with this conversation and can fuck off. Sorry, Suze.

"Mom, I just remembered I have a walking tour to meet up with, so I need to go. Don't worry about me. I'll rethink my list. You're right." There is no walking tour, but I can't handle any more of this conversation. I either want to cry or bang my head against a hard wall instead.

My mom takes a deep sigh of relief and says, "Oh Dabney, I think that is for the best. Your dad and I love you very much and only want what's best for you."

"I know, Mom. I'll talk to you later."

I end the call with my parents and bury my head with my pillow. If I push hard enough, I might be able to stop my breathing for a while…

But I have a list to accomplish. To hell with my parents. They may love me, but they have no idea what it's like to be me.

CHAPTER 11

I take a nap after my utterly defeating conversation with my parents. I wake up to find I feel much better and am ready to go downstairs and help with happy hour, once I have touched up my hair and makeup.

I go downstairs and find Carole and Pauline already there, ready to drink and socialize.

"Dabney, we're so glad you're here." Carole says as I pour her glass of wine.

"We leave first thing tomorrow morning." Paulina says as she picks up a strawberry and dips it in her Prosecco.

"Oh ladies, I'm going to miss you so much."

"We're going to miss you too, Dabney. But good news! We both have Instagram things now! So now we can follow your goings on when we're back home! Isn't that exciting?"

Carole and Paulina both open their pages to show me what they've done so far. It's mostly selfies of them drinking, but it's adorable regardless. I'm impressed that ladies in their late 70s even know how to start an Instagram page. I don't think my mom still understands what I do or what Instagram is.

After I've made sure Carole and Paulina have food and

wine, I chat with some of the newer guests until happy hour is over. Then I clean up and put the wine bottles away for Sam. Since they won't be at full capacity until tomorrow, I told Sam earlier to go home and enjoy the family. Thankfully there were no plumbing disasters this time.

I go over to the pub to order some dinner. Technically, I am eating dinner alone, sitting at the bar but I don't think I can really count this as finding a new restaurant and eating alone. That would be kind of cheating.

Not feeling wonderful, I just order a chef salad and a Coke. Tilda has left for the day, but the new lady is working. She brings out my salad and brings me my drink. I decide to check in with Ruby since I'm feeling kind of lonely and unsure about my grand new plan of bettering myself.

"Sorry, Dabney I don't have much time to talk. I'm about to start my class. How are you?"

"I'm great!" I lie. I don't want to tell her my parents completely depressed me.

"How about I get back with you in a few hours?"

"Sure."

I hang up and poke my head back into the kitchen to see Simon.

"Need any help? I'm free tonight!" I try to sound cheerful.

"Not really, Dabney. We have Donno working tonight and then Deacon is about to go out and sing so things slow down a bit when he's on."

"Oh, okay. I'll go out and wait for him to come on."

Simon plates some food and he follows me out of the kitchen to take the food to a table. "I'll come out and sit with you for a bit. I'm due a break." Almost sensing my need for company, Simon takes a spot next to me at the bar. "You seem a bit out of sorts, what's up?"

"I talked to my parents today that's all," I say glumly.

Simon takes a sip of his water and says, "Ah, it didn't go well?"

"No. I made a list of things to better myself and they completely shot everything down. They don't even think I can go a day without makeup!" I shriek, somewhat loudly, but the pub is lively tonight, so most people didn't hear...I think.

I show Simon my list. He smiles as he reads it., "So you want to drive here in Ireland? Where are you getting a car?"

"Well, I could rent one? Or I could use someone else's since I don't have all my car insurance information or an updated driver's license?" I have deep fear of the DMV and when my driver's license expired a couple years ago, I conveniently forgot. Thankfully, I always have my passport with me for identification.

Simon is flabbergasted, however. "Are you serious? You don't even have a license? How can you not have a license?"

"Because I don't ever drive in Chicago. I can take the L or rideshare service or just walk anywhere I want to go... and I really hate getting my driver's license photo."

Simon rolls his eyes and says, "But you can drive?"

"Of course, I can drive. Don't be silly."

Simon continues to look at me for a second, perhaps not entirely convinced I can drive an actual car.

"Well, I think this list is great, Dabney. I hope I get to be the new friend you cook a meal for."

"Don't get too excited. There's only one meal I can actually cook. Finding a new one might be a challenge."

"Ah, but that's what your list is all about. Challenging yourself and learning you can do it."

"You're right. I'm just not going to tell my parents anymore about my plans." They have lost their open communication privileges. From now on, my mom and dad are on a need to know basis.

"I'm sorry they weren't supportive. Give them some time. Once they see how well you do, they might come around and see you've grown up some."

"Are your parents supportive of you?"

"My parents have been dead for over twenty years. But I like to think they would be."

"Oh, Simon, I'm sorry for your loss."

Simon looks to the other side of the room and says, "Hey, it looks like Deacon is about ready to go."

Deacon comes out and introduces himself. As always, his music is amazing, and I get my phone out to record him live for my Instagram.

He notices and smiles at me. I guess like Tilda said, he's used to strange women getting their phones out for him.

I can see that my post is already getting excellent

feedback. Good for Deacon, I think to myself.

"Well, since Deacon is singing, I best get back to my work. Have you decided what you're going to do first?"

"Yes. I'm going to turn off my phone tomorrow. The only thing I will use is my Kindle for reading. There's no internet on there so I don't think that's cheating."

"Okay then. I'll plan on meeting you in the lobby to-morrow evening at 6:00 for our date since I won't be able to reach you any other way."

"Ooh! Sounds, wonderful." Simon sneaks a kiss on my cheek and goes back to work in the kitchen. I float on cloud nine for a few minutes then go back to my room and go to bed to dream of more kisses

from my Irish stranger.

***

I wake up feeling refreshed and much more positive than I was the night before. Simon helped me put things into perspective and to forget about my par-ent's misgivings.

I go to check my phone but then remember I'm doing the no cell phone thing today. I have only been awake for a minute and it's already killing me. Maybe I started off with the most difficult thing first?

I start to panic, realizing that nobody besides Simon even knows I've sworn off modern technology today. I never got back in touch with Ruby. Since my parents were so upset about me even doing this list of things, I wasn't going to text them and let them know I was indeed going through with it. My mom would call me immediately and tell me to stop this nonsense and take a brewery tour instead, but don't drink because I need my wits in the strange and unknown city of Dublin.

I decide to not worry about what my mom is going to think and get dressed. I choose some comfortable clothes today. Leggings, ballet flats and a long grey t-shirt with cardigan. My makeup is neutral today to match my ensemble. I do a quick dark eye with light lip gloss and go downstairs to check in with Sam and Maura. I truly have today off to do whatever I want which is great, except I can't do anything because I'm not using my phone. I suppose I could call people the old- fashioned way if I need to. But I don't know who I would call anyway.

Maybe I should try to keep myself occupied with a scary movie to watch by myself?

No, I need my phone to check the times and locations. I don't even know where I'd go. I'd best wait to go on an adventure to the movies when I have my phone to use as backup, in case of an emergency and all.

"Good morning, Dabney! Fancy a coffee?" Maura asks as she brings a tea and coffee to a table of new guests.

"Good morning, Maura. Yes please."

I sit at the table, not really sure what to do. Normally in this situation, I would browse social media on my phone. Check current events or something. I look around to see everyone else is busy enjoying their breakfasts. There are a couple of people who are sitting alone, seemingly content and not anxious to look at their phone one bit. I envy them immensely.

Maura brings me a coffee and I go up to the food tables to get some breakfast. Sam and Cassie always have a nice display of yogurt, fruit, different breads, and pastries along with a display of meats. I take some strawberries and banana with a yogurt and go back to my table to finish my coffee. A family sits at the table near me. The two teenage girls, looking bored with their phones, sit there while their parents bring them some plates of food.

"Don't they have pancakes?" One of the teenager says, disappointed.

"No, dear, they don't. This is Ireland. Maybe they don't eat pancakes here."

The other teenager just wants coffee. Her mother says she can't just drink coffee for breakfast.

There is a whole discussion about nutrition and needing fuel for the body. I must say, the family is quite entertaining. I almost forget about not having my phone... until one of the teenagers gets very excited because some boy named Tyler F. not Tyler S. liked her Instagram post from last night. Tyler S. always likes her posts, but Tyler F. is way pickier and also, he's more popular.

They must have noticed me listening to them because they stop and look at me.

"Oh um, I like your phone case. Is it Kate Spade?"

"Yeah." Teenager 1 says. She has long straight blonde hair and is rather skinny.

"Are you American, too?" Teenager 2 asks as she puts her wavy blonde hair into a ponytail.

"Yes, I'm from Chicago. Where are you from?" I ask, hoping my fear of them doesn't come out in my voice.

"We're from Florida. Our parents made us come to this cold, dreary place with them. Who takes their kids to Ireland for Spring Break?" I want to say I would have loved a trip to Ireland for Spring Break, but I don't. We had to go to the family cabin in Wisconsin on long school breaks. While the cabin was familiar and comfortable, I think it would have been exciting to see a new and different country as a teenager.

"We do and you should feel fortunate you got to come with us." The parents return from their second round of food plating in time to silence the sulking teens.

"Good morning. I'm Dabney. How are you liking Ireland?" I ask the adults, who are hopefully not as angry and depressed as the two teenagers.

"Oh, it's wonderful. Especially this B&B. Very charming and quaint." The mother says while trying again to get her kids to eat food.

Teenager 2 continues to sip her coffee. "The rooms are tiny and the wi-fi is weak."

"They do a nice happy hour in the evenings," I tell them. "I've been helping out since one of the owners just had a baby."

"We were out late yesterday on a walking tour and then dinner, so we missed it. Girls did you hear about the happy hour?" The dad says.

"Duh, Dad. Happy hour is for grown-ups. We can't drink, remember? You made that clear last night." Teenager 1 says.

These kids are a bundle of joy. If I thought toddlers were scary, teenagers are downright terrifying.

"Well, I guess I should head back to my room. It was nice to meet you all." I'm practically running away from the table of demon children as I speak. I decide to go back to my room for a bit to relax and read.

An hour into my book, I'm dying of boredom. Not because the book isn't good, it is. It's a mystery-romance that is full of intrigue and sex. But I'm wishing I could check my phone. I have turned it off to make sure I don't accidentally use it. The temptation is strong.

I decide I will go for a jog around the neighborhood. I haven't exercised at all since I have been here. I have however, eaten plenty of Walkers crisps and fries from the pub.

I put on my running clothes and shoes and go outside. I opt for my bright pink camouflage running pants, pink sports bra and black tank top. I go outside and take a deep breath. It's a lovely, sunny day. Perfect weather for running. I get around one block and see Tilda is outside with the twins.

I stop jogging. "Hi! Tilda. I didn't know you lived so close."

"Hi, Dabney! Out for a run?"

"Yep. I've sworn off my phone and social media today. It's part of my make myself better bucket list"

"You made a list? That's great, Dabney!"

"Yeah, but my parents aren't so keen on it. I don't think they have a lot of confidence in my ability to follow through with any of it, even though most of it is basic stuff."

"Well, nobody probably thought I'd be able to get

naked in front of an art class, but I did it. There comes a point when you have to do what you need to do and not worry about other people. No offense to your parents."

"I know. I'm already off to a great start. I haven't looked at my phone once today. I turned it off for the day."

"I hear you have a date with Simon tonight."

"How did you hear about that?"

Tilda laughs. "News travels fast around the pub. Deacon told me."

"It's nothing formal. I'm leaving soon. Just a nice night out with someone I guess."

"Okay, sounds fun. So, what else is on your list besides giving up your phone for a day which, by the way, sounds torturous." Tilda asks as she throws the ball for her dog to run and fetch.

I ramble off my things to her, hoping she doesn't find them to be too superficial. If she does, she isn't letting on.

"Those all sound like great things for you to do. I don't think your parents should be worried at all."

"I've also decided something else. I'm not leaving until I finish them."

"Oh, now that's a big deal. Maybe you should add more things to your list so you can stay even longer!"

I laugh at the idea but wonder if I shouldn't. I've been here a week and only have a week left to go. I have loved my time here. To be honest, I don't really feel ready to go back to Chicago and Ruby's sofa.

"That's not a terrible idea. Maybe I will. I'm having a wonderful time right now."

"Well anytime you want to some babysit the kids, now you know I'm just around the corner."

"Duly noted. I hope you're not offended by me having them on the list. It's just, it was really difficult, and I feel like I should give myself another chance at kids." Maybe if I am mentally prepared, I can deal with them better.

"I'm not offended at all. My kids are super sweet but a handful. I'm with them every day!"

I say goodbye to Tilda and continue my run. I wave to people I pass on the street and almost totally forget that I don't have my phone to play music while I run. It's a peaceful run and by the time I get back to the B&B and my room I feel exhilarated and relaxed.

I run a bubble bath into the claw foot tub. Normally, I would turn my phone on and play music, but my phone is still off, on purpose. I get in the tub, lay back in silence and enjoy the peacefulness—until someone knocks at the door. Who on earth could be at my door? House-keeping maybe? But they came when I was out running.

I get out of the tub and put on my bathrobe to answer the door. Expecting a stranger, I crack open the door. My mom would probably not approve of that, but oh well. Luckily, it's not a stranger.

"Simon? What are you doing here?"

"I know I'm early. I was out and about and thought I would bring you these." He hands me a small bouquet of tulips with a vase. "I also wanted to check on you. I know it must be difficult going without a phone all day long."

I open the door to let him in, which may or may not be a bad idea.

"Well if you must know, I've been doing fantastic. I talked to some new guests this morning. Something I never would have done if I'd had my phone. Then I went for a run. I haven't gone for a run the entire time I've been here. All because I had time to remind myself to exercise. I even saw Tilda on my route."

"Did I interrupt your time away from your phone?"

"Oh no, that's okay. It's a nice interruption. Have you had lunch yet? We could go out and find something to eat.

"I would but I have a couple things to do before our date tonight."

"Oh, okay. That's fine." I'll just figure out what to do by myself.

"Why don't you go find somewhere to eat lunch? You could mark another thing off your list."

"No, I don't think I could do that without my phone."

"What? But look at what you've accomplished so far."

"True. I've spent several hours now sans phone and I've survived. I just don't think I can do it without my phone. How will I know how where to go? Or how to get there? Or the menu to review ahead of time to make sure I even want to eat there? These are all things I use my phone for."

"Very well. I guess I should get going. I'll see you tonight at 6:00, right?"

"Right. Can you tell me where we're going, so, I know what to wear? Is if fancy? Or casual? Or semi-casual?"

"You can wear whatever you like. But I'm not telling you. It's a surprise."

"Ooh, a surprise! I love it already!"

Simon leaves and I get dressed. I put on a comfy blue and white t-shirt dress and denim jacket with my white sneakers. It's still a while until our date, I go next door to the pub to get a salad to go. The B&B has a terrace that is nice to use for an outside break. It's secluded with brick from the two buildings that are covered in vines and pretty flowers. I know this doesn't count as eating alone somewhere new, but I think it is a nice way for me to get used to being by myself. And without a phone no less!

I find some things to do until it's finally time to get ready for my date. I look over at the pretty tulips Simon brought me. Things have taken such a turn from the first day we met at the airport. I don't think either one of us liked each other much. But here we are, getting ready for a first date. Maybe or maybe not fulfilling our sexual destiny.

Since Simon said I can wear whatever I want, I choose to wear my dark blue skinny jeans and long flowy, pink floral blouse. I don't know if we have to walk anywhere, so I pick out my tan Tory Burch wedges and a khaki belted trench cape to wear with it in the event I get chilly.

Now, for my hair and makeup. I load my body with good smelling lotion. Luckily, I had enough time to shave my legs before Simon called on me today. I had a professional waxing of my naughty bits before I left Chicago, so they are fully prepared for a visit tonight. I curl my hair and do my redo my makeup from this morning but add some pink lipstick, rather than the neutral gloss I wore earlier. I have to say I am very impressed with myself. I really like my outfit and look. I wish I could take a picture of it to post but I can't...

I get my purse and go downstairs to meet Simon. I forgot that happy hour might still be going on. I suppose if Tilda knows about the date, everyone else does too.

I see Sam clearing the plates. I don't see Simon, so I offer to help him.

"Hi Dabney. You don't need to help me. Besides, aren't you going on your date tonight?" His question confirms my suspicions. Everyone knows.

"Yes, but he's not here yet. I can help put some things away. Was happy hour busy tonight? Did you need help?"

"No, it wasn't too bad. But man, there's a couple teenagers that are really nerve wracking. They tried to get some wine for themselves until their parents realized what they were doing. I offered them some Cokes, but they looked at me like I'd just said the most insane thing ever."

"Ah yes, the teenagers from Florida. I've met them. They are terrifying and from what I've heard, quite keen to drink alcohol."

We continue to discuss the teens, who are named Rory and Devon when Simon walks in.

"Hi, I'm sorry I'm late. I was finishing up something and lost track of time."

Sam picks up the last of the dishes and says, "Hi, Simon. How's it going?"

"It's great. I'm just taking Dabney out for a special night."

"So, I have heard."

"It's just two people spending an evening together. Nothing major to talk about." I say, hoping to stop the gossip mill.

"Got it." Sam says, smiling. "I'll be sure to pass that message on."

"No need to pass anything on to anyone." I say as Simon and I leave.

We walk outside and down the street to his car that's park on the side street.

"Sorry, I couldn't find any street parking right out front."

"It's fine. My legs are able to walk me to many places even further than down this street."

"You look nice tonight."

"You look nice as well." He does. He's wearing some black jeans with a black and white striped t-shirt and a black blazer. He also smells incredible.

"So, what's on the agenda tonight?" I ask as we get into the car.

"If you don't mind, I thought I could cook for you." Simon says, driving down the narrow street. Why are streets here so much smaller than in America? I'm starting to regret my idea of trying to drive here.

"That sounds interesting."

"I hope you're not disappointed. Would you rather go out? There are plenty of good places we could go."

"No, I'd love for you to cook for me."

Simon smiles. "Good."

When we get to a large brick building Simon parks the car on the busy street. I'm not sure how gentlemanly he is so I let myself out of the car. I want to show him I am not one of those ladies who expects chivalry. I am an equal. I can open my own door. I let Jack open my door all the time. Look how chivalrous he became.

"It's an old building so we don't have an elevator I'm afraid."

"Well these wedges have done plenty of hiking up and down the Magnificent Mile I'm more than capable of making it up some stairs."

He failed to mention his apartment is on the very top floor of a building of four stories with an extremely steep set of stairs. No worries! I can do this, I think to myself, desperately hoping not to sound winded by the time we get to his door.

As we walk up the stone stairs I comment, "Your building is lovely. I like the tile downstairs."

"Yeah, sorry about the whiff of marijuana. My downstairs neighbor is a bit of stoner. He's an artist and says it makes him more creative."

"Is it legal here? It is in some states where I'm from."

"Nope. But he hasn't been caught and I'm not going to report him."

He lets me into his apartment. Of course it's very

clean and tidy. He has a huge bookcase full of books, some vinyl records, and a stack of comic books to the side.

"You have a lot of comic books. Do you collect?"

"It's a hobby of mine. I've been busy lately though, so I haven't done much with them."

I go to sit down, and a huge cat jumps up and lands on my lap.

"Cleo, now that is rude. She didn't say if she liked cats yet. Do you like cats?"

"To be honest, I've never had a cat. My mom is allergic, so we always had dogs."

Simon puts on some music and I start to feel nervous. This is the first time I've been in another man's apartment since I met Jack. It's a strange feeling.

"Right, well let me get started. I've prepped everything, so I just need to cook. Would you like some wine?"

"Yes, please!"

I walk toward the small but open kitchen and sit down at the counter to watch him cook. He's at ease and comfortable. I sip my wine as he puts out some appetizers for me.

"Dates and bacon because those were a hit the other night and veggies with hummus dip. I'm making chicken satay over rice with roasted veggies."

"Wow that sounds delicious! I've never had a man cook for me before."

"Really? Never? Not even your husband?" Simon asks, perplexed.

"Oh heavens no. He can barely make a sandwich. He's had people do things for him so much he can barely function. It's a wonder he made it through law school."

I watch Simon mix up some peanut sauce as the chicken cooks on the grill. He does everything so fast. The rice cooks in the rice cooker while veggies roast in the oven. All of a sudden, I see him pull out a big platter, toss the seasoned rice on the platter, spread the roasted veggies on top and lay the chicken skewers on each side as he drizzles peanut sauce on them.

"Simon! This is beautiful!" I am thoroughly impressed.

Simon brings the platter of food to the table, which is already set with napkins and plates. I bring my wine with us and he fills a glass for himself. The candles are lit with dim lighting in the rest of the house.

"Simon O'Connell if I'm not mistaken, I think you might be wooing me with your scrumptious food."

"Dabney Corrigan, you might be correct."

We take a few bites and then go back to candlelit conversation.

"So, I must ask, how have you survived all day without using your cell phone? I'd like to give you trouble about it but, honestly, I don't think I could do it myself."

"It's been great! I feel so liberated and free! I might do it more often actually."

Simon looks at me strange and says, "Really?"

"God no. It's been awful. I have no idea what Instagram posts have done well or not. I don't know if anyone has tried to text me. I've gone radio silent and I'm someone who does not go radio silent. I'm always on social media or something."

"Maybe going radio silent isn't a bad thing." Simon can say this because he has an unhealthy aversion to social media. He doesn't understand what it's like to not have it all day.

"I hope you're right," I say, not convinced. "I'm not sure what's more exhausting. Being on my phone all day or not being on it at all."

"I guess you'll find out tomorrow when you get back on it."

"I guess I will. But tonight, you have me all to yourself," I say smiling.

Simon puts his napkin down and stares into my eyes. "Lucky me," he says softly.

I take a big sip of wine to calm down. But I can't. I can feel my heart pounding a mile a minute. I hope Simon can't hear it.

"Um, so who is that lady in the picture frame behind you?" She's a pretty lady, with crystal blue eyes, just like Simon.

"That is my Gran," he says thoughtfully.

"Oh, does she live nearby to you?"

"No, she died a few years ago, unfortunately."

Great, Dabney. Way to ruin the moment. Why do I keep asking him about dead family?

"I'm sorry."

"It's okay it's not your fault. She lived a good life, but I miss her terribly. Anyway, would you like dessert? I have some pound cake and strawberries with whipped cream. Which now that I say it, sounds like I'm trying to be a cliché romantic. But it's my favorite so I promise I didn't have any preconceived notions."

"It sounds wonderful. And don't worry. I didn't think you had any preconceived ideas. What happened the other morning was spontaneous. Nothing needs to happen." Although I did shave my legs soooo...was it a waste?

"Do you feel like a walk?" Simon asks suddenly.

"A walk? Sure." Truth be told I really would like some of that dessert, but a walk is probably the better choice.

While we go down the nine hundred flights of stairs, I wonder if I'll die going back up them. Simon opens the large, wooden door and we enter the lively street. It's a nice evening. There's no rain so quite a few people are out.

"I love to walk down these streets and just people watch," he says, looking around at the myriad of people.

"You like to walk alone?" We are so different. While I do walk around alone, because it is necessary a lot of times, I would much rather walk around with another person. Yet, Simon seems perfectly happy with his own thoughts.

"Yes, it's peaceful. I also like walking with you though." He smiles and takes my hand.

"I guess I walk alone when I go places in Chicago, like when I went to work or the grocery store. But I don't know if I would just go take a walk by myself for pleasure."

"So, do you ever take a walk for pleasure?" Simon asks, waving at an elderly gentleman standing in his doorway.

"No, I don't suppose I do. I go running though. I guess that's kind of like walking." That's one thing I like to do alone. I don't like running with other people just in case they are faster than me.

"I think if you learn anything from this trip, Dabney, it is to embrace loneliness. Take the quiet time to listen to yourself. You might be surprised how profound your thoughts might be."

"I can assure you my thoughts are mostly what I should wear tomorrow or if I'm hungry."

"Why do you do that? You downplay how deep you can be?"

"Because I'm not that deep?"

I can tell he's starting to get frustrated.

"Okay, okay. You're right. I do need to embrace being alone. I can do better."

"Sometimes I feel like you're playing a part of someone who has been told all their life they are superficial. You are more than that."

I don't really know what to say. How can someone who has only known me for a matter of days, think he has me so figured out?

"But what if I am superficial? Are you okay with that?"

"It's not up to me. It's up to you."

This walk is not going the way I thought it would go. I thought it would be a romantic opportunity to chat about our feelings. Perhaps Simon will say how beautiful I am and then spontaneously wrap my chilly body in his arms and kiss on the street in front of everyone. But he doesn't. Instead he tells me how wonderful I am and that I don't value myself enough. That's not romantic at all!

"I'm getting cold. Maybe we should go back to your apartment."

Without flinching, Simon takes off his blazer and puts it on my shoulders as we turn to go back to his place.

"I'm sorry. I didn't mean to preach." He stops me in the middle of the street, and as though he could read my mind, he lightly touches my face, reaches down and kisses me.

"Well that's better. I was wondering when you were going to do that." I say, kissing him back.

"Do you want to take this back to my apartment?"

"Yes."

We briskly walk back Simon's apartment, climb back up the nine hundred flights of stairs and shut the door quickly.

He kisses me more voraciously than when we were on the street and I can feel his hunger. It's been a very long time since I've been this intimate with someone. Simon scoops me up and we walk toward his bedroom.

"Are you sure we should do this?" I ask in a moment of clarity. Or is it confusion?

"What? Are you serious? Yes, I think we should do this. Do you?"

"Yes!"

We do' this' and it is incredible…

I sleep over at Simon's and after some morning sex, I check my phone.

I turn it back on and wait to see if I've missed something. I can't imagine there is too much I've missed since everyone I talk to knows where I am.

"Oh my god, Simon. I have like a bazillion views of Deacon's performance. People are asking who he is and how they can download his music! Does he have music to download?"

Simon brings me a cup of coffee. "What? I don't think so. I think he just sings it in the pub."

"Look at some of these comments. I even have DM's about him. This guy says he's a record producer. How do I know if he's legit?"

"Google him."

I google the guy and he is definitely legit. I see a list of well-known people he has worked with…assuming I'm not being duped by an impersonator, which I don't think I am. When I look up his Instagram profile name, he has A LOT more followers than me.

I take a deep breath.

"Simon, I think I just made Deacon famous."

CHAPTER 12

Simon drives me back to the B&B and I get ready for the day. Sam and Cassie want me to help out with happy hour tonight, which I am more than happy to do. I kind of enjoy it. It's a nice way to socialize and meet the new guests. I've been here a week now, so I feel like a regular.

I have been so preoccupied with Deacon's instant fame that I have ignored all the other messages and phone calls. One from Ruby, apologizing for not getting back to me earlier. One from my mom, not apologizing to me but asking me to call her back because she wants to know what I think she should get my sister's husband for his birthday. I also have another text from Jack, which I am going to ignore. I am done with his weird games. Only my loser ex-husband gets divorced and engaged in the same month, while still continuously texting the first wife.

I decide to call my mother back later. My brother-in-law's birthday present is not a top priority. I text Ruby back to let her know it's fine and I'll chat with her later. I don't know if I should be honest with her and let her know my vacation romance has taken a delightful, yet unhealthy turn. She might be happy for me, but also extremely worried that I'm getting myself into something that will be hard to get out of. I am not sure she's not wrong.

But for now, I need to figure out how to let Deacon know I've made him famous by posting his performance the other night. I'm somewhat nervous. Maybe he doesn't want to be famous. What if he's perfectly happy with his life the way it is? Running a pub, singing in his spare time, and hanging out with his family?

I walk next door to the pub which is somewhat quiet and use the opportunity to chat with Tilda. If anybody is affected by this, it's her.

I see Tilda busy wiping down the ketchup and vinegar bottles at the bar.

"Hi, Tilda. Do you have a minute?"

"Sure, what's up?"

"Okay, so you know the other night when Deacon played? Well, I posted it on my Instagram page."

"Oh, that's nice. Did your friends like it?"

"Why don't I show you." I show Tilda the post and point to her the number of views, likes and comments. "That's not all. I've had about twenty messages from people that work in the music industry or know somebody that works in the industry. In fact, I have a message from someone that wants to sign him to their record label!"

Tilda takes my phone and studies the Instagram posts. "Does Deacon know about this yet?"

"No, in fact the only people I've talked to about this is you and Simon."

"Ooh, things are going quite nice for you and Simon,

eh?"

"Yeah, they are actually. I'm not sure what we're going to do when I have to leave though."

"Just see where things go for now. But back to Deacon. This is insane. I can't believe this many people have responded to a five-minute video. I mean, don't get me wrong, I know Deacon is a fantastic performer. I've often thought he deserves to be famous. But I'm just in shock it's actually happening. He needs to know about this." Tilda goes back to the kitchen, where Deacon is prepping for lunch.

"Hi Dabney, I didn't know you were here. How's it going?" Deacon asks, coming out of the kitchen. "What do you have to show me?"

"Well—the other night when you were performing, I posted it in on Instagram. Since then, I have thousands of views, comments and likes. I also have messages from the people in the industry asking more about you. In fact, I have a serious record producer that wants to come from London to visit with you. I looked him up and he's a major player in the industry."

Deacon looks at me dumbfounded. "What?!"

"I know. I wasn't sure if you guys would be happy or upset that all of this was happening."

"Well, I'm surprised, for sure. But this is exciting. I've never actually met with anyone serious about me before. He said he wanted to come from London?"

Deacon looks as shocked at I was this morning.

"Yep." I have his contact information in his message. I give the information to Deacon. "I think it's to his personal assistant so you should get through fine."

"Tilda, can you believe this?"

"Yes! Of course, I can! You are the most talented man I have ever met. I'm shocked, too, but I know you deserve this. Whatever happens, I think we need to see it out. We'll just make Dabney stay longer if we need more help at the pub. She has incentive now. Right, Dabney?"

"Uh. Right?" I'm not sure if she's joking or serious. I go along with the comment regardless. To see Tilda and Deacon as a team and see how supportive Tilda is, even knowing their lives might change forever, makes me wish I had something like that. Jack never would have been supportive like Tilda. It's obvious that their love and commitment is real.

Deacon takes his phone out. "I'm going to call him now. Let's find out if this is really going to happen before I get too excited."

"So, were you serious? Do you think you need to hire me? I still have a list of things to accomplish before I go home, don't forget."

"Obviously, it's all up to you. I have no idea how this will all turn out, but you have an open door at The Stag's Leap. I think I speak for Sam and Cassie as well. You fit in well here, Dabney."

"Thank you, Tilda. That means a lot. I'll be honest, I didn't have any idea what I was doing when I came here, and I still don't. If I don't' come home when I'm supposed to, I think my family and friends will think I've lost my mind.

"Well, I thought this trip is supposed to be about

you?"

"True. I've accomplished a lot so far. I went an entire day yesterday without my phone."

"Impressive!" Tilda says, raising an eyebrow. "I can't wait to see what you do next."

Deacon rushes back and says, "I talked to him. He's coming tonight. Tonight. He's getting on a plane and coming TONIGHT. What am I going to do? Am I ready?"

Tilda takes his face, kisses him and says, "Of course you are ready. You have been ready for as long as I've known you."

Deacon instantly calms down and says, "Can Lauryn stay and watch the kids tonight? I need you here, Tilda."

"Oh, I'm not sure. That's a long day and I think she has something tonight. She mentioned needing to leave at 6:00."

Deacon's face falls. Then I realize I can watch the kids.

"Wait, what about me? I don't need to be here. I can stay with the kids tonight. I'm supposed to do happy hour tonight but that's over at 6:00. Would Lauryn be willing to give me a few minutes to get there?

"If not, I'm sure I could talk to Sam or Cassie to see if you could leave a few minutes early. Are you sure, Dabney? I know the last time was tough." Tough might be an understatement but if I am going to prove to myself that I can take care of children, for a short period of time at least, I need to get knee deep in it. Just not literally. I still have mud stains from the last time.

"Yes, I am absolutely sure—as long as you trust me to watch your kids. You need to be here, Tilda. I assume there is no mud inside your home."

"No mud—last time I checked."

"It's on my list, remember? *Babysit Tilda's kids again.* I need to do this. I need to prove to myself that I can be with kids and not be a complete disaster. I also really want to help you guys."

Tilda texts Cassie, who says of course I can leave the happy hour five minutes early.

"I'm sure that's fine with them, Dabney. I really appreciate this."

"Not a problem. I will meet your nanny at 6:00 to take over. I am actually excited!"

Feeling satisfied that I am on track to making myself a better person, I go back to my room to take a nap. I didn't get a lot of sleep last night, after all.

I wake up to Ruby calling me. Feeling groggy, I answer.

"Dabney? How are you?"

"Hi, Ruby! I'm great!" I say enthusiastically. Maybe a bit too enthusiastically. My best friend can read me like a book.

"Oh no Dabney. What are you hiding?" Ruby asks, taking a deep breath.

"I'm not hiding anything. What do you want to know?". How does she always know when I need to tell her something? I suppose that's a sign of a best friend.

"What do you want to tell me?"

"Oh, Ruby we could do this all day long. Yes. Yes, I did."

"Seriously?! You did?? Part of me is concerned, but how did it go?"

"It was fabulous. Much better than Jack, which surprises me because I always thought Jack was good. Maybe I just told myself he was because he was supposed to be. You know, his reputation and all."

"Or maybe he was too busy fucking his clerk to pay attention to your needs." Ruby stops and says, "Oh, sorry, Dabney. That was insensitive."

"No, no you're probably right. But enough about him. Ruby, we had a great night. He brought me flowers earlier that day, he made me dinner, we took a walk and talked. Like, we talked, Ruby."

"Dabney, what are you getting yourself into?" Concerned Ruby returns.

"I don't know. I just know I'm having a great time. He makes me happy. He's different from Jack. He's honest with me. He calls me out on things."

"But Dabney, you guys are from two different countries. What if you fall in love? Then what?"

"We'll figure it out. Right now, we're just getting to know each other and having fun."

"So, what else has been going on? I saw your video of the cute guy in the pub. He is a great singer! Is he single? I might come visit after all."

"Sorry, he's happily married. But he's so good, isn't he? I think I made him famous, Ruby. A bunch of people have messaged me about him, and a record producer is flying from London tonight to meet him. Can you believe it?"

"What?! That's bananas!"

"And Ruby, I've made a list of all my flaws and such. I'm going to fix them. And Ruby, I've decided something else. I'm not coming back until I fix them. I'm not coming back home until I'm a better person."

Ruby goes silent for a moment.

"Dabney, have you thought this through? What kind of flaws do you have on your list?"

"Only seven."

Ruby coughs and says, "Only seven? Are you sure?"

"Yes, Ruby." I furrow my brow. "Are you implying I have more than seven?"

"Maybe? Tell me what you're going to fix."

I rattle off my list and Ruby seems content with what I've come up with. She seems a little more concerned about the driving part, which I don't understand because she has driven with me and she knows I'm an excellent driver. How hard can it be drive on the other side of the road?

"Anyway, Ruby, I'm going to babysit tonight and get a really good feel for how I can be with kids. This will be my second time around with them."

"So, you babysat once already, and they let you babysit again?"

I laugh. "Ruby, I'm beginning to think you don't have a lot of faith in me."

"No, no. That's not it. I'm just surprised that's all. You don't have a lot of experience and I thought kids terrified you."

"They do, Ruby. That's why I'm doing this." Am I not

being clear as to why I have made this list in the first place?

"Okay. I can respect that. Just be careful. I'm here if you need anything."

"Thanks, Ruby. I'll be fine."

I get off the phone with Ruby and get ready to go downstairs for happy hour. Since I am going straight from happy hour to Tilda's I make sure I am wearing a kid friendly ensemble. Some comfy leggings, a dark shirt in case they spill something on me, and sneakers. Kid friendly and hopefully kid approved.

The Terrifying Teens are the first to arrive with their parents. I have Cokes ready for them and a keen eye in case they try to sneak some booze. They don't seem interested though. Instead, they've got their eye on an attractive chef who has arrived with the appetizers. Something tells me it's not the appetizers they are after.

"Hi Dabney, I've got tonight's snacks for you." We keep it totally professional, although he does give me a wink and a sly smile.

"So, have you heard? I'm going to Tilda's tonight to babysit! After happy hour. I'm going to check another to do off my flaws list. Isn't that great?" I carefully arrange some wine glasses on the counter for the guests as I talk.

"Yeah, that's wonderful. I was hoping you would take a bit longer to get it completed though."

"Don't worry. I still have plenty to do. I can't become a better person overnight," I say joyfully.

"Ah, that's true. It does take some work. Even for the best of people."

"Did you also hear about Deacon? That record producer is coming tonight."

"I did hear. I can't believe it. A lot is happening really fast," he says, and I feel like there is more to our conversation than just Deacon's up and coming singing career.

"It is." We look into each other's eyes for a brief time and look away quickly when we realize that the Terrifying Teens have noticed our interaction.

"Right, so I'll see you later?" He asks.

"Um, I have to get up early for breakfast. Maybe tomorrow?"

"Yes, that's what I meant. Of course." Simon blushes and I see his soft side coming out again. Never would I have imagined the grumpy guy I met the first day here would turn into a blushing romantic who cooks for me and brings me flowers.

Once Simon goes back to work, I get back to pouring drinks for the guests. I've met some new people, but nobody has the pizazz of Carole and Paulina. They have barely been gone, but I really miss them. Plus, they aren't as scary as those girls who now seem to be approaching me.

"Hi, would you like a Coke or something?"

"Yeah, I guess. So, who's that guy you were talking to? Is he your boyfriend?" Teen 1 inquires promptly.

"I thought you were staying here. Why are you working?" Teen 2 asks, somewhat horrified.

"Wow, a lot of questions." I start to perspire. "Well, yes I'm a guest here but I'm helping the owners. Cassie just had a baby a month, so they had to scramble for help. And as far as the guy goes, we're just friends. He's the chef at the pub next door."

"He's hot." Teen 2 says as Teen 1 nods in agreement.

"Well, yes I think he's attractive as well. He's quite old and sometimes grumpy if you must know."

"Huh, he didn't seem grumpy just now. He seemed like he liked you." Teen 1 rebuts. I can't seem to get much past these two. They are quite observant.

"He likes me? Oh no, like I said, we're just friends. Purely professional. Anyway, how about I get you those Cokes."

I give the two girls a can of Coke each and try to send them on their way. Thankfully, their parents intervene to tell them they have reservations at a nearby restaurant and they all have to leave now. Thank goodness. I think I sweated my makeup off.

I get through happy hour, clean up quickly and leave for Tilda's house. I knock on the door and the nanny answers. She is young, perhaps in her early twenties, with light red hair and pale blue eyes. Her hair is pulled back in a loose braid.

"Hi, I'm Dabney. I'm taking over for you tonight," I say anxiously. I am still not a hundred percent ready for my evening but still proud of myself for tackling it.

"Yes, come in. I'm Lauryn. I'm sorry to rush out, but I have to get back home to help my mother with something tonight. The kids have eaten their dinner. Tilda usually lets them have a sweet snack after dinner. Logan and Livia have finished their homework." Then she whispers, "Logan is in a bit of a mood. Didn't like his homework but he did it. He usually finds something to watch or play in the evening. Livia will help out with anything you need. I really have to be off though."

"Sure, I've got this. Have a good night."

"You, too. Good luck." I suppose she is just being nice but why would I need luck? Does she doubt my ability to take care of four kids?

I walk over to Logan and Livia, who I have had yet to meet.

"Hi, I'm Dabney." I look around at Tilda's house. It's extremely cozy with neutral tones and throw blankets draped over sofas. She has a fireplace with a huge mantle that boasts pictures of her family.

"Hi." Logan says, looking up from his comic book briefly as he sits sideways in the oversized chair.

Livia smiles. "Hi, I'm Livia. Do you know how to make cookies?"

"Um, I suppose. I haven't made cookies in a long time though. Do you?"

"No, but Lauryn was supposed to make cookies before she left, and she didn't." Livia says, sounding quite disappointed.

"Oh well I'm sure she can make them tomorrow."

"No, she won't be here tomorrow. It's my mom's day off so she'll be here instead."

"Maybe your mom will make them." I am starting to perspire again and wonder if the sweet but inquisitive girl can see my fear.

"Maybe. But it's hard with the twins. They want to

help her and it's a disaster. One time they dumped the entire bag of chocolate chips on the kitchen floor when mom was trying to mix everything. We ended up having chocolate chip cookies without chocolate chips."

This reminds me of the twins, I look around to find out where they are.

"Where are Brennan and Brianna? I just saw them."

"I don't know. Maybe in their playroom."

"Where's that?" I ask, not seeing a playroom anywhere nearby.

"Oh, it's upstairs."

"The twins go upstairs by themselves?" I ask Livia. The stairs are over on the other side of the room and I am having a difficult time figuring out how they were able to slip past me so quickly.

"No," Livia says.

"But they just did?" I ask, feeling somewhat confused.

"No, I mean they aren't supposed to, but I think they did. Do you want me to go get them?"

"It's okay. I'll be right back."

I go to the stairs, where a baby gate is open. Did Lauryn not close it? Or did the mastermind twins figure out how to get past it?

I make my way up the dangerously steep stairs of the presumably old home. The steep stairs are probably why they aren't supposed to go upstairs alone, right? Because they can fall and break their necks, right? Good lord. I've been here five minutes and I've already almost killed them. The dog, George, has followed me every step of the way and probably thinks the same thing.

"Brennan? Brianna?" I shout running now. I find them, drawing on the chalkboard, perfectly fine. Phew. But wait, what is that? I see scissors on the play table. They're kids' scissors but scissors all the same. Probably for Livia to do crafts I assume. Maybe they were just left out...

"Oh my god." I look at Brianna's hair. There is a huge chunk of her hair missing! "What is happening? How did this happen?"

"I cut Bree's hair!" Brennan exclaims proudly.

Holy shit. I'm over. I'm over. She's never going to forgive me. I'm never going to master children and I'm never going to be a better person. I suck at children and that's just the way it is.

"Oh no, not again." Livia says, as she arrives at the disaster. Oh, and it's a big disaster. There are light brown pieces of hair all over the wooden playroom floor.

"Wait, what do you mean not again? This has happened before?"

Livia picks up the scissors and puts them back in the bin labeled Arts and Crafts.

"Yep, a while back. But it was Brianna who cut Brennan's hair. That's why his hair is so short. My mom had to get someone to fix the big chunk Bree cut out of it. I'm not sure how we can fix this one. Brianna isn't a boy..."

"Livia, what am I going to do? Your mom is going to be so upset with me. The first time I babysat they were a muddy mess and then today I let them go upstairs and play barbershop!"

"Mom was upset, too, when it happened before." The pretty little girl says casually. She has a long ponytail that bounces around as she walks around the playroom.

"Did Lauryn get in big trouble?" I mean, she didn't get fired so that's a positive thing. Right?

"No, why would Lauryn get in trouble? It was my mom's fault. She turned her back for a second and they were upstairs getting the scissors and then *you know what* happened." Livia makes a motion like scissors slicing through the air. Snip. Snip.

"Let's get you two downstairs. Livia, what time do they normally go to bed?" I find the portable vacuum cleaner that is hanging on the wall and clean up the pile of hair on the floor.

"Their bedtime is 7:30. I think you have a while, Dabney." It's only 6:15.

"Oh my gosh, Brianna! What happened to her hair?" Logan looks at me, expecting an explanation, which is fair. His baby sister looks like she just stepped out of a punk rock bar circa 1980.

Livia steps in to explain. "They got hold of the scissors again."

"I think we need to hide them." Logan suggests, which may not be a bad idea.

Then, I get a stroke of genius or insanity.

"Hey, let's make cookies. Livia, do you think we have all the ingredients?"

Livia's eyes light up with excitement and says, "Yes! Look! Lauryn has everything out already. She ran out of time."

The twins just hear cookies and jump up and down, repeating, "Cookies! Cookies!"

"Okay, it's been a long time, but I think I can figure this out. If Logan, you can help me keep an extra eye on Brennan? Livia, will you help me keep an extra eye on Brianna? The baby gate is secured."

I look at all the ingredients and try figure out how to use the Irish oven which is different than American ovens because they use Celsius, while the measurements are all metric, but I follow the directions closely. I mix it all together and lo and behold, I have made cookie dough. According to the taste testers, the cookie dough tastes correct. All we need to do is put them in the oven.

"So, kids what do you think? Are they as good as Lauryn's cookies?" I ask, taking a bite of my accomplishment.

"They're yummy." Livia says, snuggling closer to me.

Logan nods in agreement, "They're good."

The twins seem to also agree that the cookies are delicious, because they're covered in chocolate and cookie crumbs with no noticeable complaints.

Once Brennan and Brianna have finished their sweet treats, I get them cleaned up and ready for bed. Livia let me know they sleep in their bed together. Once they are settled, I read them a story and let them go to sleep.

"Okay, two down. What time do you guys go to bed on school nights?"

"I go to bed whenever." Logan says.

Livia, in protest says, "Logan that's not true. You have to have lights out by 9:00."

Logan smiles, knowing he's been busted. "Okay, it's 9:00. I usually go up early and read or watch something."

I let Livia get ready for bed. Then I let her watch a kids show before lights go out at 8:30.

Exhausted from the evening I just had, I sit down finally and check my phone. Yet another text from Jack.

Dabney, I need to talk to you. Please call me. I've been trying to reach you.

Ignore.

After watching some crime drama on the television about a priest from what looks like the 50s who solves crimes, I can't keep my eyes open and fall asleep on the sofa.

Deacon and Tilda come wake me when they get home.

"How did it all go?" I wearily ask as I try to smooth down my hair.

"He seemed really impressed with Deacon. He has a lawyer who will put paperwork together, but I think they're going to offer him a contract!" Tilda says excitedly.

"Deacon! That is so awesome! Congratulations."

"I'm still in shock to be honest. Never in a million years would I have thought this would happen. Thank you, Dabney, for getting me out there. I don't know how to repay you."

"No need to repay me. Just get me front row seats at your first concert."

I leave to walk back to the B&B, feeling happy and

content with my lively evening. One more thing to check off my list.

CHAPTER 13

I wake up in the morning feeling exuberant. I have a busy day ahead, so I do some yoga in my room and get ready. My yoga has made me feel extra calm, which leads me to match my makeup to my feeling. I don't even add mascara to my freshly moisturized face of foundation, cream blush and eyeshadow.

The day could not look nicer outside. I bounce down the stairs to the dining room to help Sam get the coffee set up and ready to go for our guests. I say 'our guests' now because I don't really think I'm one of them anymore. I have worked several times for Sam and Cassie therefore, I am more of an 'employee' type person now. He even made me a name tag.

"Good morning, Sam!" I say walking past him in the kitchen area.

"You're chipper, this morning." Sam groans as I snatch a cup of coffee from the coffee urn.

"Rough morning?" I look closer at Sam, who looks positively exhausted.

"Yes. Miles was up all night. Cassie and I take turns feeding him and trying to get him to sleep. The pediatrician says it's normal colic, but it's miserable—for all of us."

"I can't imagine having to stay up all night with a baby. I need seven hours of sleep a night at least or I have to add extra eye cream and a lot of coffee to my morning regime."

"Just wait till you have kids, Dabney. Everything you think you need in life completely changes."

I don't have the heart to tell Sam that it's possible I may never have kids. Not because of any tragic health concern, but rather, I don't think I will ever settle down and get the courage to have them. I proved to myself that I can fix a situation with cookies, but to do that every single day? I just don't think I have the mental and physical fortitude!

In a change of subject, Sam whispers to me, "The Terrifying teens have arrived. I'll rock, paper, scissors you."

"I've got it Sam. You have enough to worry about."

I take a deep breath, tighten my posture, and approach the delightful young ladies.

"Good morning! Can I get you a coffee or juice this morning?"

"Can I get a 200-degree soy vanilla latte with one Truvia and a straw?" Teen 2 asks with, what I can only surmise, complete seriousness.

"Um, what?"

"She's just being bitchy. This isn't Starbucks, Devon. You have to drink regular coffee like the old people." Teen 1 says in her all-knowing tone. God, I really hate these kids.

"Oh my god, Rory I'm not." She whines to the sister, Devon. She looks at me and says, "Fine. I saw you had cappuccinos. Can I have one? Just please make sure it's hot. I can't stand a lukewarm coffee."

"Oh, and me too and can you bring more Truvia? There isn't any in here." Rory asks as she looks through the small bowl of sweetener packets.

"I don't think we have Truvia. The artificial sweeteners are filled in this little bowl right here on your table."

"Ew. I don't like the pink one and Truvia isn't artificial. It is plant based. Ugh. I guess I'll have to do regular sugar."

Devon is horrified. "Rory, you can't do regular sugar. It's poison."

"I have some honey if you would prefer a more natural sugar?"

Rory and Devon look at me like I have just offered the most ridiculous thing ever to them. Not knowing how to even respond to anything they say or do, I simply walk away to go make their probably lukewarm cappuccinos.

Sam is bringing out another carafe of juice and looking a bit perkier. I think being busy is helpful for him. Although I am sure he would not scoff at a quick thirty-minute nap or two. To be honest, I don't think I would either. My beautiful, sunny morning has now exhausted me.

I bring the teens their coffees and move on to the other guests, all of whom are much friendlier and not as angry that we do not have Truvia.

Sam and I make it through breakfast. Then we have a

quick bite of breakfast after all the guests have moved on with their day.

"I heard that Deacon has had a rise of fame. All because of an Instagram post?"

"Yes! It's unbelievable! I am so excited for him."

"Cassie said there might be a lot of travel around Ireland and some of the U.K."

"Oh, well I suppose that's to be expected."

"Sure, I just can't imagine how much pressure this will add to Tilda's load. She might have to add more employees to the pub or at least hire another nanny." Sam says as he spreads the cream cheese on his bagel.

"Another nanny? Oh my," I cringe because I don't have to imagine that would cost a lot of money.

Sam, seemingly reading my expression says, "She has plenty of money, she inherited a few million for her great-aunt. But I don't think she wants to be away from the kids so much."

"It sounds like she needs some more help at the pub, then."

"Maybe you should stay and go work there."

"People keep suggesting I stay. I have a life in Chicago, you know." Just because I'm divorced and somewhat homeless doesn't mean I don't have something planned. I just haven't figured out what that plan is yet.

"Sorry, I didn't mean to imply that you didn't have a life there. We just like having you around."

"No, I'm sorry. I shouldn't fuss at you. I have actually been considering extending my stay. If I'm getting a discount on my accommodations, I think I would only be financially out for airline fees."

I tell Sam about my list of things to better myself as I pick up our plates and coffee mugs.

"That's great. Then I think you should definitely extend your stay. At least for a couple weeks. By that time, Cassie will be able to get back to working more. I have to tell you, Dabney, Maura and I really appreciate you helping us. So does Cassie for that matter."

"Well, it's settled then. I will call the airline today and change my flight dates."

"And I'll let Cassie know. She'll be excited to hear your news."

I call the airline to change my return flight from a week from now to an open date. I know I have only been here a week, but I simply don't feel like two weeks is long enough to fulfill the needs I have for this trip. I feel like I am finally for once, living on the edge!

I'm working the happy hour again tonight, but since I have some free time until then, I look at the list I wrote on the back of the B&B welcome letter. I decide maybe it's time to go to a movie by myself. I'm feeling brave and energetic today.

I look up local movie theaters on my phone. To my dismay I don't see any scary movies.

"Hmm. Maybe a drama or action movie..." I say aloud. I book my ticket online for an early afternoon showing, then decide to read for a while. Back home I don't read enough, instead I spend most of my days online.

When it is time to go to my movie, I call a taxi and

head over to the movie theater. It's a new complex in the city that has several different movies. I hope I chose the right one.

I see a few older couples together and a few other solo movie goers. I don't feel quite as self-conscious. I go order my drink and popcorn and find my theater.

There are plenty of seats and I choose one in the middle of it all. A few more people join me in the middle of the theater, which I assume now is the prime spot. Thankfully, nobody has chosen to sit next to me. I am so uncomfortable at this point I don't need any extra pressure of social interaction. Not that we probably would have much…given it's a movie and all.

I recline my seat, get comfortable and wish I brought my glasses. I rarely wear them since I just need them for driving, which I rarely do. Unfortunately, I also need them for watching movies that are on big screens but far away. Oh well, it's not too blurry.

The lights go down which makes me feel less anxious. It's dark now. I don't have to worry about being judged. I'm the only person in the movie theater who is alone from what I can see, which isn't that far to be honest.

Halfway through the movie, I realize it's not just a drama-action-thriller, it's also a love story between a man and his best friend, his dog. They are so in tune with each other, it makes me wish I had a dog. I mean, they listen to you with very little judgement, give you a good excuse to go outside and walk and don't cheat on you with prettier owners. They are quite loyal.

Then, without any emotional preparation, the dog is killed by the international bad guy! What the hell? How did this happen? What kind of movie is this?

Suddenly, I find myself blubbering in the movie theater. I am actually crying in public, with other people sitting near me probably hearing every sniff and snort. I can't control myself. Everything comes out. Every emotion that I have held in from my husband cheating on me to why mother made me wear bows in my hair every single day of elementary school. Why? Why can't I have a healthy relationship with men? Why do I feel I am less than, if I don't wear name brand clothes? Why didn't my mom let me play soccer instead of doing cheerleading every year?

Any single thought that runs through my head causes me to blubber more. It's therapeutic and completely embarrassing.

I stay for the end of the movie and bury my head in my sweater and phone while every single person leaves the movie theater.

Once everyone has left I go directly the ladies room, which is of course busy because other movies have been let out around the same time. I find an available mirror and touch up my makeup. My puffy face is a bit less splotchy and my nose has gone back to its normal color.

I google how long it takes to walk, what the path is and decide maybe a good and quiet walk will do me some good. I begin walking for a bit and I realize I know this neighborhood. It's Simon's neighborhood. I decide to text him to see if he's home. I can't remember if he works today or not.

He texts me back right away and says he's home. Of course, I have no idea exactly how to get to his house, so

I let him know where I am and he meets me.

"Well what a surprise! Is everything okay, Dabney? You look upset?"

Oh, wonderful. My 'I've just been crying for an hour' face has apparently NOT gone away.

"I'm great. I just saw a sad movie is all." I tell Simon what movie I saw, and he seems confused.

"Isn't that an action movie? Where the guy goes and kills everybody that's done him wrong?"

"Yes, but it's more complicated than that. You'll just have to see the movie to know what I'm talking about."

He runs his hand through his black hair. "Oh, I see. Okay, well I'm off today. Do you want to come upstairs for a bit?"

We make our way up to his apartment that is still clean and tidy...and I caught him off guard. That's a good sign, although I wonder what he thought of my messy room the other night. Perhaps I should add, *Be a tidier person* to my list.

"What were your plans today?" I ask, taking a seat on his sofa.

"I popped out to the grocery and ran a few errands. Not much. Planned on texting you, possible irresistible seduction. Possible drinks after. I dunno." He sits down next to me and plays with my hair, that I didn't really do this morning, I just gave it a quick blow dry and straighten. It was actually a fuss free morning for once and I kind of liked it.

"Oh, those sound like nice plans." I breathe deep. I try to be cool, but I can feel my heart beat rapidly and I'm sweating a little bit everywhere.

Then, Deacon moves my hair off my shoulder and softly kisses my neck. I'm in trouble. I lean my head to the side a bit to make sure he has ample room to nuzzle. It is difficult to resist him, even if I wanted to, which I don't. We kiss for a while. When he carefully runs his hand up my shirt I suggest we take it to his bedroom, but we don't make it that far and end up having spontaneous sex right there on his sofa.

As we snuggle for a bit, I tell him my plans about staying a little bit longer and maybe working for Sam and Cassie a bit more.

"Dabney, this brings me to my next question." He sits up and takes a deep breath. The blanket we're using only covers below his torso, showing his toned upper body and every breath.

I can't help but know where he is going with this awkward, deep breath of a question.

"Where are we going with this?"

And there it is. The tricky question that either leads to more spontaneous sex or an uncomfortable silence that becomes tense and perhaps even argumentative.

"I don't know" is all I can say.

"Can I be honest with you then?" He softly takes my hand. "I've had a wonderful time with you. What I thought might be a spring fling with a pretty blonde girl has turned into something more special."

"So if I leave, do you want to see where this goes? But how can we have a relationship if I'm in Chicago?"

"Don't go back to Chicago. Stay here."

"But what about my life in Chicago?"

"What is your life in Chicago, Dabney? You don't really talk that much about it. You've mentioned your Instagram but that can be done anywhere. You don't have a place to live right now and your ex-husband is getting married to someone else."

I want to rebut his statements, but I know deep down he's right.

"I don't know what I'm doing, Simon. I've lost myself and I'm desperately trying to find out where I am. I will say this though, coming here and getting to know you and everyone here has lifted my spirits to no end. I am happy here."

"So, stay happy here."

"It's not that easy. My mom would kill me if I moved away this far."

"It's not her life now is it? You can make your own decisions."

"But what about her suitcase? I need to return her suitcase." I laugh at the thought of that damn suitcase. It caused so much trouble the first day I met Simon, yet here we are.

"I'll buy your mum a thousand ginormous suitcases if it means you don't leave."

"Simon O'Connell, that might be the most romantic thing I have ever heard."

"So, will you consider it?"

"Give me some time? Let me focus on perfecting my flaws? I'm not saying no, but I can't say yes. Not yet anyway."

"Fair enough. I know it's a big decision. The fact that you're considering it gives me hope."

Simon lifts me up from the sofa and we continue our discussion in his room, with very little talking.

CHAPTER 14

It has been a few days since I've babysat Tilda's adorable, yet extremely challenging children, and I have to say I have avoided Tilda quite well. She has not mentioned her child's extreme haircut in text or phone call, and I am hoping I can dodge an awkward conversation as to how it occurred. There is a good chance I will not be watching her kids again any time soon.

It's also the last breakfast of the Terrifying Teens. Sam let me know they check out today and I could not be more pleased. They aren't terrible people, just slightly awful. Perhaps as they mature they will be tolerable and not a menace to society's happiness.

Apart from the typical annoyance of the teens, this morning's breakfast has gone off without a hitch. I have really gotten used to my gig at the B&B and still enjoy it. I can make an excellent cappuccino and have even learned how to make a pretty leaf on top thanks to YouTube videos. I have taken a few excellent photos of my work and put it on my page. My page, which I have not been giving a lot of attention to. Which means I make a lot less money since I'm not posting anything to it.

I make yet another cappuccino for Devon, who has found her own Truvia and brought it to breakfast with her. Rory has decided since yesterday to not consume dairy or anything like dairy and has now taken to drinking green tea only. Thankfully, we have that.

As I walk away from my thankless delivery of beverages, I hear an odd sound from their table.

"Rory?" Devon says, in an oddly concerned tone.

I turn around, and see Rory is choking. Maura looks at me in horror. Then I remember my First Aid class that I took in college.

I get behind Rory, stand her up, wrap my arms around her torso and thrust my clasped hands into her, trying to push out the air and get whatever is lodged in her throat out. Eventually, it works. Rory spits out a huge strawberry and begins to cough.

"OMG. You saved her life, lady." Devon says, in shock.

Rory, who is still trying to catch her breath nods in agreement.

"Thank you, Dabney." She says, looking at my name tag.

"You're welcome." I say, somewhat shocked myself.

Maura brings over a glass of water for Rory and she takes slow sips.

This possible loss of life has suddenly humbled the teens and their dispositions change dramatically. They quietly finish their breakfast and instead of just taking off upstairs, they actually say goodbye.

"We're leaving today, but thanks again Dabney. That was really scary, and you were there in an instant." Rory says.

"Yeah, we'll definitely give you guys five stars and

an awesome review. Your cappuccinos are really hot." Devon says and two young ladies leave to go back to their room.

"Dabney, that was really excellent. I need to learn how to do the Heimlich Maneuver." Maura says while picking up the last of the breakfast dishes.

"Well, it probably isn't a bad idea. I'm sure Sam and Cassie would pay for you to take a First Aid class."

Maura nods. "I haven't told anyone here yet, but I got into University! I am going to have to quit after the summer."

"Oh, Maura that's great news! Congratulations!" I say, giving Maura a big hug.

"Thank you. I'm very excited. I just feel bad leaving Sam and Cassie. I have been here since they opened."

"I am sure they'll miss you, but they'll understand." Sam and Cassie seem to be very easy going people.

"I guess you should stay and take my place!" Maura says, cheerfully. Is there some sort of secret meeting where people are trying to get me to stay here?

I laugh to Maura. "I've extended my stay a bit longer, but I'm not sure about the Fall!" To be honest, I'm not really sure about anything at this point.

"That's great! I'm so happy you can stay longer!" I can tell Maura is excited.

"Listen, I've been thinking, what if we give Sam and Cassie a long weekend break and we run the B&B for them. It might be a few long days, but I think we can handle it. Sam looked so tired the other day."

"Oh, I don't know Dabney. That's a lot of responsibility. Have you checked people in and out before?"

"No, but it can't be that hard, can it? You can teach me."

Maura thinks on it for a bit and then says, "Well, you're right. Sam has been looking rather exhausted since the baby came. I imagine Cassie would love the extra help, having him at home and all. Okay, let's do it. That's if Sam and Cassie are on board with it!"

"I can't imagine they wouldn't be. I mean, I did save someone's life today. That should show I'm capable of taking care of a Bed and Breakfast for a weekend." Right?

I pop over to the pub, where I know Tilda is working and see if she still remembers the haircut incident. If she doesn't mention it today, then I think I'm good.

"Well hello! I haven't seen you in a few days! Have you been avoiding me?" Tilda smiles and pours a beer for a customer.

"Oh, well, I've, um, been quite busy." That would be, busy trying to stay away from Tilda so I don't have to explain her adorable daughter's edgy new haircut.

"Ah, yes. So why didn't you tell me when I came home the other night that my daughter looks like the hedges were taken to her hair?"

"You seemed so happy and excited about Deacon, I didn't want to worry you. Plus, I thought the haircut was rather cute and cutting edge for a kid. Brennan was very proud of his work."

"Uh huh. Well, I suppose Logan or Livia told you that the same thing happened to me a while back?" Tilda asks me while wiping down the counter.

"Livia may have mentioned it. But the point is they are safe, and sound and I made them cookies, and everyone was very happy. Right?"

"Yes, they seem to like you. Just next time, if there are any things that go awry, let me know. You don't have to be afraid of me! I'm not scary."

"No, you aren't. I just don't want to disappoint you I suppose."

"Well enough of that business. How are things with Simon? He seems rather the smitten kitten with you."

I can feel myself blush at the mere mention of him.

"They are going fantastic. He wants me to stay..."

"Wow, those are bold requests. How do you feel about that?"

"I really like him. He's the first person I've let in since my divorce. But it's a scary decision. Moving to a different country? We've only known each other a little over a week." When I say it out loud, I wonder if we're taking things too fast. But I am having such a great time, I decide not to wonder too much. I need to just live in the moment.

"Tell me about it. But you know what? I knew Deacon was the one and I knew we'd be happy here. What do your friends and family back home think?"

"I haven't broached the subject. I'm afraid they would think I've lost my mind." My parents would definitely think I was unstable.

"Hmm. Maybe be honest and give them the benefit of

the doubt. I'm sure they want you to be happy. You just have to decide where that is."

I ponder what Tilda has advised and I let her get back to work. I walk back to my room at the B&B and review my list of flaws to perfect. I need to decide what I should do next. I'm actually halfway done!

I really do need to plan this out. If I'm going to work for Sam and Cassie full time for a weekend, I won't be able to do much of my list. I certainly am not ready to go make up free.

I would like to find a recipe and cook a meal for Simon. I wonder if he would let me use his kitchen. I'm sure he would. I use my phone to find a cooking website to get some ideas. Maybe another pasta dish? Or should I cook something American for him? Hm. But what is American food nowadays? They cook burgers at the pub.

I find myself getting overwhelmed at the idea of cooking for Simon. He's an excellent chef. He's trained. My mom never let me in the kitchen, although she is a pretty good cook herself. I wish now I had made her teach me some things.

I decide to give her a call. It's early, but my mom wakes up very early. She likes to drink her coffee first thing before the sun rises.

"Hi, Mom. Did I wake you?"

"No, of course not. Is everything okay?" She asks, concerned.

"Oh, yes everything is great actually. I am really enjoying myself. In fact, I've decided to stay an extra week or two."

"An extra week or two? Dabney, is that practical? Don't you have to get back home and figure out your life?"

"I can figure out my life here, Mom."

"Do you have enough money to stay that long?" I decide to not get into the whole thing where Jack gave me a bunch of cash to make himself feel better.

"I do. And I've been working a bit here. The owners of the B&B let me help in the mornings and evenings in exchange for a discounted rate. It's very casual here. But they're very nice. They're American."

"Hm. I don't know how I feel about that...but it's your decision I suppose."

"Well I also called to see if you had any good recipes to share. I have a friend I'd like to cook for."

"A friend, Dabney?" Mom responds again with her concerned tone.

"Yes, Mom. He's a friend who I've gotten to know while I'm here. I've had a really nice time with him."

"What does he do?"

"He works at the pub next door."

"Oh Dabney, I have all sorts of red flags. He probably does this all the time. A pretty girl comes to visit for a few days. He thinks he can have a fling and then she's off on her way and he can move on the next one."

I am speechless. One, it never occurred to me that Simon would be remotely like that. Two, my mom has yet again shot down anything positive I want to do.

"Mom, you know how I've made a list of things I want

to do before I go? One of the things is to cook a meal for a friend. The only thing I know how to make is chicken piccata. I want to make something new. Something I didn't make for Jack."

"Well how about tacos? We used to always do taco night for you kids. That's not too difficult."

"Can I find tortillas in Ireland?" I wonder aloud.

"Make them yourself. It's easy. Flour, water, and oil. They have that in Ireland. I can email you my recipe for taco mix. If you can't find tortillas, I doubt you'll find taco mix. I think I have a recipe for tortillas I can give you as well."

"Thanks mom."

"Dabney just be careful. I know you think I'm over-protective, but I don't want to see you get hurt."

"I won't Mom. Don't worry."

Feeling satisfied with my phone call with my mom, I go downstairs to see if Maura needs any help.

"Most of the people have checked out already but I have a few things that I could use help with. Sam is coming in later to check some guests in before happy hour. I think it's a big group. We need to put together the welcome signs for the rooms."

The welcome signs are a nice touch. They're just printed out on nice cardstock with the guest's name on it. They leave it on the bed with a cute bag of candies and bottled water. It made me feel welcome—especially since I was there by myself.

Maura shows me the list of people checking in later and I create a welcome sign for each room.

"Okay, now what?" I ask feeling proud of my accomplishment.

"Well, do you want to help me with the bottles of wine? I need to inventory and let Sam know how much we need for next week's supply order.

"Absolutely." I go through each box and count the red and white. I think they should have Prosecco and wonder if I should mention that to Sam.

By the time Maura and I finish our few things to do, Sam has arrived to set up for happy hour. He still looks exhausted, but not as much as he did the other day. Maura and I give each other a look and decide now is the time to tell him our plan.

Sam furrows his brow with concern. "I don't know, ladies. That's a lot to put on your plate. Dabney, you've barely worked here. Do you think you could manage?"

"Of course, I can manage. I just need to know how to check people in and out. What else is there to do?"

"We need to make sure all the rooms are cleaned and ready to go. We have a cleaning team that comes in each day, but we still have to make sure all the rooms are stocked with everything. We have breakfast and clean up, happy hour and clean up. And we have to be here for the guests when they have questions."

"Sam, we can do a weekend of that, I'm sure." I say confidently.

Maura adds, "But obviously only if you're comfortable."

"Okay, I'll let you ladies take over for a weekend, but expect me to be checking in on you by text."

"Absolutely! If that makes you feel better." I say excitedly. I am so happy to be able to give Sam and Cassie an entire weekend with their family.

"So, Dabney, how long do we have you for then?"

"As long as you need me, Sam."

Maura clears her throat and says, "Now that we're on the subject Sam...you might need Dabney longer. I got into Uni in Cork. I won't be here in the Fall, I'm afraid."

"That's great news, Maura!" Sam is enthusiastic until he realizes that means Maura is leaving.

"We're going to miss you, Maura. But I know you're going to go on to do great things at University."

"Um, in answer to your question, I don't know that I'll be here for Fall—"

"Dabney, you can stay as long as you need to."

"I just wish I knew how long that is..."

CHAPTER 15

My alarm goes off extra early this morning, giving me plenty of time to prepare myself to be Bed & Breakfast worker extraordinaire. I tip toe to the bathroom so as not to wake Simon, who stayed over even though I told myself he shouldn't. I just couldn't resist. I love having him sleep next to me.

"Good morning." He whispers to me when I come back from my shower.

"I hope I didn't wake you," I say while I dress. Sam and Cassie don't have a uniform, so I settle on my nice skinny jeans, a long tunic shirt and white sneakers. I decide not to wear my bracelets because they make a lot of noise when I pick up the plates and cups. I quickly apply a thin layer of makeup over my moisturizer and put my hair up in a quick top knot.

"No, you didn't wake me. Are you excited for your first day as a real employee?"

"What do you mean, real employee?"

"You know, the boss has let you be in charge. You're not helping out as a guest. You have a lot of work to do today."

Simon isn't wrong about that. No wonder Sam looks exhausted all the time. He's been doing this with a newborn and not having Cassie to work with.

"I am absolutely, positively ready. Sam and Maura have shown me the computer system, I know the routine for breakfast already. Plus I have Maura to answer any questions I might have."

Simon gets out of bed and walks toward me. "I am so proud of you, Dabney." Simon wraps his arms around me and kisses me on the forehead.

"You know what? I'm proud of me too."

"But this isn't on your list. Will you have time to do all that as well?"

"It's just a weekend. I have been meaning to ask though. I'd like to cook a meal for you. If you like that is. I would need to use your kitchen, though."

"That would be wonderful! Yes, absolutely you can use my kitchen. What are you going to cook for me?"

"It's a surprise. Well at least until I might need you to take me to the grocery store. You know what? No, I can do that on my own. I'll take a taxi."

"Nonsense. I'll drive you to the store. It's easier that way."

"Do you know your next day off? We can do it then."

"Yes, it's Tuesday.

"Tuesday it is then! But for now, I must get downstairs to start my job." I kiss Simon and tell him to leave whenever. I'm so excited that I don't even care about sneaking him out.

I get to the kitchen to find Maura hasn't arrived yet. I'm a bit early though. I decide to start prepping the fruit plate and the meats. We are out of apples, so I only put out bananas, oranges and strawberries.

Maura arrives shortly after I have most of the plated items on the buffet.

"Good morning, Dabney. You've done a lot so far!" She says, taking off her jacket. "I'll get the juices filled and put those out."

I'm really impressed with Maura. She's only nineteen, but very mature and responsible. I was not that mature when I was her age. In fact, when I went away to college the first year, I almost dropped out. I partied so much most of my classes were failures. I can't imagine Maura being that reckless. In fact, I almost think she could manage the B&B without my help…almost.

Maura gets out the hot plate. "Do you want me to handle the omelet bar?"

"Yes, definitely. I've never made an omelet and doubt I could learn in a few minutes."

"It's not really that hard but I don't mind. You handle the coffees."

"Got it! I can definitely do that."

We handle breakfast quite well considering it is a full house. There are a few families, but the rest are mostly couples. Although there is one solo guest that I am intrigued by. She is sipping her beautiful cappuccino and reading a book. Her jet black hair is pulled back in a bun. She's definitely Irish, given her accent, although I don't know if she's from around here or not. I am not expert enough to determine dialects yet.

"Can I get you another cappuccino, Miss?" I ask, trying

not to interrupt her solitary bliss. I wish I could look that serene when I'm alone. I imagine people can smell the anxiety seeping from my pores.

"Oh, yes please." She says, joyfully.

I make another cappuccino with lovely foam art and bring it over to the lovely stranger.

"Are you staying here by yourself?" I ask, hoping it doesn't sound creepy.

"Yes, but I'm planning on meeting someone."

"How nice! I recently took my first solo trip. It was totally worth it. It's nice to have some quiet time to reflect, you know?"

"I do. I'm Christina by the way."

"Nice to meet you! I'm Dabney, but I guess my name tag has already revealed that."

I leave Christina to finish my work and get back to Maura, who seems quite busy with omelets.

"Can I help, Maura?"

"Yes, can you bring me more eggs please? We've had a lot of orders this morning."

I bring Maura more eggs and help her clean up her station. There is only one hot plate to make the omelets, not that I would be much help anyway. Instead I help by getting all the dirty dishes to the dishwasher and tend to the guests that are not waiting in their omelets. Hmm. Possible note to Sam...Are omelets a necessary part of breakfast? They seem to add a lot of work...

Once breakfast is over, I take all the tablecloths and napkins off the tables and put them in the wash. Then set the tables with the other set for tomorrow's breakfast. Maura cleans up the omelet bar area.

Once we have everything cleaned up from breakfast, we go to the front to process some checkouts. We call a taxi for one group of guests, handle an online charge dispute and have a completely smooth checkout for our final guests.

At this point in the day we've only had three texts from Sam wondering if everything is going well. I don't take it as a slight, only that he wants to make sure we don't need anything…and perhaps ensuring his business isn't burning to the ground. It's fair.

Maura goes to the empty rooms and starts to pull sheets for housekeeping, who is running behind. I hold the fort down at the front desk and answer questions like, 'does a shuttle take us to the airport?' That would be a no. 'Is the pub next door open for breakfast?' That would be a no and a follow up question from me. What's wrong with our breakfast? Not really. I don't ask it, but I would like to know. I was also able to let a guest know that the bus line does run down our street and does stop at the supermarket and pharmacy.

My new friend, Christina comes downstairs to ask about the pub as well.

"Do you know how late the pub next door stays open?"

"On weeknights it's open until 10:00, but on the weekend they stay open until 11:00. It's a family run pub so they don't stay open really late. Are you concerned about noise?"

"Oh no, nothing like that. Just curious. Do you know

much of the staff?"

I find her question odd, but perhaps she's curious if we are a friendly establishment or connected with The Stag's Leap for some reason.

"I have not been here long, but I will say I've gotten to know most of the staff quite well."

"Hmm. Do you know the chef by chance?"

"Simon? Yes." I say, still confused. "Why?"

"Oh, just curious. I've heard the food is very good."

Ah. Maybe she's a food blogger or something. I should let Simon know so he's prepared tonight.

"The food there is excellent. The chef also does the food for our happy hour. Don't miss that! It's from 4:00-6:00 right here in the lobby area." I say proudly.

"That sounds lovely. I won't miss it."

Christina, who is now even more mysterious to me walks out the front door with her bag. Off to a new restaurant. Perhaps to eat alone with little hesitation or disdain?

Maura offers to take happy hour tonight. Since I don't have any responsibilities for the time being, I hang out in my room and catch up on social media. I have decided to take Simon's advice and stay away from anything Jack may have posted.

I call Ruby to see how she is. I miss not having her around. Even though she works a lot, I still get to talk to her quite often—especially since I started living with her. We have our coffee mornings at her apartment. Ruby is rather quiet when she first wakes up, whereas I am ready to start chatting right away. I probably drive her crazy but that's our friendship I suppose. We've been friends since high school and although our career paths took very opposite turns, we have remained close.

"Hi, Dabney how's it going?"

"It's good. How are you?"

"Busy. I have never ending papers to grade. Teaching four classes is so much work. I'm never going to assign papers instead of an exam again! But whatever. How are you doing? I miss you."

"Well, that's what I wanted to talk to you about. I'm staying a bit longer than I thought."

"What?! How much longer? I am having to go to my yoga classes alone now and my partner is a 70-year old man. Do you know how awkward it is? It's awkward Dabney. Very awkward."

Ruby and I started taking a yoga class about a year ago together. She likes yoga because it's calming and helps keep her centered. I like it because it's great exercise and keeps my abs and butt looking firm. Unfortunately, it's a partner centric class, so when someone goes alone, they have to partner up with someone they don't know possibly.

"I'm sorry. It's just, well, I'm having a great time here. I do miss you though. I miss you a lot. But I'm doing this list to better myself and I still have things to do and I said I wouldn't leave till it was done. And I think I'm falling for someone." I cringe as I say it.

"Oh Dabney. You're falling for the chef?"

"Yes."

"Have you told your mom?"

"God, no! I haven't completely lost my mind. She has no idea I've hooked up with anybody!"

Ruby catches my admission. "You've hooked up with him again?"

"Yes, and it is wonderful. Every single time. If Jack can get engaged less than a month after our divorce, then I can hook up with any hot dark haired, blue eyed Irish guy I want."

"Listen to you! Okay, I'm on board. With just this one guy though. Not the other part. Also, um, Jack is engaged???"

"Yes."

"How do you know?"

"I saw her Instagram post. It's public."

"Dabney, I'm sorry. That is so wrong. Especially since he's been harassing me about you."

"Huh?"

"Yeah! He came to the apartment yesterday asking when you were coming back and where were you staying and all that. I told him I had no idea what he was talking about and he should probably leave before I spray him in the eyes with the Chanel No. 5 he bought on your honeymoon."

"He's been calling and texting me too. I don't know what his problem is. I'm sorry he has been bothering you since I left. He's lost his mind obviously."

"I don't know what his deal is, but don't worry about me. I can handle it."

I tell Ruby about my new job. She seems to be somewhat on board since it keeps me busy.

"I just hope you're not being too distracted from life. I mean, you have to come home at some point, right?"

"Yes, yes I'll come home." I decide not tell Ruby my thoughts on that since I don't really know what they are. It's less complicated that way.

I finish my chat with Ruby and relax for a bit with my phone. Once I've had a nice rest, I check in on Maura for happy hour. Then I decide to go next door for a bite to eat and see Simon.

It's fairly busy when I walk in. I see there are no open tables. Christina spots me though and waves.

I walk over to her. "Hi! You made it to The Stag's Leap, I see."

"Yes, it's really cute." She says, then takes a sip of her beer. "Have a seat, if you like. I feel bad taking up an entire table by myself."

"Have you ordered yet? They make a delicious stew here. And their hamburgers are good, too." I talk up the food as much as possible, in case she's a food blogger. "Has your friend made it yet?"

"I'm hoping to meet up with him tonight actually."

"Great! Tell him to come by! The more the merrier. The owner is an excellent musician. He might have a recording contract soon, in fact!"

"Wow that's amazing! I didn't know they had music here as well. What a great little pub."

That's right, food blogger. This is a great little pub.

Christina's food comes and I order a salad with a side of fries.

"You're right, this stew is delicious. I have to give my compliments to the chef!" Christina waves over the new server, Jules, who brought over her food.

"Can you please send the chef out when he has a moment? I want to let him know how wonderful his stew is."

Jules looks at Christina funny as though that's never happened before, but nods and says she will. I am excited because it's a chance to see Simon and introduce him to Christina.

I see Simon come out of the kitchen and Jules points over to our table. He looks closer at us and then his face drops. What did she tell him? Was she confused and thought Christina was complaining rather than complimenting?

Simon slowly walks over to the table. But instead of greeting me with a happy smile, he looks over at my new friend and says, "Christina? What are you doing here?"

Um, he knows her? How?

"Hi Simon. I finally tracked you down." She stands up to give Simon a hug while I look on completely bewildered.

"How do you know Simon?" I ask after the uncomfortably long hug ends.

"Dabney, Christina is an old friend." He finally answers in an awkward tone.

"Old friend? Simon and I go way back. He was my first love until he broke my heart by breaking up with me."

"I had a good reason to break up with you. Do we have to talk about this here?"

"You're right. Dabney doesn't care about all this. Let's talk tonight. After your shift?"

Simon looks at me and then looks at Christina and then says, "I have to get back to work. We have orders that are backing up. I'm really busy."

"So, were you pretending to be a food blogger so you could find Simon?" I ask Christina.

"Food blogger? I never said I was a food blogger." She laughs at the idea, and then I realize, she never did say that. I just assumed. I mean how was I to know she was actually here to see my vacation boyfriend?

"Is he the person you've been waiting to meet up with?"

"Yes, why?" Christina asks me as she momentarily breaks her eye contact with Simon, who is extremely uncomfortable standing in front of the two of us.

"Simon, is this your girlfriend from a few years ago that you broke up with?"

"Dabney, I'm sorry but I really have to get back to the kitchen. Can we talk about this later?"

He gives me a kiss on the cheek and practically runs back to the kitchen.

Christina looks at me with a serious glare and says, "Oh, well this is awkward now isn't it?"

"Yes, I'm sorry but I didn't know who you were looking for. Simon and I are, um, well, we're seeing one another." I take a bite of my salad and wait for her reaction.

She looks at me with disapproval. "How long has this been going on?"

"Christina, why are you here exactly?"

"I don't see how that is any of your concern. You're just the help. I'm your guest don't forget."

Oh my god. She just called me 'The Help.' I want to punch her in the face.

"I am not just the help. If you must know, I am a guest too. I'm helping Sam and Cassie at the B&B so they can have a break. I can quit whenever I want."

"Look, I don't mean to cause any trouble. I just wanted to catch up with Simon. I haven't been able to reach him since he moved, changed his number and pretty much fell off the face of the earth. I finally tracked him down here."

"Was he hiding from you?"

"No, he wasn't hiding from me," she replies in an offended tone. "I'll be honest, Dabney, I don't want to talk about it with you."

"Okay, I get it. I'm going to go. I don't really want to talk about it with you either."

I leave the pub and go back to my room. I send Simon a text to let him know I'm going to bed because I have an early morning and I'll talk to him tomorrow.

Maybe old girlfriend drama is a sign that this whirlwind romance is about to die down.

CHAPTER 16

I barely slept a wink last night. But unfortunately I have work to do, so it's up and at em. A commitment is a commitment. I can't let Sam, Cassie or Maura down.

I take a long, hot shower to try and wake up. It's an extra layer of eye cream morning for sure. Once I've done my hair in a simple ponytail, I finish my makeup with a quick layer of serum, moisturizer, eye cream, primer and foundation. I get dressed in my yoga pants and long t-shirt with sneakers and go downstairs to start work.

My routine is the same as yesterday, but this time Maura is here first. She's setting up the coffee.

"I'll take a cup of that." I say, bringing my cup to the coffee urn.

"Long night last night?" Maura asks.

"No, but I didn't sleep well. Simon's ex-girlfriend showed up and guess who she is?" I anxiously whisper.

"Who?" Maura whispers back.

"Christina! Our really pretty and cool guest from yesterday!"

"Are you serious?!"

"Yes!" I whisper again.

"I'm sorry, Dabney. Simon seems like a nice guy though. Maybe he can explain everything to you later."

"Yeah maybe so. It's fine, really. I need to stop being so silly and get serious about what I'm doing with my life. Look at you. You're so focused and you're much younger than me. I think it's time I grew up and figured things out."

"Ah Dabney, you'll be fine. Let's get this food out before the guests get here, eh?"

I get through most of breakfast before Christina comes downstairs looking perfect with her shiny black hair and perfect bun. Has she ever heard of letting her hair down or perhaps putting it up in a messy top knot? I decide to be professional though. I'll act as though nothing has bothered me since last night.

"Good morning, Christina. Can I get you a coffee?"

"Hi, Dabney. Yes please. A cappuccino."

I go make her cappuccino, but she doesn't get a pretty picture today. It's just a plain normal and somewhat messy cappuccino for her.

"Dabney, can I talk to you for a minute?" Christina asks when I drop off her coffee.

"I'm actually quite busy." I look around for a table that needs me. Unfortunately the dining room is kind of empty. Everyone has finished their breakfast and either have left already or are getting ready to.

"It'll just take a minute."

"Okay," I say, feeling extremely uncomfortable as I shift on each foot.

"When Simon broke up with me, I thought my world was ending. We talked about marriage. Did he mention that?"

She waits for an answer, but I don't have one because Simon hasn't mentioned much of his past at all. Just that he was in a relationship that it ended.

Christina continues. "I had no clue he was going to break up with me. He just said he couldn't do it anymore. That was it. We didn't contact each other or carry on any drama. It was just over. I left to go work in London and never heard from him again. Then I realized one day, it wasn't over. Not for me. I was never able to get over him and I don't think he was able to fully get over me. I need us to give our relationship another chance."

"What do you want me to say. That it's fine. You should just go be with Simon and I'll go back home and forget it all?"

"Yes. That's exactly what I want you to say and do. Simon is the love of my life. For you, he's just some fling."

"That's not fair. You don't know anything about us."

"Us? You've only known him a couple weeks? You just got divorced! He's a rebound fling."

"How do you know— Okay—listen, I don't think this is appropriate to talk about here. I have to get back to work."

"Sure, go back to work. But remember what I said, Dabney. We aren't over and you're just getting in the way."

Christina leaves while I'm left trying to figure out what is happening. Of all the weekends this all had to take place. It was the one where I promised to work to make sure Sam and Cassie have a break. I can't just go see Simon whenever I feel like it. Or go bury myself under my covers with a bottle of wine.

"Holy shit, Dabney. I listened to all of that. She's barking mad." Maura says, coming up to me.

"What if she isn't? What if it's true?"

"Nah, she's barking mad. I can tell. But you need to talk to Simon. We have some cleanup to do and one checkout, but that's it. I can handle that if you need a break."

"Thanks, Maura. I appreciate that." I text Simon right then.

We need to talk. Now.

A few minutes later Simon comes to the B&B and finds me in my room.

"What the hell, Simon? What is happening? And how does she know about my business?" I ask as I let him in. Thankfully, Christina isn't on my floor.

"I am so sorry Dabney. I had no idea she even knew how to find me."

"Are you still in love with her?" I want the bad news out of the way first.

"Dabney, is that what you think? No. I'm not."

"Well she seems to think you are. She pretty much said so. She said you broke up with her for no reason."

He sits down on the sofa like he's carrying the weight of the world "I think it's time you hear the story."

"Okay so tell me."

"My parents died when I was young. My Gran took care of me after that. She was like a mother to me. When she got sick, I couldn't bear to leave her in a home. So I quit my job to take care of her full time. She was everything to me. Christina couldn't understand that. My Gran was dying, and that was all I could handle. We broke up, Then Christina moved to London. I never heard from her again after that."

"Were you going to get married?" I ask, folding the clean clothes from my laundry pile.

"We talked about it, but I never proposed Dabney."

"If I wasn't here, would you think about getting back together with her?"

He goes quiet. Like he's thinking about it.

"It's okay if you want to go back to her. I understand." I say finally.

"No, I don't want to go back to her. I know it seems complicated, but I really like you. I want to see where we go with this. I wouldn't have asked you to stay if I wasn't serious about that."

I let out a deep breath because I believe him. I really believe him.

"Okay. That's all I need to know. I'm sorry if I doubted you, Simon."

"Are you kidding me? You have nothing to be sorry about! Are you okay? I'm sure this was an awful shock for you."

"I'm okay. It was awkward though, for sure. Did she happen to say when she's leaving?"

"No, she didn't."

"What am I going to do? I can't keep serving her cappuccinos and acting like everything is normal. She wants my boy—"

"Are you about to call me your boyfriend?"

"Um, no. I don't know. Are you my boyfriend?"

"I am if you want me to be."

I sit down next to Simon on the sofa. "I suddenly feel like I'm in middle school asking you to the dance. This is so juvenile. Yes, I want to be an official couple because I'm falling for you Simon O'Connell."

"Good." He says, taking off my shirt, "Because I'm falling for you Dabney Corrigan and there is nothing anybody can do stop me."

Simon leads me to my bed and begins kissing me all over my body. I let him, because there is nothing else I would rather happen than Simon devour every inch of me. I want to forget the awkward conversation with his ex-girlfriend. I want to forget my feelings of not being good enough and insecurity that I am not the object of his desire. At this very moment, he is proving that I am and that is all I need.

We lay in bed for a bit, then I say, "I really need to get back to work. Maura let me have a break, but I don't know what she has going on downstairs."

"I need to get back home as well. I work tonight."

"I wish you didn't. I wish we could just run away for a while and leave all this mess."

"I know. I do have tomorrow off. How about we spend

the day together? You can make me your surprise meal." He says, kissing the top of my head and softly rubbing my arm.

"Hmm. Sam will be back. I just have to get up early to help him with breakfast and some morning work since Maura is off tomorrow. Can we meet up around lunch?"

"Sure. I'll come get you. Then we can get your groceries and you can finally tell me what you're making me."

"It's not that exciting, trust me. But it will be made from the heart. Remember that if it doesn't taste very good."

"I have no doubt it will be delicious."

"You have clearly not eaten any of my cooking, dear Simon." I give him a kiss. "Lock up when you leave. I'll see you later."

CHAPTER 17

Once Dabney left the room, Simon got dressed then took a look in the mirror. The dark circles under his eyes were evidence of his sleepless night. He had no idea his ex-girlfriend, Christina was back in town. What had she said to Dabney? He didn't talk much to her when he had the opportunity. Although he did regret giving her any personal information about Dabney. What was he thinking?

Before leaving he made Dabney's bed. He wasn't sure was a priority to her, especially since housekeeping might come in and do it for her, but it was important to him. His Gran had taught him to make his bed every morning. It was a good way to start the day off fresh and tidy. He could tell Dabney didn't have the same tidiness that he did, but it didn't matter to him. She was still something special.

Although everyone knew he was a frequent guest of Dabney's, he still felt inclined to tip toe down that stairs, especially since Christina was somewhere possibly in the building. He had no interest in talking to her. It was over, despite what she seemed to think.

As he made his way down the stairwell, he heard a familiar sound. Shit, he thought to himself. Was it a coincidence or was she waiting for him? Did she know he was in Dabney's room?

"Good morning, Simon. Or is it afternoon? Being on holiday makes me so flighty when it comes to time and schedules. Is the same true for your friend? She is on holiday, isn't she?"

"What can I do for you, Christina?"

She walks to Simon stopping so close to him his personal space in complete invasion mode. "I would like you to give me the decency of hearing me out. Why can't you at least listen to me? This girl is going to break your heart. Watch."

Christina caught his stare and refused to let go. Simon was almost mesmerized by her. Not in a sexual way, but her passion almost weakened him.

"Stop. Stop it. I'm sorry you are confused about your feelings for me. It's over Christina. It has been over for many years. You can't just show up expecting things to be something they aren't. Perhaps something they never were."

She was affected by those words, he could tell. He didn't really mean them. He did have feelings for her many years ago. But when she made him choose between his Gran and her, it dissolved anything he may have felt for her.

"I'm going back to London in a few days. I have some business to catch up on while I'm here in Dublin, but I'll say goodbye once I'm done. Who knows? Maybe this time you'll come with back with me to London."

Not a chance, he wanted to tell her. Not a chance. His life was here. His new life—which included Dabney Corrigan.

CHAPTER 18

Although Maura and I had a decent weekend proving to Sam he could take a weekend off once in a while, I am happy to see him back. Taking care of an entire B&B is a lot of work and I have a lot going on in my life. I don't think I am quite ready for the responsibility of complete adulting.

Simon picks me up as promised at noon. First we go to the grocery store. As expected, I don't find any tortillas, so I get the ingredients to make them. My mom sent me a recipe for everything, and I made a complete list of what I needed.

The only thing I forgot was dessert. I look around the bakery section to find some yummy looking tarts that we can nibble on afterwards.

"Well I think that's it. I've found everything I need on my list."

"I can't wait. Let's get some wine as well."

"In America, we typically drink margaritas with tacos." I am reminded of my usual Taco Tuesday nights I have with Ruby. We go to the local Mexican restaurant that has $2 tacos and $4 margaritas. She doesn't have to teach on Tuesday nights, and it has become a fun tradition for the two of us. I have also just realized I told

Simon was the surprise is.

"Ah so I'm getting tacos, am I?"

"Oops. Busted."

"Well margaritas it is." Simon looks up the recipe on his phone and we get ingredients for them. I think it's going to be a fun night. We have completely forgotten our drama, or at least given the impression we have.

We go back to Simon's. I start to put away some of the groceries. It feels quite normal and comfortable, as though we have always done this.

"So, have you heard from your ex lately? Is he still bothering you?" Simon asks, unloading the last bag of groceries with me. I can tell he's used to working in a kitchen. Everything he pulls out of the bags is methodically placed on the counter. Spices are organized together. Vegetables are put in their own spot next to the spices and then the meat is in its own special section on the counter.

"What's with our exes harassing us?" I pull out my phone to find Mom's recipe. "Actually, to answer your question, no I haven't. I have stopped engaging with him so maybe he finally got the message that I want nothing to do with him. Although Ruby said he did bother her the other day."

He stops. "What did he do?"

"He was asking when I was coming back and stuff like, Where I was staying? That sort of thing. Ruby wouldn't tell him anything though." I trust Ruby 100 percent to not divulge any important personal details. She has kept the best of my secrets throughout our friendship.

"Why does he want to know where you're staying? Do you think he would contact the B&B trying to reach you?"

"Ew, I can't imagine he would go that far." I say, mixing up my taco seasoning. "To be honest, I don't know why he keeps bothering me."

"Who knows? Maybe he realizes he made a mistake and that you are absolutely perfect." Simon takes my hand and kisses it.

"You've seen my cleaning skills. You are about to see my cooking skills, so I know you don't think I am perfect."

"You're perfect enough for me. If you were mine, I never would have taken that for granted." Simon mixes together everything to make our drinks as he smiles warmly at me. "His loss is your gain. Now shall we try out the margaritas? I know it's early but I'm feeling festive."

Simon and I pour our drinks and sit on the sofa together. It's cozy and relaxing. We watch a mindless, funny show on Netflix and sip our drinks. Is this what it could be like all the time with Simon?

Once it gets closer to dinnertime I begin cooking. Simon sits at the counter watching me like I did when he cooked.

"I feel like I'm on a cooking show or something. I'm a bit nervous."

"Don't be. I just like watching you move." Simon takes a sip of his drink and continues to watch me as I chop the vegetables for the tacos and Pico de Gallo.

"Have you had tacos before?" I ask getting the meat out to cook.

"Actually, yes. I went to Mexico once on holiday. Playa del Carmen I think it was."

"Wait, you've had real Mexican tacos?" I have a sudden sinking feeling. I doubt that my tacos will be anything like those from Playa del Carmen.

"Yes, but I'm excited for your version."

"Okay, well, this version will be from the cooking repertoire of the suburban Chicago housewife." I remember my mom made tacos every single Tuesday of our entire childhood. I got really tired of them. Now, as I cook them, I see why she did it. It is easy. Of course, her tortillas were usually already made. "Simon, normally, tortillas are circular. These tortillas have taken a more, shall we say oval-ish form."

I taste one. I must say, they are quite edible. I am rather impressed with myself. I never would have thought I would ever make my tortillas.

"Not a problem, my dear." He says, tasting one. Then he gives me a thumbs up.

"Maybe I should've had one less margarita." I'm feeling extra relaxed.

"Nonsense. The margaritas make everything better."

I finish our taco dinner and we eat. I think I did quite well, considering I had to make my own Pico de Gallo and tortillas.

"Dabney, I am thoroughly impressed with you." Simon takes a bite of his taco and smiles at me.

"Thank you, Simon. I appreciate that."

He stops for a moment then he looks at me and says, "You underestimate yourself."

"Maybe I do."

Our eyes lock for a long time, before I am interrupted by a series of texts.

"Who is texting you?"

I pick up my phone to see what's going on. "It's Sam. I hope everything is ok." Sam doesn't normally text me unless there is an issue. If he needs help for some reason, we're in trouble because I have had several drinks.

"Oh my god." I stare at my phone in shock as I read the text messages from Sam.

"What is it?" Simon puts down his margarita and sits up straight with a worried expression.

"Jack is here." I can barely get the words out of my mouth. "I mean, he's here at the B&B looking for me!"

"What?! He's here? I don't understand. Why would he be here? You said he wouldn't follow you here."

"I have no idea. What am I going to do? I don't want to see him, but I don't want him pestering Sam and everyone at the pub."

"I'll go with you, but we'll need to get a taxi or walk. I don't think I can drive."

Simon calls a taxi, and we head to the B&B. When we get there, I see Jack sitting in the lobby area with Christina of all people.

"Oh fabulous." I say aloud and from the expression on Simon's face, he feels the same way.

"Dabney!" Jack stands up and rushes over to me. "Thank goodness you're okay." He looks a mess. He hasn't shaved for a few days; his hair is overgrown, and his khaki pants are wrinkled and stained. He must have just stepped off the plane...a few days ago by the looks of it.

"Why wouldn't I be okay?" I ask, confused.

"I've been trying to reach you for days and you won't communicate with me. Can we have a moment—alone?" He looks at Simon as he's talking.

"Whatever you need to say, you can say in front of Simon." I say with my head held high. At this point, I have no secrets and it might be good for Simon to see what kind of person I have been dealing with.

"It's okay, Dabney. Maybe you should have some privacy."

Simon walks over to Christina, who is sitting in the lobby area where we do happy hour. She has a Cheshire grin on her face that says, *I told you so.*

I lead Jack back to the dining area, where we can speak in private since nobody sits in there after breakfast usually.

"Jack what the hell are you doing in Dublin? How can you think this is remotely appropriate?"

"Like I said, you wouldn't return any of my calls or text messages."

"Yes, because we are divorced. I'm trying to move on with my life!"

"I understand. But some things have happened that I think you should know."

"Jack, I already know. You're engaged. It's fine. I'm over it."

"No, I mean yes but that's not it. She took all my money and left me, Dabney. I'm broke."

"What?" I want to laugh but I am more shocked than anything. "How did she take all your money? Isn't it in a trust?"

"Yes, but I let her have access to my bank account and cards since we were engaged. She said she needed it for the house remodel we're working on."

"You bought a house?"

"Yes, but we didn't get far. I thought she was paying the contractors, but she wasn't. She was just taking the money for herself."

"Look Jack I'm sorry for this, but what does it have to do with me?"

"I came to apologize, Dabney. I never should have gotten involved with that She-Devil. I was under a trance and I'm sorry. I'm sorry for hurting you, for breaking your trust. I'm sorry for everything, Dabney. I love you. I want your forgiveness. I want you back, Dabney."

I am dumfounded.

"How on earth can you think coming here and telling me all this would automatically prompt me to forgive you."

"Because, what we had was real. We were husband and wife!" Jack raises his voice in desperation.

"Yes, and then you fucked your law clerk!" I shout back at him.

"Do you know how many nights I spent alone because I thought you were busy at work? Like an idiot. Do you know how stupid I felt that night? I brought you dinner. I worried about you. I loved you and you threw it away."

"I am sorry. I will never not be sorry." Jack says quietly.

"Good. I'm happy to hear you say that."

"There's something else." Jack says, finally.

"What." I say with a deadpan stare. I am done with surprises.

"I need that money back. The money I gave you."

"The money you insisted I take?"

"Yes, I'm sorry, but she took everything. My parents paid for me to come here. They're trying to get some money put together from overseas accounts, in the meantime I'm destitute. My credit cards are maxed, my bank account is empty. I'm living off a credit card my parents gave me."

"Well thank goodness you have your wealthy parents to fall back on. Most of us don't have that."

"I know, Dabney. I know I'm privileged and you're working class."

"What are you talking about? My dad is an accountant, he went to Northwestern. He's not working class. Not that there is anything wrong with that."

And now I remember another reason why I've grown to dislike my ex-husband immensely. He's such an elitist. When I met him, I was attracted to that kind of behavior, I think. I tried to be like him, which was why I bought the designer shoes and handbags. I spent money on the most expensive makeup. Because I thought that's what I was supposed to do.

I've learned I don't want to be like that anymore.

"Jack, I've already spent some of it, and you don't deserve to have any of the rest back anyway."

"You're right, I don't. I'm sorry. I shouldn't have asked." Jack runs his hands through his hair and says, "I'll let my parents pay for the flight back. I assume your flight has already been paid for?"

"Yeah, but why does that matter?" I say, leading him back out to the lobby area where Simon is talking to Christina.

"I thought you would want to come back with me?"

"Why would you think that?" I can't help but laugh at his assumptions. Who exactly did he think he was married to? A complete pushover?

"Well, um, I don't know. I thought we would reconcile. We have history together Dabney. I don't want to just forget about that."

"No, Jack. I'm not going home with you."

I walk over to Simon and put my arm in his. "Simon, I think I need a drink. I know it's your day off, but can we go to the pub?"

"Of course, we can go."

Jack stops us in our tracks. "Wait, this is Simon? Your 'friend' from way back? The one who called me all cocky and thought he would get in the way of us?"

"Us? There is no 'us' Jack!"

"Yeah, I'm Simon. What do you want to do about it?" Simon steps up to Jack, getting between us with the manly testosterone stance.

"You have a lot of nerve, dude. This is my wife."

"Ex-wife, I believe. And wasn't it because you were caught fucking another with woman?"

Jack's face gets red and his veins begin to bulge.

"I'm not leaving here without you, Dabney." Jack says, quiet but firm.

"Then you're going to wait a while, mate." Simon smiles at him.

"Oh yeah? Says who?" Jack asks, in the cocky tone when he gets defensive.

"Says me." I say getting in between the two men, now.

Simon looks at Jack and says, "The lady has spoken."

"The lady doesn't know what she wants. She's confused and you're making it worse."

"Alright, I've had enough of this. You guys need to take this outside." Sam says, obviously getting annoyed with the level of testosterone in the room. "I need to go home, and I can't do it if it looks like a fight is about to break out in my Bed and Breakfast."

"Fine, let's take this outside." Simon gestures to Jack towards the door of the B&B.

I look at Christina, who looks back at me as though to say, *Are they really going to go outside and fight?*

"Wait, you guys, this is ridiculous," I say following them out the front door.

"No, Dabney. I'm willing to fight for you. This idiot can't be more than a few minutes of a fight. I can take him."

"Simon, I don't want you to fight him. He's not worth it." We are now on the street since that's where this has taken us. To the streets like ruffians.

Simon, who is about to reply back to me suddenly gets hit with a cheap shot by Jack who has wasted no time in this nonsense.

"Oh, is that how you're going to do it, eh?" Simon is furious now and takes a shot at Jack, getting him right in the nose. There is blood everywhere. The two men are trying to get each other in head locks, blood getting all over the place as we all watch in both awe and horror.

Christina looks at me exasperated. "Do something! He's bleeding all over the place!"

"I'm trying! I can't break it up!"

Then, as I literally try to get in between them, I get shoved to the ground by Jack. An obvious mistake, he stops, giving Simon an opportunity to get a shot in. Jack falls to the ground and Simon is left victorious. In a sense, anyway.

He stops then, not realizing what had happened.

"Enough." I say as Simon lays down next to me—on the street, out of breath.

"This is ridiculous! You are grown ass men. I'm done with both of you, right now. I'll be back with something for your faces though."

I go into the B&B to get a first aid kit. Once I have found it I run outside and help clean them up. Then I walk away. Leaving them on the street to fend for them-selves.

I find a small café that's still open in the evening and go in. It's quaint, with black and white tile and soft pink walls. I spot a case in the front with a display of delicious looking pastries like almond croissants and lemon tarts. However, the chocolate cake is calling my name. I walk over to the table, sit in the large wooden bench seat and try to get comfortable. I feel like the table is swallowing me up in my solitude.

"May I have a coffee and piece of chocolate cake, please?" The lady, who looks to be in her sixties, takes my order and brings me my coffee and cake.

I slowly eat it while thinking about what kind of day has taken place. It started out so lovely. A nice grocery trip with Simon, some cooking, fun and drinks. Then it's ruined by my ex-husband showing up unannounced.

I don't understand why he would want to get back together with me. Why did he cheat in the first place? I never really got a solid answer to that question and I probably never will.

But I don't care. I don't need it. I don't want to get back together with him. Not for all the Louboutins

in the world.

I stop and wonder if me sitting here, eating my dessert counts as eating a meal by myself. It's not that bad, really. I am finding it somewhat relaxing eat and be with my own thoughts. As I finish my coffee, I see Simon standing at window looking at me. Can come in? he mouths. I nod yes. So much for being alone.

He comes in and takes a seat at my table. "I've been looking for you."

"Well I don't know that I wanted to be found. I've been having a nice piece of cake and cup of coffee by myself."

"I see that. I hope I'm not upsetting you by being here."

"No, you're not."

"I'm sorry about my behavior, Dabney. I shouldn't have gotten into a fight with him. It was stupid."

"Yes it was, but I understand. It's a guy thing. When you feel like doing something, you do it. Women are different. We think about how we want to do it, then have an internal conversation about doing it and then don't do it. You don't think I wanted to punch Christina in the face every time she mentioned your name? But I didn't because I am a civilized human being."

"I think she was horrified by our behavior as well. She left and went to her room. But not before she told me which one. That woman is relentless."

"She probably thinks I'm going to leave you for my ex-husband, and everything will be perfectly in line for her to get you back."

He takes a deep breath. "Are you? Going back to him?"

"Simon, how can you even ask me that? After everything we've talked about? No, I'm not leaving you for him."

He puts his hands in his face for a moment, then rubs his eyes that now look pretty rough. I'm fairly certain there will be a black eye in an hour.

"Maybe we should take a trip somewhere. We can take a couple days in the country. I can teach you to drive."

"I know how to drive, asshole. I've just never driven on the wrong side of the road."

"Yikes. Who says our way is wrong?"

"Me."

"Got it." He says, knowing to give in at this point in the conversation. The Simon I met earlier in my trip would have argued with me.

"In the grand scheme of things, maybe my flaws list is stupid. Who cares about driving? Or eating alone in a restaurant."

"You did. It was something you were afraid to do, yet here you are."

"I'm with you."

"But you weren't. You left us idiots on the street and took care of yourself."

"I did, didn't I?"

"How about we go back to the B&B, apologize to Sam and head over to my place?"

"Okay, I do owe Sam a huge apology."

We walk back to the B&B. Sam is still there, perhaps waiting to see if anyone comes back.

Sam accepts my apology and says a couple days away is probably a good idea. Especially since Cassie is thinking about getting back to working a little bit and I probably won't need to help out as much as I did have. I'm not sure if those are my walking papers or he's just being accommodating.

I am afraid to ask...

CHAPTER 19

I look out the window as we drive out of the city to the luscious green Irish countryside. I have no idea where we are, but I feel stress free albeit somewhat curious.

"Where are we going?"

"It's a secret."

"But you said I definitely did not need to pack any formal wear."

"That's right. Why did you pack formal wear on a solo trip to Dublin anyway? Where did you think you were going to go?"

"I don't know. What if I met someone who invited me to an important awards ceremony? Or a wedding? Or I just woke up one day and said, 'I feel like wearing a fancy dress today.' It could happen, you know."

Simon smiles at me. "Yes, now that I know you better, you're right. It could definitely happen. But to be clear, I don't have a wedding or awards ceremony planned so your casual clothes are completely appropriate."

"Fair enough."

We continue to drive, listening to music and talking about random things that are mildly important. It's relaxing and for the first time in what seems like forever, I feel I can let my hair down. In fact, I've done more than that.

I have gone on this trip makeup free.

Well not completely. I have packed makeup. I only agreed per my list to spend one day makeup free. I am not a complete bohemian.

I fall asleep for a few minutes and wake up as the car stops.

"We're here." Simon says, turning off the car. I open my eyes and see a small cottage.

"Is this where we're staying?"

"Yep. I rented it for the weekend. It's just you and me. No people walking down the hallway or stairs. No neighbors on the other side of the wall. We have the entire place to ourselves to do whatever we please." Simon's blue eyes sparkle and he flashes a devilish grin.

"I don't suppose your plans are to play cards all weekend?"

"I think there are a few fun games we could play with cards." He says, still grinning.

Simon takes our bags out of the car and carries them to the front door. Thankfully, Simon had a few extra weekend bags I could use since my ginormous suitcase doesn't fit in his car.

After we carry all our bags to the cottage, Simon checks his phone for the code to the electronic door key, puts it in and we enter the cottage.

It is larger and more spacious that it appears from the

outside. It has a grand fireplace with a decorative mantle along with a large, cozy sofa near it for relaxing by a fire. A television hangs above the mantle, but you wouldn't know it was a television on first glance because it actually displays art. Very chic.

The floor plan is open concept, leading me to believe the cottage has been remodeled to make it fresh and new looking. While I've been looking around the cottage, Simon has started unloading bags of groceries in the kitchen.

"I would love to have a kitchen this large to cook in."

"You cook in a big kitchen at the pub."

"Yes, I do. But it would be nice for my home kitchen to be like this. I'm somewhat limited as to what I can do in my tiny apartment kitchen."

"Oh, I don't know. You made me a lovely meal in your tiny kitchen."

"As did you. Too bad we were interrupted by your ex-husband."

"Let's have a glass of wine and toast to new beginnings." I get out the bottle of Prosecco Simon packed in the cooler and find some glasses in the cabinet.

Simon helps me open it, then he pours a glass for each of us.

"To new beginnings." He says, eyes fixed on mine.

"Yes, and to new adventures."

"Speaking of adventures, I thought we could utilize the hiking trails they have nearby. It hasn't rained for a few days so they shouldn't be too muddy."

"Too muddy? I didn't pack hiking boots. I only packed my white leather sneakers."

"They should be fine. I think you'll enjoy getting some of that good old Irish fresh air."

Hmm, I think. It is a nice day and I have gained a pound a two—I have been doing a lot more eating and drinking and a lot less yoga and cardio lately. But if I am being completely honest, I would much rather sit outside on the back patio and drink some wine in the garden. I don't tell Simon this, however.

Consequently, after we finish our drinks, I change into more "hiking appropriate clothes" while Simon packs some waters and snacks in a bag for us.

We find the hiking trail and begin our walk. It's not as bad as I thought it would be and to be honest, it's kind of romantic. As we come to a couple of areas that are a bit steep, Simon takes my hand to make sure I don't slip. We continue walking along the trail until we meet an opening in the trees. There is an open area of green grass and flowers. I can't believe my eyes. It is so beautiful.

We find a spot to sit and admire the view.

"Did you know it was such a breathtaking view?" I ask, staring out into the openness.

Simon takes out two waters for us. "No, I've never been here before."

We're quiet, almost too quiet. It feels like Simon has something on his mind.

"A penny for your thoughts?" I ask him finally.

"I am taking in this moment, with you. Have you thought more about what you should do? How long to stay?"

"Honestly, I can't stop thinking about it. I don't know what to do. I feel like things are kind of crumbling suddenly."

"They aren't crumbling with us...are they?"

"No, I think we're building up the right way. But I don't know if Sam needs my help anymore or wants it after all the drama with my ex-husband. God, Jack always ruins everything!" I shout in frustration.

Simon rubs his face where Jack punched it. "The fucker takes cheap shots as well."

"It is kind of funny though that his fiancée left him and took all his money."

"That's karma."

We continue to sit on the light blanket Simon put down for us to relax on.

"You never answered my question, Dabney." Simon whispers in my ear softly. "Do you want to stay?" He moves the hair off my neck and kisses it.

"You know how to be persuasive, don't you?"

"Dabney, I'll do whatever it takes to keep you with me. That's if you want me to."

"I think I do." I say, softly holding his face while I kiss him. I want him to devour every inch of my body right here with his soft lips.

I help him take off his shirt as he unhooks my bra. As I begin to take off his pants, I hear voices as the bushes start to rustle.

"Shit! There's people coming!" I say, trying to get my

boobs back in my unhooked bra.

As Simon zips up his pants, a group of people appear from the trail.

Unfortunately, he has welcomed them minus a shirt.

They look at us in horror, since it is obvious what we were doing.

"Lovely day isn't it?" Simon remarks to the couple, who aren't sure what to do.

"Um, yes. We were going to have a picnic. This is our favorite spot in the area. Lots of families come here for the view." The man is obviously concerned and shocked.

We both stand up and start picking up our belongings. "Yes, I could see how this would be the perfect spot for that. We were just leaving though." I say, handing Simon his shirt, which he proceeds to wrap around his waist.

"It warmed up quite a bit, eh?" He says as we leave the two horrified people.

We jog down the trail laughing hysterically at the embarrassment of being caught trying to have sex in the middle of a picnic area.

"Maybe we should stick to indoors." Simon says as he puts his shirt back on and I adjust my bra.

"It's your fault. You started it."

"Me? You're the one who ripped my shirt off." He says, incredulously.

"But I couldn't help it. You were kissing my neck. What was I supposed to do? Not reciprocate? That would be rude."

"Quite true."

When we get to the car, I instinctively look at myself in the mirror to reapply my makeup. Only I don't have any makeup on to reapply.

"It's such a strange feeling, not wearing makeup."

"What do you mean? You don't always wear makeup, do you?"

"With the exception of going to bed and first thing in the morning, have you ever seen me not wearing makeup? I never not wear something on my face. Foundation, blush or something." I don't add that I even make sure my makeup is done when I go to check the mail or walk to get a quick coffee somewhere. I even make sure my makeup is done first thing in the morning if I'm expecting a delivery.

"I'll be honest with you, Dabney. I didn't even realize you weren't wearing makeup. Maybe that should tell you something."

"It tells me that you aren't paying close attention to me, perhaps?"

"No. Not the case at all."

"It tells me I should wear more makeup so that you notice when I am?"

"Nope. It should tell you that you're beautiful regardless and don't need to depend on it," Simon says sweetly as he pats my knee.

"I don't depend on it. It just makes me happier." I say, wishing I had some lip gloss to blot on my lips. Hmm. Perhaps I should have specified in my list what I could and could not use. A lip gloss can be essential for the prevention of dry lips.

"Regardless of your future opinion on makeup use, I am proud of you. I know this day could not be easy for you, given your fondness for cosmetics. What do you have left of your list to complete? Are you a perfect person now?"

"Shockingly, I might be." I laugh at the thought of being a perfect person. "I only have one thing left. I have to drive on the wrong side of the road."

I watch Simon's face twist into a smile when I say 'wrong.'

"Well there is no better time like the present." He pulls over to the side of the road then he turns to me. "Shall we?"

I cringe. "I hope you're offering sex Simon." I think I would rather have sex on the side of the road than drive right now and that is saying a lot given our previous spontaneous encounter.

"Very funny. I thought we could complete your list. You'll be done. All you have to do is drive. Seems simple enough to me."

"But I have to mentally prepare myself. I don't think I'm quite there yet." I haven't told Simon that I actually have not driven a real car for several years. When I moved to the city. I got rid my Honda Civic. Driving in the city made me nervous and parking was too expensive. I also haven't told Simon that my driving record is less than stellar. In my defense, I didn't realize I needed glasses for a while, which may have been the reason I may have had some fender benders. Okay, I was in denial that I needed glasses. Street signs began to look fuzzy and sometimes at a distance fire hydrants looked like dogs, but I was so focused on being able to wear my designer sunglasses when drove, I ignored the obvious indicators.

Aha. I don't have my glasses with me. I left them at the rental cottage and my fuzzy eyesight lately hasn't been the best.

"Sorry Simon but today isn't a good time. I need glasses to drive. While my sight is perfect for close up, I cannot, in good faith, see safely to drive your car."

"I don't think I've seen your glasses." I don't tell him I don't wear them because I hate them—despite how fashionable they have become. So far, the fuzzy hasn't caused me too much trouble. Maybe a headache once or twice a week. That's it. I can manage.

"Exactly." I reply to Simon, "because I can see you up close."

"You don't keep them with you though?" Simon seems confused by my story.

"We were going on a hike. Why would I need my glasses?" I feel like I have provided a solid excuse as to why I can't drive his car.

"Okay, fine. But let's plan on doing a drive tomorrow morning." Simon pulls back on the road and we continue to our rental cottage.

"Why are you in such a hurry to get me to finish this list? After all, my plan was to go home once I finished it. I thought you wanted me to stay."

"I thought your departure plan changed once you fell for the devilishly handsome, me?"

I stop and stare at him for a minute. His grand description of himself is not exaggerated. The way his left cheek dimples when he smiles. His crystal blue eyes are like an ocean wave that gushes over me. His black hair shines with blue tones when it hits the sun. But most of all, it's just him. That grumpy guy that I first met has completely mellowed now that I have gotten to know him.

Simon catches me staring at him. "What?"

I smile. "Nothing. I just can't help but agree that you are devilishly handsome."

"Glad we can agree on something."

"Why were you so grumpy that first day we met? I feel like you are so different from that guy."

We have parked at the cottage now, but I feel like he's not ready to go in. Have I prompted an uncomfortable conversation?

"Dabney, I'm sorry. That day was difficult for me. It was the third anniversary of my Gran's death. I usually take the day off, go visit her grave and spend the day thinking of her. Clearly, a Saturday as a chef in a pub is not a practical time to take off. When I met up with you, I was impatient and not thinking about being an inviting representative of our country."

His openness and honesty have humbled me to the point of guilt. Could I have handled the situation better? I didn't know he was hurting. How could I?

"I'm sorry, Simon, for anything that I did to cause you any further aggravation."

"Don't be sorry, Dabney. I was acting like an ass. It was just a difficult time for me. I haven't completely dealt with her death I guess."

"I have no idea what you're going through. I still have my parents and grandparents. Although they are getting up there in years. One pair of grandparents have moved to Florida, so I don't see them as often. They got tired of the Chicago winters."

"My Gran was all I had. My father's parents died when I was little. My mother's father died before I was born. I never knew him. I only had stories from my Gran."

Simon's pain and longing for his grandmother makes me feel guilty. I don't call my grandparents enough. I rarely go visit them. I am so caught up in my own life in the city that I can't seem to make a quick trip to Evanston to see how they are. It's so close in the grand scheme of things.

We eventually get out of the car and go back into the cottage. Since I'm a bit dirty from walking along the trail, I change into some other clothes while Simon starts prepping for dinner.

"Are you going to cook for me?"

"I am. It's how I show my love for people."

We stop. Stare at each other. Then stare some more. I can't breathe. I wonder if Simon can't either.

He stumbles over his words. "I'm sorry. I didn't mean that. I mean, I did mean that, but I didn't mean to tell you that. I know it's early and I don't want to come across as a crazy guy. I'm sorry."

I walk up to him slowly, nearly in tears. It is early, it's crazy in fact. He has known me for only a couple of weeks, silly to think something so serious in feeling could be felt so soon. Yet, I can feel his sincerity.

"Simon, it's okay. It's okay to feel that way. Your honesty is what draws me to you." I kiss him softly and he pulls me even closer to him.

"I just need time. I need to time to figure out what I'm feeling." I say as we passionately embrace in the kitchen.

"No rush. I just don't want this to end."

"I don't either." We continue to kiss.

He takes my hand and I follow him to our bedroom. It's only our bedroom for the night but it feels like it could be ours forever.

Simon is so different from other men I've slept with. He takes his time. He is thoughtful. He is attentive. He doesn't worry about his needs first.

Once he has determined I have gotten everything I need for the moment, we lay in bed for a while in total bliss. He caresses the top of my breast as I lay on his chest.

I look up at him. "This is happening so fast Simon, but it feels so right." I don't want to go back to Chicago. I want to stay right here in this moment.

"So, what are we going to do?"

"I don't know."

"You're welcome to stay at my apartment while you figure it out. It's not huge, but it has to be bigger than what you're in right now."

"True. But I don't want to impose."

Simon laughs. "Impose? Hardly. I love having you with me. When we're apart, all I think about is you."

"Me too." I admit, sheepishly. "But I have stuff in Chicago. I can't expect Ruby to just keep everything in her apartment. I at least need to see if my parents will let me keep some of the stuff at their house. Maybe I need to go back to Chicago for a few days and then come back for good."

He sits up. "Does this mean you've made a decision? A real decision?"

"But how does it work? I can't stay in the country forever on the basis of romantic adventure. That man at the passport section of airport will not take kindly to that declaration." I shudder as I remember his grumpiness. If I thought Simon was grumpy, that guy was downright cantankerous and definitely not welcoming.

"You'll have to apply for a work Visa."

"Ugh, work. Do you think I can mend my fences with Sam?"

"I'm sure Sam will see this wasn't your fault. You can always get some work at the pub as well."

Instead of Simon cooking, we forgo the groceries in the kitchen and decide to order pizza and stay in bed for the rest of the night, drinking wine, and eating our pizza. It's quite romantic. We discuss our plan for me to stay; and how to go about getting a Visa so I can legally work in Ireland.

Our morning starts late, as we stayed up late, paying little attention to bedtimes. But we have to be out of our rental cottage at noon, so we shower and get ready to leave.

Simon packs up the car and I follow him out. He hands

me the keys.

"What is this for?"

"You have your glasses, right?" He asks walking over the passenger side of the car.

"Yes, but you want me to drive home? I don't know where I'm going."

"We have navigation. I can help you. I thought you were ready."

I don't want to admit to him that I am beyond NOT ready. I am terrified.

"Of course, I am ready. I've been ready." I fumble through my purse for my glasses. Thankfully it isn't a particularly sunny day, so I don't need to wear my fashionable sunglasses instead.

I get into the driver's seat and take a deep breath. Simon stares at me.

"I like your glasses. You look quite studious with them on. Are you a librarian perhaps?" Simon quietly laughs. I choose to ignore him.

"Ahem. Right. Let me just get situated here." I adjust the seat and the mirrors to get everything just right.

Simon puts on his fashionable sunglasses for this non-sunny day. "Dabney, are you stalling?" How can he be so calm? He is about to release his main source of transportation to someone who has had five fender benders, several parking tickets and only a few speeding tickets. Good lord, maybe my mom is right. Maybe I am a terrible driver!

"No, I am not stalling. It's safety first, Simon. Mirrors

have to be adjusted. Seats have to be just right so I can reach the breaks and gas pedal." I adjust the seat back and forth a few times to ensure I have it in just the right spot and then adjust the mirrors again to match. "All right, then. Let's go." He says, impatiently.

"Okay, so full disclosure. I haven't driven a manual before. I can only drive an automatic." I cringe, thinking of all the times I have watched the contestants on *The Amazing Race* struggle because they can't drive the rental car provided for them. Fussing at the television. It has been on my mind to learn, but again, I don't drive in the city!

"Dabney, are you kidding me?" Now he's laughing. He is actually laughing at me.

"It's not funny. Just tell me what I need to do. I'll do it."

"I wasn't planning on teaching you how to drive."

"I know how to drive." I say, in a dark tone.

"Okay, okay. Let me give you the basics." Simon shows me the clutch and how to put it in gear to drive. I practice in the driveway for a few minutes, pushing the clutch down as I change gears.

And then I sit. I'm still petrified.

"Dabney, we have to leave at some point."

"I know." I take a deep breath and turn the ignition.

When the car starts I take another deep breath. I need to get into yoga breathing mode. I can do this. I am a competent woman who is more than capable of driving a car.

And then I stall the car.

"It's okay. Just try again." Simon touches my shoulder to comfort and calm me.

I try again and back out of the driveway in super speed mode.

"I'm doing it!"

And then I stall the car. Again. On the road. As our heads bob back and forth.

"Dabney, quick before another car comes." Simon is a bit less comforting and a lot more rushed.

"I'm trying!" I take a deep breath and start the car. Again. I put the car in gear and we start moving.

"That's it! You're doing it! Now keep going up into the next gear. Wait, Dabney, you're on the wrong side of the road!"

We are so focused on the driving part, I forgot I was in Ireland.

I rush over to the left side of the road, thankfully, before another car comes driving past us. There is a lot to focus on.

"You're doing great, Dabney. Keep going down this road for about eight kilometers." Simon relaxes and looks down at his phone.

"How many miles is that?" I ask, having no idea what the conversion is.

"It's only about five miles I think."

"Five miles! I didn't agree to five miles." My knuckles are so white that my hands are beginning to cramp up.

"Dabney, it's just driving. You might want to slow down though. I think we're driving a bit fast."

As we pass the speed sign, I realize I am driving too fast. The last thing I need is a ticket when I'm trying to stay in the country.

Several miles go by and I find I have relaxed a bit. I have done it. I have completed my list! Not wanting to tempt fate, I see a place where I can pull over.

"Wait, you're going to stop now?" Simon looks up from his phone, disappointed.

"Um, yes. I have completed my goal. Now I would like to be driven the rest of the way, thank you."

I pull over and come to a sudden stop. Clearly, I have not completely mastered the art of driving a manual automobile.

"Fair enough. You did great, Dabney. I'm really proud of you."

"I am too! I even got used to wearing my glasses! But now they're going back to my purse so I can put my sunglasses back on."

"I don't understand how you can justify not wearing your glasses more often if your eyesight is as bad as you say."

"It's not that bad. It's just kind of blurry is all."

We eventually get back to the B&B and there is no further discussion of whether or not I should wear my glasses permanently.

"I suppose we need to decide if you're coming back to my place or are going to stay here for the night."

"I guess I need to chat with Sam."

We enter the bed and breakfast, only to see our two least favorite people enjoying a glass of wine together.

"Dabney, why is your ex-husband chatting over wine with my ex-girlfriend?"

"I have no idea, Simon. No idea."

CHAPTER 20

I feel sick to my stomach as Simon and I approach our respective exes. I assumed they were both leaving but, yet here they are, enjoying each other's company.

"Jack, what are you doing here? I thought you would be back in Chicago by now?"

"Or you would've been asked to leave given your behavior," Simon adds.

"Oh, don't be silly. Jack and I have been chatting and we don't think we accept the fates that you two have dished out for us." Christina gives us a sly smile as she sips her wine.

I rub my face and say to the un-dynamic duo, "I don't understand. It's our decision who we want to be with."

"Dabney, this ridiculous fling you have is just a fantasy. You belong in Chicago with me. We can renew our vows, and everything can go back to normal."

"Are you delusional? Are we really having this conversation again? I am not going to get married to you again! We're divorced because you cheated on me!"

I look at Simon who appears to be just as baffled as me.

"We'll leave you to your drinks." Simon guides me over to Sam, who has just finished pouring some drinks for guests that arrived for happy hour.

"Hi Sam, how are you doing?" I ask, picking up a glass of wine.

"Hi guys, how was your trip?" Sam pours a glass for Simon, who is fidgeting with his hands, seemingly uncomfortable.

"I'm surprised you didn't ask Jack to leave, given his behavior the other night."

"I know. He's paid up until the end of the week and to be honest, I didn't want any more drama. There isn't going to be any more drama, right?"

"Absolutely not." Simon reassures Sam, while glaring over at Jack, who seems to be completely at ease. He is relaxed, sipping his wine, and having a long conversation with Christina.

"Look at them over there. Ruining our evening while they drink their wine and laugh at one another's stories. Why don't they hook up and leave us alone?" I ask, bitterly.

The fact that Jack paid up for the week means he either wasn't planning on leaving quickly in the first place or added some days due to my not intending on going back to Chicago with him as he planned.

I let Sam know that I'm going to move out of my room, but I would like to keep working for him if he needs me. Sam gets in touch with Cassie, who agrees to having me do five days during the week, starting with breakfast.

But I still need to get my work Visa. And I need to tell Ruby and my family I'm staying here.

First things first, I'm calling Ruby. I find a private spot in the office to make my call.

"Hi Ruby!"

"Dabney, how are you? Ready to come home yet?"

"Well, that's what I am calling about. I have decided to stay here. Indefinitely."

The phone goes silent. I've killed Ruby.

"Ruby? Are you there?"

"Yeah I'm here. I'm just in shock. Do you hate my sofa that much?" To be honest, her sofa is terribly uncomfortable. Super chic, but like sleeping on a pile of plywood and metal springs.

"No silly. I love your sofa and you. But I need to see what else is out there in the world for me. I really like this guy—"

"No Dabney. A guy?" Ruby whines in what sounds like serious pain.

"Ruby. It's not just for a guy. I'm happy here. I like it. I have work I can do, and you know I am partially responsible for making a musician famous. I think I'm meant to be here."

"I thought this trip was to find yourself. So far I feel like you have found yourself in the same situation you did three years ago."

"Are you saying I'm going down the same path that I did with Jack? Ruby, Jack and Simon are two very different people. And speaking of Jack, did you know he came here??"

"What?? No! Why is he there?" Ruby chokes out, possibly spitting out some herbal tea.

"To bring me back! He wants to marry me again. His fiancée took all his money and he's temporarily destitute. He asked for the money he gave me, Ruby. What a loser."

"I'm glad you think so. Jack Van Horn is a loser. That dude deserves everything that comes to him. But what about this Simon guy? How well do you really know him? You're uprooting your life for a guy you've only known a couple weeks. Are you sure you want to do this?"

"I'm living life, Ruby." I say solemnly.

"And there's no way I can persuade you to do the opposite?"

"I don't think so."

"Okay then. What do you want me to do with your stuff? You packed most of your things on your trip, but you still have some things like shoes and clothes. Do you want me to ship them?"

"I was thinking I should come back for a few days to tie up loose ends. But not with Jack obviously."

"Honestly, Dabney, I could ship your things for less than the amount of money you have to spend on a plane ticket. Have you told your parents your exciting news?"

"Nope."

"When do you plan on telling them?"

"I dunno. Maybe Thanksgiving when they expect me to come to dinner?" That's only several months away. I could avoid my parents until then, maybe?

"Dabney."

"I know, I know. I'll tell them. I'm just not excited about it."

"They're your parents. They'll never be satisfied with your decisions." Ruby hits the description of my relationship with my parents spot on. They are never happy with anything I do. The one time they were, was my marriage to Jack but that went to shit fairly quickly. Maybe their judgement isn't the greatest after all.

After we say good-bye, I go back to the lobby of the B&B to find Sam and Simon chatting. Simon is helping Sam pick up some empty wine glasses. Jack and Christina continue to sit in their cozy spot. I still can't help but feel like there is something more between them. It's so confusing.

My thoughts regarding Jack and Christina are interrupted, however, by Tilda running over to Sam and Simon.

"Oh Simon, I'm so glad to find you. I need help. I have about twenty fangirls that have shown up to listen to Deacon sing tonight. They've brought with them a half dozen guys and I am drowning." Then Tilda looks over at me. "Dabney, have you waited tables before?" She asks in desperation.

"Yes! For a day or so." I suppose bringing people coffees count a bit. To be honest, my experience as a server is limited. I waited table for a very short period of time because I kept bringing the wrong food to tables. Maybe I needed glasses back then?

"Can you please come help me?" Tilda pleads.

242

"Of course, I can. Just tell me what you need me to do."

Simon and I follow Tilda over to the pub where every seat is filled and then some.

"Is this because I posted Deacon's performance schedule on Instagram??" I ask sheepishly. Deacon generally sings four nights a week, while Donno or Simon fills in for him in the kitchen. I figured I could drum up business for the pub while getting Deacon more exposure. Simple enough, but it seems Tilda and Deacon weren't quite ready for the extra, extra business.

"You posted his schedule? I guess it is!" Tilda pours multiple beers and puts them on a tray. "Here, can you please take these to table five? It's the one with the four giggling young ladies."

I look over to see several tables of giggling young ladies. I believe Deacon officially has fanbase…

I bring the drinks over to table of fangirls drooling over Deacon as he sings his first song, *The Waves*. He ferociously strums his guitar as his voice glides across the room. I listen to the words and wonder if his song is about him and Tilda. It's so upbeat and romantic.

His next song is about a loss of love and wanting to get through the regrets. Damn he is an amazing songwriter as well as a singer. I am kind of fangirling at my new friend. He is that good! I look over to see an older man in the corner, taking notes. I wonder if it's the record producer, or someone from his company. I want to go talk to him but Tilda waves me over to come back.

I blush as I say, "Sorry, I got distracted by Deacon."

"Yes, he has that effect on people. Especially women." Tilda laughs and hands me another tray of drinks. "Can you bring this over to table six? It's the two guys and girl swaying back and forth." I look over and sure enough, there they are, swaying to Deacon's music.

"Oh my gosh. I can't believe you get to work here." A young man, with perfectly coiffed hair and a hint of clear lip gloss says to me as I hand him his cocktail. "Do you know him? Like, for real?"

"Yes, I suppose I do. He's quite nice."

The three of them look at each other and giggle more.

"Is there anything else I can get you?" I ask because I remember that's something you're supposed to do when you're a server.

"His phone number maybe." The young lady, with long brown hair and warm brown eyes says. Then she takes a chug of her beer.

I just laugh a little. "I'll be back to check on you."

I take more trays of drinks to tables for Tilda. Once the drinks are delivered, I go to the kitchen to see what needs to be taken out. I still haven't quite figured out the table numbers, but I know a few so I just count and ask if it's their food once I get there. Everyone is in such a good mood they don't take notice of my ineptness.

Tilda waves me back over.

"Dabney, thank you so much for your help. I don't know what I would've done."

"Well I suppose it's partly my fault. I didn't know my post would have this effect."

"Your fault? Dabney, this busines on a Monday night is exactly what we need. I just wish I'd had a heads up, but I'm not mad at you. I'm grateful."

"Shall I go check on the tables to see if they need anything else? More drinks or food?"

"Dabney, that would be wonderful. Thank you."

I smile, feeling pleased I can help. I want to tell Ruby about my experience tonight. If I was sitting around at her apartment in Chicago, I wouldn't be helping anybody but myself...to a package of cookies probably, feeling sorry for myself.

Deacon finishes his first set. "I'm about to take a break but thank you so much everyone for coming the pub tonight. We appreciate your patronage. Now go get another pint," he says to his admirers with a wink.

I decide to approach the table of the single, older man with graying hair. He is wearing glasses and still taking notes and periodically typing something on his phone. Not bothering to look up, he doesn't seem terribly interested in interacting with me.

"Hi, can I get you another drink? Or something to eat?"

"No, thank you. Just here to do some work." The man continues to look down at his notes and phone while mildly ignoring me.

"Are you here for Deacon?"

The man, barely looking up from his phone "Yes."

"He's got a good crowd here tonight," I say trying to continue our awkward conversation.

Finally, the man looks up and around at the room. "I see that. If this says anything about his talent, he'll have more than this soon." The man goes back to his notes, then follows up with, "Actually, can I please have a Diet Coke?"

"His wife is very proud of him." I gesture over toward Tilda, at the bar.

"Oh, well we'll be keeping that under wraps. The ladies don't want to lust over a guy who's married. It also creates drama for the wife."

"But that's who he is. Doesn't it matter to be authentic?"

The man laughs. "You obviously know nothing about the business. We create what the public wants. His demographic wants a single, hot man. They do not want a married father of four."

I walk away, feeling a sense of panic. Does Tilda know this? Does Deacon? How can he become famous by being someone he isn't? How is that good for anybody??

I march back to the kitchen to check on food orders and find Simon. I am extremely concerned at what I have just heard. How can he keep a married man like Deacon, 'under wraps' when his wife is the amazing Tilda? Mother of a million children, boss to some rather decent people and bucket list extraordinaire?

"Simon, I don't know about this. I just talked to that record producer. He wants Deacon to pretend he's single. He doesn't want anybody to even know about Tilda and the kids!" I'm whispering. I can't imagine Donno is interested in our conversation, but I still want to keep it all under wraps.

"Really? That's shady." Simon hands me the plate of chips for table four.

Deacon comes back to the kitchen, wiping his face with a towel. "Woo! Busy night, eh?"

"Deacon, you were great! The crowd out there loves you," I say, trying to hide my shock and disbelief at over what I've just learned.

Deacon waves in the air, bashfully. "Aw, they're just here for the drinks."

"Deacon, they are all here for you. Trust me. I've gotten the third degree from practically every table out there."

He laughs it all off and puts an apron on to help in the kitchen.

"Dabney, the chips. They're getting cold," Simon gives me a gentle nudge.

I take the chips out to the table with a bottle of ketchup and malt vinegar. My excitement has faded. I can't talk to Simon about it while Deacon is working in the kitchen, so I go back to the bar.

"Well Dabney, I think we're caught up for now." Tilda takes a deep breath, wipes down the counter and fills up some bowls with pub mix for a couple sitting at the end.

"Tilda, how do you feel about all the girls drooling over your husband?"

She laughs. "I think it's funny."

"But it doesn't make you jealous?" I ask, incredulously. I think if Simon were in Deacon's shoes, I'd have a hard time with it.

"Jealous? No. I know he's my husband. He comes home to me at night. Most of his songs are about us. If anything, I think it's cute. He deserves to be drooled over."

I can't help but admire Tilda's maturity over the situation. Maybe I'm a bit envious too. Deacon's songs are super romantic.

"But what's going on with his record contract? Are they going to shape his image differently?"

Tilda shrugs. "I'm not sure. How different could they shape it?"

"I don't know, like pretend he's a single guy looking for love?"

Tilda stops for a moment when we're interrupted by an obvious fan.

"Can I have another shaken martini, ma'am?" Then the fanboy asks, "Is Deacon going to sing anymore songs?"

Tilda begins to make his drink. "Well, I can ask him. He typically does one set and then maybe another toward the end of the night if people are still here."

"There was a song he sang on the Instagram page I saw. It was about his hometown or something? An old flame? It was so romantic." The fanboy fans his face with his skinny hand. Tilda and I look at each other and can't help but laugh.

"I'll go back and tell him there's a request for the hometown song," I say to the cute fanboy. It's kind of sweet that all sorts of people are excited for Deacon. "By the way, are you a follower of my Insta page?"

"No, why would I?" Fanboy asks with a touch of sassy

attitude.

"Well my dear, because it was my Insta page that got Deacon all of this attention."

The fanboy takes out his phone and looks at his account. Sure enough, the young man's face softens a bit, and he asks in shock, "Are you Dabney??"

"Yep!"

"Are you going to post more about Deacon?" The fanboy leans on the bar and takes out his phone, possibly live streaming our conversation for all I know.

"Maybe." I don't feel like getting into my whole life story about how I don't know when I'm going back home or if I'm going back home. I mean, I think I'm staying, but who knows what'll happen tomorrow, right?

"I suggest you do post more about Deacon. That'll triple your followers." Tilda hands the fanboy his martini and he walks back to his table.

As much as I'm tempted to get my phone and post some things, I have to focus on helping Tilda.

"Do you want me to go back and tell Deacon he has requests for an encore?"

Tilda nods her head. "Yes please, tell him his fans are waiting for more."

I walk back to the kitchen to find Deacon and the rest of the guys taking a break at the small table in the kitchen.

"Well Deacon, I'm sorry to interrupt your break, but your fans are requesting more songs. Something about a hometown song?" I laugh, trying to remember what the fanboy said. I've listened to Deacon sing several times now, but I still don't know all his songs by heart. Perhaps I need to relisten to my Instagram posts.

"My fans?"

"Yes! They're all still here and they're asking for more songs."

Deacon appears to blush a bit but gets up from his seat.

"Well boys, I guess I need to figure out more songs to sing for my fans." He laughs as he takes off his apron and picks up his guitar.

"Wait," I say. "Why don't you let me introduce you?"

"What? I don't need an introduction." Deacon quietly laughs as he begins to walk towards the kitchen door.

"Just wait. Let me do it."

"Okay?" He says, still not convinced.

I walk out of the kitchen towards the microphone. The fans see me and stop what they're doing immediately.

"Hi everyone. Someone said they wanted more Deacon Brody. Is that true?"

The room explodes in hollers and whistles.

"Well then! Let's not waste any more time! Deacon Brody everyone!" I holler along with the fans as I clap excitedly and walk back over to the bar with Tilda.

Deacon sheepishly comes out from the kitchen and sits on the stool in front of his microphone.

I look over to see the music producer guy typing on

his phone.

Then I look over at Tilda, smiling so proud with love and admiration. I want to tell her the plans the universe has for Deacon, but I don't. I don't know how, and I don't know if it's my place.

So, I sit on a stool at the bar marveling at my new friend's early success and hoping the love he and Tilda has is stronger than anything else that's coming his way.

Simon comes out from the kitchen and sits next to me. "Are you coming over to my place tonight?" he asks in my ear.

I sway back and forth to the music and say, "I wouldn't want to be anywhere else tonight."

CHAPTER 21

The next morning I wake up next to Simon, who is still sleeping next to me in his bed. I have so many things revolving around in my head.

Do I tell Tilda what the music man said? When should I tell my parents that I'm not coming home? Is it smart of me to move in with Simon this early in our relationship? Will I be able to get rid of Jack and his new partner in chaos, Christina? Furthermore, what are they doing? Why *are* they still here? Do I feel more complete now that I have worked through my list of flaws? Does Simon know yet that I have terrible gas first thing in the morning?

All questions that I do not have answers to...

I see Simon begin to stir in bed. "Dabney, you seem very deep in thought this morning. Do you need coffee?" Simon asks as he yawns and stretches casually.

"I dare say yes I do." I slowly get out of bed and make a coffee from his Nespresso machine, while also making one for him.

"Thank you, my dear. I knew there was a reason for asking you to stay with me." Simon sits up and takes the coffee I made for him. "So, what had you thinking so hard on this early morning?"

"Everything." I don't think I have the time or energy for everything on my mind.

"Are you worried about last night?"

"A little. Don't you think it's crappy that Deacon might have to pretend he is someone else?"

"Yeah, but I wouldn't worry about him and Tilda. I've never seen two people more in love. Especially with four kids. They'll be fine."

"I don't know. I mean, I agree. They're definitely madly in love. But when I mentioned the idea of Deacon's new image and pretending to be single, she got a weird look on her face." I'm filled with guilt and gloom.

"Hmm. I wouldn't be too concerned until it actually happens. I would stay out of it, to be honest Dabney." He puts his coffee down on the side table and takes my hand. "So, is that all that's bothering you?"

"No. I have a few other things on my mind. Like, what are we going to do about Christina and Jack? Why do you think they're still here? Don't you think it's odd?"

"I have no idea what is going on there. It's strange, for sure. Christina could definitely be manipulative when we were together, but I never knew her to be conniving."

"Jack is acting weird, too. It's like he has suddenly gotten totally jealous now that I've moved on."

"They need to move on and find something new to be involved in because you and I aren't going anywhere." Simon kisses my forehead, gets up from the bed and says, "Except to the kitchen for more coffee."

When Simon returns with his second cup of coffee, I continue to talk about my long list of worries.

"Another thing I'm worried about—how to tell my parents." I have never been good about open communication with my parents, especially my mom. If I was, I would've played soccer instead of going to dance recitals.

Simon sits back down on the bed. "Have you talked to Tilda about working more at the pub?"

"I didn't get a chance to talk to her about the possibility of more work last night because it was so busy." Deacon's fans are not only enthusiastic about him, they also drink a lot of beers and cocktails.

"I think you did an excellent job, jumping into work and all. I can't imagine she would take issue with you working more, but I'm rather partial I suppose." Simon moves closer to kiss me on the cheek.

"You think I did well?" I'm not completely convinced at my success last night.

"Yes! I also heard you get the pub crowd excited for Deacon's second round at performing. You're underestimating yourself again, Dabney."

"I almost spilled a tray of beers on an entire table of people, but caught myself at the last second."

"You'll get used to it. Did you like working last night though?"

"I did. It felt good helping Tilda as well." I pick up my phone. I should text her and see if she has time to chat."

"Good idea. I'm getting in the shower. Care to join?" Simon pops off the bed in his paisley boxers.

I get out of bed and walk towards Simon. "Maybe another time. I need to text Tilda and then get back to the

B&B. Will you give me a ride?"

"Of course. But this is my sad face." Simon puts his arms around my waist and kisses me before he concedes and walks to the bathroom. As much as I want to get in the shower with him and do what I think he wants, I really must focus on other things at the moment.

I text Tilda, who responds immediately. She is at home and says I can come by to chat if I like. I let her know I'll by in an hour.

Simon drops me off at the B&B where I take a quick shower before walking over to Tilda's house. Luckily, I have been able to dodge Jack and Christina. I am not ready to deal with those two yet today.

I approach Tilda's door and ring the doorbell. It takes a couple rings, but Tilda eventually answers.

"Hi Dabney, what's up?" I see Brennan and Brianna hanging around her legs. She guides me to the sofa in the living room dragging the twins along with her. They laugh the whole time.

"Dabney!" The twins shout. "You going to make cookies again?"

"Hello my dears! No, not today I'm afraid. I'm here to talk to your mama." They are so cute that I almost wish I was making cookies for them, which says a lot about them. I turn to Tilda. "Well, as you know, I've been here a while trying to find myself and such. I thought you might want to know...I've decided to stay. But I need a job offer to apply for a work Visa. Would you be interested in hiring me?"

"Dabney, that's great news! Of course, I would be

happy to hire you. I need help. You saw what it was like last night. In fact, I was curious if you did any more Instagram posts?"

"I have some video, but I didn't know if you wanted me to do that anymore."

"I don't mind. It seems to drum up business. My husband is suddenly a popular man." Tilda says, walking over to the kitchen to give the dog, George a treat.

"Did you get a chance to talk to that guy? The music guy?"

"No, he doesn't have much to do with me. If I'm being honest, I don't think he cares for me much." Tilda says, filling up a cup of milk for Brennan.

Knowing what I know, I imagine he doesn't care much for Tilda at all. Jerk. He obviously doesn't know that Tilda and Deacon are two lovebirds matched in Heaven.

"You know Tilda, I wouldn't worry about what he thinks. I'm sure he's off to London soon?"

"Yes, but he's taking Deacon with him. He leaves tonight." Tilda suddenly looks sad. "I know I should be excited, and I am. But I'm going to miss him terribly. We haven't been apart since we first got together. It's going to be hard."

"We'll all be here for you. I'm sure Deacon will miss you as well. How long will he be gone?"

"A month," Tilda says softly.

"A month?!" I'm alarmed. "What is he doing for a month?"

"They have a small tour planned for him. They didn't

waste any time getting the word out. He has plenty of his own songs to sing. He even had to start a bunch of social media pages. In fact, if you could retweet or repost any of his stuff that would be helpful for him. You seem to have a solid base."

"My base grew a lot when I posted about Deacon."

"Yep, he's meant to be a star. I just hope that star includes all of us."

I can feel Tilda's apprehension about Deacon's new success. I don't have the heart to tell her that it's not supposed to include them at all.

Tilda and I agree on the days I'll work for her. Simon will be much busier now that Deacon is on the road. That's okay because if I work, it means I get to see him a bit. I am determined to help Tilda as much as I can. I feel somewhat responsible for her situation.

Once I leave Tilda's, I walk back to the B&B, hoping to avoid the exes.

I'm not that lucky.

Christina is coming downstairs as I enter the main lobby area. She looks lovely. She is wearing a snug cardigan over a flowy mid knee dress. It's perfect for the Irish spring weather we have today. Her shiny black hair is down for the first time since I have met her. Not a hair out of place. I used to be like that. But now that I have relaxed in my fashion and style, I feel sub-par to the 'perfection' that is Christina. In comparison to my casual ensemble, Christina is wearing a pink shift dress with tan wedge sandals. She has bright floral scarf around her neck and a tan handbag that almost perfectly matches her shoes. I hate to admit but she looks fabulous. I would totally wear her outfit.

"Hi, Dabney! Did you just get back from a workout?" She asks, looking at my casual attire and messy up do. I was in a hurry this morning to meet up with Tilda. Old Dabney would have been late in order to get her hair and makeup precise. I simply added some dry shampoo to my hair and quick layer of tinted moisturizer, blush and mascara to my face. I hardly look like I've been exercising though.

I ignore her comment. "How are you Christina? Off to somewhere exciting?" I try to sound polite. It's difficult. I really dislike her now.

"I am lovely, thank you for asking Dabney. I am going to meet a dear friend for lunch," Christina says joyfully.

"Well, don't let me stop you. Have a nice time, Christina." As I walk over to the stairs. I see Maura roll her eyes at me in solidarity, which makes me smile.

I get back to my room and begin to tidy up. I didn't give Sam and Cassie an exact date of when I would leave, but I think the sooner the better. I'm sure they would prefer to have their room available for an actual full paying guest.

I text Simon to let him know I'm ready to pack up and move in indefinitely. He texts back a thumbs up. I was hoping for a more enthusiastic response, but maybe he's busy.

I still wonder if I am ready to tell my parents my new life plans. I decide I'm not and choose to go out for a run instead. I find my ear buds, arm strap for my phone and get the rest of my running clothes on. I need to get back to my intense workouts. When I lived in Chicago I went to a spinning class nearly every day. On days I didn't spin, I ran around the city. I love working out. It helps me clear my head on days when it's full of everything. It also keeps me thin enough to fit in my designer clothes, that I cherish. When I was a kid, my mom would always make me wear my sister's hand me downs or wear new clothes from the local discount store. My friends would have the latest name brands while I would have the latest knock off labels. Once I got enough money to buy my own clothes, I said goodbye to cheap-o and hello to glam-o.

I take one last look in the mirror and feeling satisfied with what I have chosen, I head downstairs.

"Bye Maura, I'm off for a run." Maura waves bye to me and I make my way out to the street.

I control my breathing as I run. My mind calms. I think about my parents. I decide it's best to be honest and not wait until Thanksgiving to tell them. They will just have to deal with my choices. I am an adult. I am in charge of my destiny. I am watching Simon and Christina walk down the street together? Huh?

"What the fuck?" I come to a screeching halt and back up into an alley to prevent them from seeing me. Was Simon the dear friend she was having lunch with? Why wouldn't he tell me? Why would he have lunch with her in the first place? What is happening?

I watch them walk down the street and realize they are probably going back to the B&B. I don't want to meet them, so I decide to just keep running.

I run for nearly five miles before I am so worn out, I don't know if I can make it I back home, or whatever my room is.

Thankfully, the only people in the lobby are Sam and Maura.

Maura, busy picking up old newspapers and reorganizing the magazines looks at Dabney. "Hi Dabney, did you have a good run?"

"I did," I respond, exhausted both physically and mentally. Going for a run usually clears my mind, but this one added more stress and confusion.

Sam clears his throat and says, "Dabney, did you decide when you want to move out? Could it be today by chance? I had a lady call me directly to say she wanted to stay, and I said yes, but I'm full at this time."

"Ah, by me."

Feeling completely blind-sided by what I just saw, I can't imagine moving in with Simon tonight, but what am I going to say? Sam and Cassie have been so nice about letting me stay at the B&B longer than anticipated, I can't say no.

"Actually, I think Simon is ready for me tonight. I'll just need a taxi—"

"For the suitcase." Sam and Maura both say. My ginormous suitcase has taken on its own residence here at the B&B. Everyone knows about it.

"Yes," I say sheepishly.

"I'd love to have the room ready for her for when her flight lands. I'm sorry to rush you out, Dabney."

"No Sam, I completely understand. In fact, I'm supposed to work at the pub tonight for Tilda. Give me an hour to shower, pack up and then I'll be out."

"Thank you, Dabney." Sam pats me on the shoulder as he heads back to his office.

"I'm going to miss having you so close, Dabney. Maura tells me. You're moving in with Simon, then?" Maura asks as she walks over the computer at the front desk.

"I guess so."

Maura laughs. "You don't seem so sure."

"Oh, I am. It's just a big change is all."

"I understand. Well not exactly. I've never lived with anyone but my parents, but I know moving is a big deal."

"Yes, it is Maura. Not one to be taken lightly." Although I wonder if that's what I've done.

CHAPTER 22

When all of my belongings are packed in my mom's ginormous suitcase, I make my way down the stairs. It's a loud, bumpy journey, since I don't have Donno to help this time. But the suitcase and I make it down the stairs regardless.

I look up Simon's address from a text and give it to Maura, who calls me a taxi—an extra-large taxi. I don't even know if Simon's home. I also don't know whether to tell him I saw him with Christina this morning. Being truthful is an important part of a relationship. But how well do I even know Simon? Have I been duped?

I text Simon to let him know I am coming over. He says he has to step out, but he can leave a key under the doormat for me.

As the taxi arrives, I give Maura a hug and tell her I'll probably see her in a few hours since I'm working later at the pub. She gives me an extra hug anyway. Maybe she senses I need it.

The taxi journey to Simon's apartment is relatively brief. He doesn't live that far from the B&B, but I have no desire to drag my huge suitcase down a bunch of cobblestone and uneven sidewalks.

The taxi driver helps me get my suitcase out of the car

and I pay him with an extra tip for his trouble.

Then I remember, Simon lives at the top of a million stairs. How am I going to get Mom's ginormous suitcase up there? I can do it I tell myself. I have to do it. I have to prove to myself that I don't need anybody to help me. Specifically, I don't need a man. I am conquering these stairs out of pure choice.

About halfway up, on a small landing, I question my will to conquer. However, I realize I am as close to the top as I am to the first floor. I can't possibly quit now. Besides, giving up would mean I have to go back downstairs, which would be just as exhausting.

Huffing and puffing, I continue to make my up until I have finally reached the top. It takes me forever, but I feel pride and elation.

My legs turn to jelly when I bend down to find the key under Simon's doormat.

"Dabney? You made it!" Simon has appeared from downstairs.

"Yes, I'm here." I barely get the words out of my worn out body.

He looks so handsome with his messy black hair and adorable dimples. In his hand is a bouquet of purple tulips.

"I thought you needed some flowers for your first night here," he says, taking my suitcase from me. "I'm sorry I wasn't here to help. I didn't want you to carry this all the way upstairs by yourself!"

It seems to finally occur to Simon that I have actually carried this entire suitcase up the stairs by myself.

"You really did this?" Simon stares at me in awe as he takes the key from me and unlocks the old, creaky door.

"I did. All by myself." I feel proud smug and strong. A stark comparison to my state of mind when I first arrived in Dublin.

I look at Simon. I am struck by his thoughtfulness. He went to buy me flowers. This is the second bouquet of flowers I have received from him. Maybe he's not a scoundrel after all.

But I'm still apprehensive.

"Simon, can I get a ride with you to the pub tonight? As it turns out, Tilda needs me to work again tonight." I am trying to not sound too formal, but I'm uncomfortable since seeing him with Christina.

"Of course, you can. Is everything okay? You seem off today? I'm sorry I wasn't here to greet you and help you with everything."

"No, I'm not upset about that."

"So, you are upset?"

I don't know what to do. Is now the time to confront him about what I saw?

"Simon, are you completely over Christina?"

He looks at me with an odd expression and says, "Why would you ask that? Yes, I thought I made that clear."

"Would you be a hundred percent honest with me?" I'm twisting my fingers into virtual knots. I am nervous about what Simon's answer could be.

"Dabney, I'm not sure what's going on. Why are you asking me these questions?"

I follow Simon in his apartment. "Because Simon, I saw you today. I saw you with Christina. Walking down the street."

Simon stops walking towards me. "Were you spying on us?" he asks in surprise.

"No, of course not! I was out for a run. She told me before she met you that she was meeting a dear friend for lunch. I'm assuming the dear friend, was you?"

"Oh Dabney, it's not what you think." Simon sits down on his sofa, runs his hands through his dark hair and tries to figure out where to begin.

"Then what is it, Simon? Why would you meet her?"

"She asked me to lunch. At first, I thought to say no, but then I thought maybe I could find out why she's staying. If she was here to cause trouble."

"So, did you find out anything? It's not like she's going to be honest and tell you her evil plan." That's not what evil saboteurs do.

"Well, she did tell me that Jack has left for a different hotel or back home, I'm not sure. He made a few phone calls and then decided to leave the B&B. They had an embarrassing moment when he tried to kiss her when they were out for drinks."

I laugh at the idea of Jack putting moves on Christina. That is so typical. He declares his love for me then turns around and tries to get with another woman. Regardless of the humor in all of it, I still feel overwhelmed with everything.

"Simon, I'll be perfectly honest. I don't know if I'm ready for all of this. Maybe I should go back home. I obviously have trust issues." I sit down on the sofa with him and bury my face in my hands.

"Dabney, your husband cheated on you and you found out in the worst possible way. It's okay to have trust issues. But I promise on my Gran's grave, I would never do that to you."

I want to believe him. I really do.

"Once I get my Visa approved, maybe I should get my own place nearby. Maybe moving in permanently is a bad idea for us."

Simon says to me, "Dabney, you do whatever you need to do. But just know I'm here and I'm ready for it." He gently pulls me to him and kisses me. We make our way to his bedroom and although I'm still not sure where all this is going, in that moment, I just want him. All of him.

Afterwards we lay in bed until I look at the clock and realize it's time to get ready for work. Simon and I get dressed and I redo my hair and makeup. I want to look nice for my first official night as a server at The Stag's Leap.

Simon and I have a quiet drive to the pub, and we walk in through the back. I tie an apron around my waist and go out to meet the lady who is working at the bar. She is an older lady with soft curls that she pulls back with a clip on each side.

"Hi love, Tilda said this was your first official night, but you came and helped last night for a bit. Do you know the tables yet? I'm Doris, by the way. I've been off with a poorly back, I'm afraid. I've been working in this pub for many years though, so there's not a question I can't answer."

"I kind of know the tables," I say, not very convincingly. "Oh, and I'm Dabney." I add.

"Don't worry, you'll get the hang of it. It's a Tuesday night. We aren't usually too busy, but it's nice to have the extra help." Doris says kindly as she goes over the table numbers with me.

"Tilda said Mondays aren't usually busy either but last night was bananas."

"That's what I heard. Who knew our Deacon would run away to be famous. I've known the lad since he was in nappies. I'm so proud of him but I'm going to miss him."

"Hopefully the month goes by quickly." I still feel bad that Tilda will be without her partner for a whole month.

"Too right, love. Okay let's get to work." Doris hands me the tray that includes a pint of Guinness and a bowl of pub mix for him to snack on. Bring this over to Barney at table seven. He's the old bald man with the two empty glasses that need to be picked up. "Barney is a regular here."

"But it's only 4:00, what time does he come in?"

"About 2:00. He has a snack, a few drinks, eats his dinner and then walks home. He does it nearly every day."

Now that Doris has pointed him out to me, I realize I have seen him most times I've been in the pub.

"Here you go, Barney!" I say to the old man as I put his pint and pub mix on the table. "Can I get you anything else?"

"You're the new lass, aren't you? American?" he asks, taking a gulp of his pint.

"Yep! I am American."

That's all Barney seems to want to say so I go back to the bar to help Doris by taking the dirty glasses to the back to be cleaned.

As the pub gets a little busier at dinner time, I help Doris pour some pints while taking them to tables. I am actually rather impressed with myself. I feel like I'm meant to do this. I enjoy talking to the customers and Doris is lovely to work with. She has a mom kind of demeanor to me.

I must be missing my mom, or thinking about her because when I come out of the kitchen with Barney's order of fish and chips, I see a tall, skinny blonde lady at the bar that looks just like my mom. She's a bit fuzzy because I haven't been wearing my glasses again. But it's funny, she even has the poor posture that my mom has but will never admit to. How funny that a lady who looks just like my mom would be here, in Ireland. Small world I suppose.

I pick up Barney's empty glass and return to the bar to help Doris.

"Doris, I don't think Barney wants anymore drinks. He said he wants a water now," I say, not really paying attention to the people at the bar.

"Oh, okay love. That means he's cut himself off, bless him. One night he had one too many and ended up at the next-door neighbor's house trying to get his key in their door."

I bend down to get a new tub of dirty pint glasses to take to the dishwasher when I hear a lady at the end of the bar with a thick Chicago accent say, "Dabney?!"

Uh oh. I know that voice. And I am again reminded that I probably need a new eye exam and furthermore, need to be wearing my glasses more frequently. I stand up for a closer look to see the lady that looks like my mom with the poor posture *is* my mom.

"Mom! What are you doing here?" I screech in horror.

"What are you doing here? You're working in a pub??" my mom asks in similar horror.

"Um, yes. What's wrong with that?" I am somewhat annoyed at her shock. Is it that surprising I would be doing sort of work? Well, maybe...

"You don't live here, Dabney. You're supposed to be on vacation. And furthermore, your vacation is supposed to be over as of four days ago. You should be in Chicago figuring out your life."

"Mom, again, what are you doing here?" I ask in a whiny tone. My mom has brought me to feeling like a sixteen-year-old again.

"Jack called and said he came here to rescue you, but you scoffed at his help. He said you appeared unstable and had met some hoodlum. Maybe drugs or alcohol were a problem? He said the first night he saw you, you were drunk."

"What?! Jack didn't come here to rescue me. He mostly wanted his money back. Once he realized I wasn't the old subservient Dabney, he gave up on me and went back home."

"Yes, but he wanted to win you back, Dabney. That's what he told me."

"Oh please, don't tell me you're drinking the Kool Aid," My tone is sharp.

I can't help but feel a bit betrayed by my mom for her defense of Jack. I mean, the guy was a terrible husband. He did nothing but work and cheat on me with another woman. Granted, I did have a complexion like butter and wonderful fashion sense because he let me buy whatever I wanted, but that's not important now.

"Dabney, I'm not drinking the Kool Aid. But he's your husband," My mom says with a somewhat sympathetic tone.

"Jack *was* my husband, mom. Was. We are divorced now."

My mom winces at the word divorce and her voice softens. "Dabney, can we talk about things? Woman to woman?"

"Mom, I'm working tonight. I can't really have a serious talk while I'm working."

She sighs. "Okay, I understand, kind of. Can we meet for breakfast in the morning? I'm staying at the Bed and Breakfast next door."

"Of course, you are," I can't help but say aloud.

I have Simon make my mom a salad which she takes it back to her room with a bottle of water. Because of the day I've had, I don't even try to introduce her to Simon. I'm not ready for that.

I am a bit of a mess most of the night, but I make it through. I am utterly exhausted. It has been one very,

very long day

"How did your night go?" Simon asks. He's doing one last wipe down of everything before we leave.

"My mom showed up." I say, still in shock.

"Your mom? Owner of the infamous ginormous suitcase? I have to meet her."

He starts to run out of the kitchen when I say, "She's not here. I sent her back to the B&B to rest and eat her dinner."

"Ah, she was the salad with grilled chicken."

"Yep."

"Only an American orders a salad for dinner." He goes back to the grill to give it one last wipe down.

"That's not true."

"It is around here."

I roll my eyes "Can we just go home."

Simon's face softens and he says, "Home. I love the way that sounds. Of course. Let me see if Doris is ready to lock up."

Simon and Doris lock up and we leave to go to his apartment.

I can't wait to wash up and get in my pajamas. It has been such a long day. I set my phone alarm for 7:00 so I can meet my mom at the B&B for breakfast. Simon holds me until I fall asleep hoping for calming dreams and peaceful slumber.

CHAPTER 23

I wake up before my alarm goes off. Simon is still sleeping so I quietly go into the bathroom and step into the hot shower. I don't know why I am so nervous to talk to my mom. She's just my mom. I think I just don't want to argue with her anymore.

Years of harsh discussions with her about how I should style my hair, or what type of pants look flattering on me since I have a flat rear end. Or maybe I should pick a career that doesn't require as much imagination as advertising. I've never had that great of an imagination I've been told.

I decide to not wake Simon and do the walk. It's chilly this morning so I wear my long cardigan, t-shirt and scarf with my white sneakers and jeans. I only wear a bit of tinted moisturizer, blush and settle for a light lip gloss. My dangly Kendra Scott earrings are enough to brighten up my outfit to look complete, along with my glasses that I've determined need to be added to my daily ensembles.

I get to breakfast a little before 8:00 to find my mom already at her table with her plate of fruit and toast. She is always early or on time. Maura greets me and brings me a coffee, just the way I like it. Coffee, cream, and one sugar. I sit down and take a big sip of coffee.

"Dabney, you're early for a change," my mom says in a surprised tone.

"Yes, since I've left Chicago, I've been trying to be on time for things. It's another one of my flaws that people seem to always point out."

"Dabney, I'm sorry. My therapist has told me I tend to point out your shortcomings when I describe you. If I do it with the therapist, I must do it even more frequently with you."

"Yes, you do." I can't help but feel a bit of vindication in my mom's response. I also had no idea my mom was going to therapy. What else hasn't she told me?

"So, tell me, what does this guy have that Jack doesn't? There must be something special about him if you're willing to abandon everything you know to be with him."

"Mom, I'm not abandoning anything. And it isn't just to be with him. I like these people. I like the lifestyle here. I wasn't happy in Chicago."

"Do you think you can make it work with Jack?"

"Jack is a cheater."

"Dabney, I think there is something you should know."

"Oh, jeez Mom. The last time you said you gave me the talk about where babies came from when I was thirteen."

"Ahem, may in continue?" She asks in her mom tone.

"Your father has been a good provider. He pays the bills every month. He showed up to all your volleyball games when you went through that sports phase."

"It wasn't a phase mom. I wanted to play volleyball."

"Yes, but you gave up dance for it. You loved dance. The only reason you chose sports was to impress that boy you liked. What was his name? Brett, Brad?"

"Brett Weisburger? He was in band. I didn't need to impress him. He needed to impress me! Anyway Mom where is this going? What does Brett Weisburger have to do with Dad?" I ask as I steal a strawberry from my mom's plate.

"Your dad has been a cheater for practically our entire marriage."

I nearly choke on my strawberry.

"What..." I can't even phrase my response as a question as I continue to cough.

"Dabney, he's had a relationship on and off with a woman that I've known about our whole marriage."

"And you just go along with it?"

"What am I going to do? I got married right out of high school. I raised you kids. I haven't worked since I was eighteen years old and that was just at the Frosty Freeze serving ice cream cones and milkshakes. Your father comes home to me every night. He's discreet. I just pretend I don't know what's going on."

I am suddenly furious with my dad and incredibly sad for my mom.

"Mom, that's not okay. The house is paid off isn't it? He's a cheater. Divorce him and keep the house. I'm sure you would get spousal support after all these years."

"It's fine. I'm over it. It is what it is."

"Are you sure? I mean, are you sure he's a cheater?"

She looks at me with the sternest stare I've ever seen. "Yes, I followed him more than once."

"Why didn't he come with you on this trip? Did he have to stay with his mistress? Sorry, that wasn't nice."

"No, I asked him not to come. I wanted to take this trip alone."

"Mom, if you've dealt with this kind of life for so long, why would you wish it on me?"

"I don't wish it for you. I just know Jack has a lot of financial stability. He comes from a wealthy family. You have everything you wish for with him."

"His mistress took all his money. She maxed out his credit cards, bank account and left town. He came here to get money from me."

"I'm sorry, Dabney. I want the best for you, but maybe I'm not the all-knowing mother I think I am."

"I'm sorry, too. All this time I thought you were controlling, but maybe you were just trying to control something in your life."

"Maybe so."

"Listen, don't go home right away."

"Oh, I'm here for the week. I'm just enjoying having some time to myself. Or with my daughter—if she's up for it."

"Of course I am but first, I think it's time you met Simon. I've moved in with him. Well at least for a while."

I text Simon, who says he'll meet us at the B&B in 30 minutes. I feel grateful that this man I am still getting to know stops what he's doing to come down and meet my mom for me.

My mom and I sit quietly for a while, drinking our coffee. I tell her about some of the places I've been while in Ireland, and she seems happy and excited about the possibility of seeing them as well.

I decide not to tell my mom about Christina, who has come down for a late breakfast. Instead I ignore her—although it's difficult because she's sitting right across from our table. I can't help think it's on purpose.

We're close enough that I see her eyes light up. I turn around to see her run up to meet Simon and give him a huge kiss!

"What the hell?" I say loudly.

"Is that the man I'm supposed to be meeting?"

"Yes!"

"Why did that woman just kiss him?" My mom asks confused.

"Good question."

I walk up to them, where Simon is just standing there, shocked. He's not moving or anything. He's like a statue.

"What is going on? Why are you kissing my man?!"

"I'm just giving him a morning greeting. I do this with all my loves."

"Simon, why did you let her kiss you?"

"I have no idea. I don't know what's going on. I was just walking over to meet up with you and your mum.

But you think I'm your man, huh?" Simon asks, with Christina still wrapped around him like a snake typically does to her prey.

"I thought you were! I don't know what's happening. I think I need a minute. Or two. Maybe an hour. Mom, can I go up to your room with you?"

"But I thought I was coming to meet you. Dabney. Wait!" Simon calls out, while I walk away in shock. I don't know what to do. How am I going to get rid of this woman? Furthermore, why do women keep sabotaging my relationships? I have always been a champion for other ladies. Why aren't they championing me for once?

My mom follows me out of the dining area and says, "Dabney, he could've pushed her away a little faster. I watched the whole thing." My mom loves to give her opinion and this time, I feel like maybe it's warranted.

We get to her room, which was my old room. When I walk in, I start to cry.

"Dabney, what's wrong?" My mom asks sympathetically as she sits down next to me on her bed. I've never seen her so motherly. Maybe the admission that my dad is a philandering fool has made her realize I'm not as bad as she once thought.

"This room just has a lot of old memories. That's all."

"Dabney, maybe you need to come home," my mom gently says as she rubs my back.

"Maybe you're right, mom." I say through the soft tears trickling down my face.

My mom and I lay on her bed and I just lean on her. She puts her arm around my shoulder and kisses my head like she did when I was little. Maybe my mom isn't as bad I once thought.

I fall asleep and wake up without her on the bed. It's 10:30 in the morning, but I don't have any motivation to move. I feel defeated. So, I fall asleep again.

My mom wakes me up, finally. She has changed out of her flats and into sneakers.

"I've been for a walk. It's beautiful weather here." My mom is downright jubilant in comparison to my dull feelings of gloom.

"Yes, I've enjoyed it." I yawn and sit up in her bed.

"I found your man. He's been sitting downstairs since we left."

"He has?" I ask, surprised that he didn't give up on me and go back home.

"Yes. I wonder if you should talk to him. At least hear him out before you leave."

"I don't know. I think maybe I should just go home and pretend this insane trip never happened."

"It's up to you. I'm not going to pretend I know best anymore. I have some things to figure out, too."

She takes her clothes out of her perfectly organized suitcase, which is smaller than the one I borrowed and puts them away in the dresser.

"By the way, mom, your suitcase has caused me nothing but trouble. How have you not had any issues with it?"

"Oh, your father has had plenty of issues with it. I just ignore him. It fits everything I need."

"Mom, I feel bad about leaving. People are depending on me. Tilda's husband just left for a month. I told her I would work for her to help her."

"Who is Tilda? How do you know all these people?"

"They're all friends I've made. Maura downstairs is a young girl getting ready to go to University in the Fall. I've worked a bit in the B&B with her. She's really smart and sweet. I've already mentioned Tilda. Sam and Cassie own the B&B. Cassie just had a baby."

"Did you finish all your things you were going to do?"

"Yep. I did. I even drove a manual on the opposite side of the road." I laugh inside, thinking about how I would call it the wrong side of the road just to annoy Simon. He was so patient with me, despite my terrible driving skills.

"Well, I'm here for a week. Why don't you let her know you've decided to go back home today? That gives her a week to find a replacement. I can't imagine it's that hard to find somebody." My mom, who hasn't worked since she was an eighteen-year-old girl, says.

I am so confused. I really don't know what to do. Part of me says to hit the road and forget about everyone. But I have a hard time with that. I have grown to like these people—a lot.

"Mom, I think I'm going to go for a walk. Maybe clear my head a bit."

"Okay, sweetheart. I think that's a good idea. I'll look through this travel guide to see if there are any good tours to take while I'm here."

I leave the room to go downstairs. I see Simon sitting

on one of the sofas, asleep. Perhaps he dozed off waiting for me to come down.

I decide to sneak past him so I can go on my walk. I need this time to figure out what exactly the hell I'm going to do.

I walk around the corner past Tilda and Deacon's house. It looks like she has started the renovation to add a room to her house. They're busting at the seams with six people. Right now, I suppose it's only five. Now that Deacon has left for his musical tour. It's hard to believe that just a few weeks ago he was a pub singer and now he has actual gigs in several cities. Thousands of people who never knew his name, are now coming to see him sing. I like to think I had a small part in that.

I walk past the small shop, where I buy my snacks and waters. Thomas, the nice man who always asks me how my day is going and talks to me about the weather, gives me a wave as he puts fruit in the boxes out front. He always remembers my name. I have made a point to remember his, as well. Something in the past I have been rather negligent about. I feel like my listening skills have improved since coming to Ireland.

Finally, I walk to the coffee shop where I pop in on my daily walks. It's a cute little shop that serves baked goods and obviously coffee. The young girls who work in there are always so bubbly, possibly from their over consumption of caffeine. Or maybe because they are simply happy people. They make my day, though, when they compliment me on what I'm wearing or how nice my hair looks.

I walk back to the B&B, where the people welcomed

me with open arms the first time I walked through the door? If they hadn't, I would probably be back in Chicago right now. Doing something or maybe nothing.

I look over to the sofa where Simon was sleeping and see he's still there. He's awake now, looking at his phone. He doesn't see me yet. I watch him run his hands though his shiny black hair. The one ring he wears on his finger shines in the sunlight. It was his grandfather's. A gift from his grandmother. The same grandmother he put his life on hold for, in order to give her the best care she could have before she died.

"Hi Simon." I finally say and approach him.

He lets out a deep sigh. "Dabney! I've been waiting for you all day!"

"I know, I saw you sleeping when I went out for my walk. I needed a chance to think about everything. It's been a crazy day for me."

"Dabney, Christina just accosted me. I didn't know what was happening. I was excited to meet your mum and then all of a sudden—"

"It's okay. I know she planned it that way. When I sit and drink my coffee in the morning, I think about what I'm going to eat for lunch. She obviously was thinking about sticking her tongue down your throat."

"I'm so sorry, Dabney."

"It's not your fault. But I have a question for you, and I want an honest answer, which I think you will give. If your Gran hadn't needed the help from you, would you have broken up with Christina? She never would've given you an ultimatum in that case. Do you think you'd still be together? Possibly even married?"

Simon takes a deep breath. His pause lets me know he is giving my question serious thought.

"Dabney, the fact that she gave me an ultimatum during one of the most difficult times in my life tells me no. If it wasn't then, it would have been another time. We weren't meant to be together."

"I believe you."

"Dabney, I love you. I don't need to know if you love me, too. I just need you to know that I love you."

His blue eyes glisten as he gazes into mine. He doesn't try to kiss me or anything like that. He just stands in front of me.

I hear a sniffle as someone behind me says, "Oh Dabney, kiss him for goodness sake!"

It's my mom.

Finally agreeing with mom on something, I wrap my arms around Simon's neck and give him a long kiss.

"Simon, I guess it's time you officially met my mom, Dina Corrigan."

Simon and I let go of our embrace so he can shake my mom's hand.

"I'm happy to meet you, Mrs. Corrigan."

"Please, call me Dina. I'm happy to meet you as well, Simon."

As we finish our introductions, I see Christina come down the stairs. Her eyes are wet, and her face is blotchy. I see the broken heart on her face and for the first time, I feel bad for her.

"Hello. I was um, just coming down to ask about checkout. I'll be leaving in the morning. I have to go back to London for work." She has clearly heard our entire conversation.

Simon walks toward her and says, "Christina, I never meant to hurt you. It just wasn't meant to be for us. We were over a long time ago," he says gently.

Christina wipes a tear away and says, "Well, you can't blame a girl for trying, right? You were worth fighting for to the end, Simon O'Connell."

Simon gives her a hug and says, "Thank you, Christina."

I don't feel a pang of jealousy anymore when they're together. I see Christina less as a snake and more as a woman desperate to get back who she thinks is the love of her life. I am sad for her because I know what she has lost.

Christina lets go of her embrace, says goodbye and goes over to the checkout desk.

In an attempt to break the tension in the room, my mom says, "Shall we go over to the pub for some lunch?"

Both Simon and I take a deep breath and respond with an enthusiastic, "Yes!"

At the Stag's Leap, I introduce my mom to Tilda and the rest of the staff there. I'm scheduled to work in the evening, which my mom says is fine. She'll find something to do while I'm working.

"Dina, will you be staying very long?" Tilda asks as she brings us our drinks.

"Oh, only for about a week or so."

Simon kisses my cheek and says, "That's what Dabney said as well."

I smile. Never in a million years would I have thought this simple little solo trip to Ireland would never end; that I would decide to stay and build a life here. But I am. Who knows? Maybe my mom will follow my lead and have a solo trip of her own. It worked for me, after all.

ACKNOWLEDGEMENT

I began writing this book deep in the confines of the COVID-19 quarantine. Feeling trapped, I decided to start writing. So, while I would like to punch the Coronavirus in the face if it had one, I must acknowledge it probably motivated me to write.

As always, I need to thank my family. Paul, you are a good husband who accepts that sometimes the house will not get picked up as much while I am writing. Luca and Lola, you see me at the counter writing and you still engage in normal life of video games and SpongeBob SquarePants. I have learned to write amongst the chaos and love every minute of it. Charlie and Jennie, you sit with me, keep me company and I love you, my furry little friends.

I would like to thank my editor, who always gives me honest feedback. I would not have a book without your help!

Finally, I must thank my friends, family, and supporters I have not met. The kind words, social media shares and shoutouts mean a lot to me, so thank you from the bottom of my heart.

I hope you enjoy The Solo Trip and if you feel so inclined, please leave a review! It helps writers a lot. Thank you!

ABOUT THE AUTHOR

Leah Battaglio

Leah Battaglio is an author of several lighthearted and fun books. When she is not writing, Leah likes to volunteer at her children's school and spend quality time with her husband, Paul. She also has two very spoiled pets who she loves dearly.

You can find updates about Leah's books at:
www.leahbattaglio.net
www.facebook.com/authorleahbattaglio

Printed in Great Britain
by Amazon